# Dangerous Tunes

Matt Ni

G000055251

**matt**
publishing

BRISTOL ENGLAND

First published in 2021 by
Matt Publishing
1 Priors Close, Bristol, BS2 8ET, UK
https://mattwriting.com

ISBN 978-0-9927774-3-2
Edition 1.01, May 2021
Edition 1.1, May 2021

Cover design by Alexandra Albornoz
https://99designs.co.uk/profiles/alexcreativedesing

*Also by Matt Nicholson from Matt Publishing*

When Computing Got Personal: A History of the Desktop Computer

Seated one day at the organ,
I was weary and ill at ease,
And my fingers wandered idly
Over the noisy keys.

I know not what I was playing,
Or what I was dreaming then;
But I struck one chord of music,
Like the sound of a great Amen.

It flooded the crimson twilight,
Like the close of an angel's psalm,
And it lay on my fevered spirit
With a touch of infinite calm.

It quieted pain and sorrow,
Like love overcoming strife;
It seemed the harmonious echo
From our discordant life.

It linked all perplexèd meanings
Into one perfect peace,
And trembled away into silence
As if it were lothe to cease.

I have sought, but I seek it vainly,
That one lost chord divine,
Which came from the soul of the organ,
And entered into mine.

It may be that death's bright angel
Will speak in that chord again,
It may be that only in Heav'n
I shall hear that grand Amen.

*A Lost Chord* by Adelaide Anne Procter (1858)

# One

A movement in the corner of his eye catches his attention. He turns towards the living room door, which stands slightly ajar. From this angle he can just see where she sits in the hall, back turned towards him, head angled slightly so her olive brown nose peeks out from tumbling cascades of jet black hair. She has the telephone tucked up against her ear. She is too far away for him to make out what she is saying but her right arm is gesticulating in an animated fashion, as it so often does. She has slipped her right foot out of its shoe and has pressed it high against the paisley wallpaper. Her dress lies in a crumpled heap across the top of her thighs.

She is not aware he is watching through the door so for a short moment he can observe her in her natural state, but then she turns and smiles. She shrugs her shoulders, almost bare but for the thin straps of her dress, and her big brown eyes hold his, widening as she winds up the conversation. It is a vision so achingly tender that it scares him. Whoever is on the line is an irrelevance; this is a moment shared by just the two of them. Over the past few weeks she has opened herself up and let him inside, but she is not his and he has no right to her. All he can do is make the most of the time they have together.

She puts the phone down, walks through the door and stands in front of him. 'Why so glum?' she asks, her lips turned down in an expression of mock concern. She takes his hands and lifts her face to be kissed, which he does.

'Looks like you are pleased to see me, after all. Shall we go upstairs?'

Jack has been to Ania's house enough times to understand the etiquette behind that question. Ania's mother and stepfather are fairly liberal, but there is an unspoken agreement that her bedroom door be left open when she has a male visitor. If it's not then her mother is likely to burst in with questions about a nice cup of tea.

Ania's bedroom is at the back of the large detached house, overlooking the extensive lawn and the trees that border the garden, and full of light from the late afternoon sun. She deftly avoids Jack's attempts to pull her down onto the bed, so instead they stand together looking

1

through the window at the sunlight filtering through the trees.

'It's a pretty cool view,' says Jack.

'Yeah, it's cool, but not as cool as the view I had in Kensington.' Ania looks wistfully through the window. 'My bedroom looked out over Holland Park and I could pop into Biba just up the road. That was really cool.'

Talk of London makes Jack uneasy. He's been going out with Ania pretty much since her family moved to Westerford, just a few weeks ago. They'd come here so her parents could relax in the leafy suburbs, and so her younger brother could go to Westerford Grammar, the school Jack left last year. Ania has signed on at an art college, which she travels to by train a couple of days a week.

She's given him few details of her life in London, but enough for him to realise she left some close friends behind, and that there was a boyfriend a few years older and more experienced than he. She has assured Jack she broke off that relationship when she met him, but Jack can't help feeling the guy's still there in the background, if only to be measured against. Last night they'd sat up late while Ania regaled him with tales of her exploits in London, but by the small hours their conversation had become more circumspect as Jack tried to conceal his discomfort.

To Jack, everything about Ania is exotic. She was born in this country but her Polish parents had escaped to London when the Germans invaded, her mother pregnant with her elder sister Magda, who still lives there. Her father returned to Poland in 1954 to fight the Soviet occupation, and was never seen again. Ania was just two at the time, and her only memory is of a big man picking her up and holding her tight somewhere filled with steam and noise and the smell of coal.

'Anyway, enough of that.' She shrugs and looks back at Jack with a soft smile on her face. 'Where are you taking me tonight, lover boy?'

'I told you yesterday. We're doing a gig down at the Scout Hut this evening. It's all set up, so we can get a drink first. It should be pretty good. Carol's singing, and you haven't seen her in action yet – she's really cool.'

'Really cool, eh? Fancy her, do you? Should I be worried?' But she's smiling so he knows she's kidding. She likes the idea of having a rock 'n' roll guitarist as a boyfriend, and she's become good friends with Carol.

'Well, she has got pretty big …'

'Tits? What, not like these little things?' She thrusts her chest out, and then dodges as Jack makes to grab her.

'Enough of that. I've got to think about what to wear.' She opens the built-in wardrobe that lines one wall of her bedroom. 'So, who else is going to be there tonight?'

'Ooh, most people I expect.'

'Will Dean be there?' Dean could be described as Jack's best friend, although their relationship is fairly competitive. Dean doesn't play an instrument, for example, but has somehow perfected that rock 'n' roll swagger to a level Jack has never managed.

'Most likely. He'll probably be with Pauline, though.' Jack instinctively adds 'though' to the end of that sentence, perhaps because he's aware Ania is no longer the new girl in town, being proudly shown off by her new boyfriend, but instead someone building up her own relationships, some of which Jack is having trouble accepting.

Ania grabs some clothes and disappears into her en suite, leaving Jack to check himself out in her full length mirror: lightweight army surplus jacket and faded Grateful Dead T-shirt together with pale blue jeans, skin-tight around his thighs and fashionably flared above low-heeled boots. Shame it's not a leather jacket, but put it together with his dark brown, shoulder-length hair, pale narrow face and skinny frame and he's looking OK for the stage.

But then Ania reappears wearing a slinky black number with a plunging back that clings to her body in a manner that suggests she is wearing little else. 'So, what do you think of this then?'

Jack is too distracted to come up with a coherent response, particularly as Ania eases it up over her shoulders to reveal that she is indeed naked underneath and runs back into the bathroom before he can react. When she emerges she is wearing the short denim skirt she'd worn when they first met and a white lacy top. 'Right, let's go then.'

oOo

Ania's house is on Riverside, which, as its name suggests, runs along the river that flows across the northern edge of Westerford. They walk down the front steps and the short drive, across the road and down a few more steps onto the path that runs along the bank. Here they turn left towards the Blue Lion, which sits on the junction with London Road about half a mile away, walking slowly to enjoy the fading warmth of the evening sun and the play of light on the woods that rise sharply from the opposite bank up into the North Downs. Just ahead is an ornate, wrought iron bench, and as they approach Ania slows down.

'Have you got a fag? I'm dying for a smoke.'

'I've got better than that,' Jack replies, opening his jacket to reveal the twisted end of a joint, peeking out of his inner pocket. He takes it out and runs it under his nose, savouring the smell. 'It's good Moroccan. Got it off Dean earlier.'

'Cool,' says Ania. 'Give it here, then.' They sit down and Jack fishes out his lighter, the one he bought on Portobello Road a few months back. It's a chunky brass petrol job embossed with an eagle motif, and the guy on the stall told him he had got it from an American soldier who had come back from Vietnam. Jack's not sure he wholly believed him but it does feel heavy and solid, and cool when he opens and lights it with a well-practised gesture, although it has a tendency to throw out a rather larger flame than required.

'Oops, sorry about that!' he says as Ania pulls back in alarm, and then leans forward to light the joint. Once the tip is glowing strongly she takes a deep drag, holds the smoke in her lungs for a few seconds and then exhales. 'Mmm, that's nice,' she says. She leans back on the bench and hands the joint back to Jack.

Jack takes a deep drag himself and then leans back, letting the smoke out slowly.

'How are you feeling about the gig tonight?'

'Pretty good,' says Jack. 'I mean, it's always weird, stepping out on stage and seeing all those people looking back at you, but once we're into the set the guitar just takes over. I know all the songs. My fingers know what to do.'

'I've noticed,' says Ania, throwing him a mischievous grin, which causes Jack to blush. She puts her hand on his thigh. 'I mean, it's great. You really get lost in your playing, and that's really cool. I could listen to you messing around for hours.'

They sit in silence, savouring the gentle fog that is seeping into their brains.

'That's such a nice buzz. I really like this Moroccan,' says Jack.

'Yeah, it's much more mellow than that black you had last week. That really blew my head off.' says Ania.

'Yeah, that was powerful stuff. Paki Black. Got it as a quid deal from some guy in Kensington Market, when I was up in town. He was coming down the stairs as I was going up, and he whispered "wanna score?" as he passed, just loud enough for me to hear.'

'I've got a friend who's got a stall in Kensington Market. Sells bongs and chillums …'

Before Ania can continue, Jack interrupts. 'London! God, I wish you'd stop going on about London!' He stops as he sees Ania's expression, instantly regretting what he has said, but it's too late. They

4

sit in silence, Ania gazing blankly across the river.

'Jack, there's something I need to tell you.' She studies the woods on the opposite bank. 'I've decided to go up to London this weekend.' She turns back to look at him. 'It's just for the weekend but I really need to see Magda. I haven't seen her since we moved here. Come on, let's not argue. I've got to work Sunday night on my project, but come around after I get back from college Monday evening.'

He knows she isn't asking permission, but he can see that she cares what he thinks. And the Moroccan is still swirling around his brain, soothing his synapses and preventing him from taking anything too seriously.

'That's fine – really, it's fine,' he says, smiling. He stands and crooks his elbow in an inviting manner. She slips her arm through his and they saunter down the path towards the pub, sharing the joint until it's burned down to the roach, which Jack flicks on a high trajectory into the river.

As they approach the building, which stands on the river's edge, Ania looks up at the sign: 'Why is it called the Blue Lion?'

'It used to be called The Purple Cockroach,' Jack replies.

'No, seriously? I've heard of The Red Lion, and The Black Lion, but the Blue Lion? Seems like an odd name for a pub.'

'Well … It's all on account of this lion, you see, used to wander about the woods up there.' Jack waves extravagantly across the river. 'It was a perfectly ordinary lion, until one day it walked under a ladder and this painter dropped a pot of paint all over it.' He pauses for effect: 'Then he got eaten by the lion. Which was now blue. The lion, I mean, not the painter. The painter would have been a sort of reddish colour, I guess … Maybe they should have called it The Bloody Painter.'

Ania looks at him quizzically: 'And the moral of that story is?'

'Don't walk under ladders, of course.'

'You're so full of shit!' she giggles as they push open the door and stumble into the pub.

oOo

The Blue Lion is the poshest pub in Westerford with its fitted maroon carpet, real wood tables, upholstered chairs and walls that, although stained with nicotine, could still be described as white. Jack is not surprised to see Dean standing at the bar and Pauline sitting at the best table in the place: the one in the bay window that overlooks the river.

'Hi there,' says Dean, 'if it isn't Jack and Annie. So, what are you two drinking?'

At first sight it isn't at all obvious why anyone would consider Dean attractive. His complexion is sallow and his midnight black hair almost always a greasy mess, but what does stand out are his eyes. They are the colour of a clear spring sky and have a natural intensity that you notice as soon as he enters the room. And then there's the way he moves, like he's Jim Morrison on stage at Winterland, but he's not putting it on: it's just the way he moves and it's just so cool.

Otherwise he's simply a scruff with his worn denim jeans and leather jacket with the word 'Hell' picked out on the back in metal studs. The story goes that the jacket once belonged to a biker and went through a biker-style, rite-of-passage ceremony that involved urination.

And it can't be denied that Dean's magic does work. His girlfriend Pauline is every bit the hippy chick with her tight, threadbare jeans and loose white gypsy-style top, and her round face with its high cheekbones framed by unruly ringlets of black hair that tumble about her shoulders. And there's the fact that Ania seems quite happy for Dean to call her Annie, something Jack is careful to avoid as she usually hates it.

'Mine's a pint,' Jack replies.

'I'll have a half of lager,' says Ania. She joins Pauline at the table.

'So, you playing tonight?' Dean asks Jack, once he's ordered.

'Yup, with Black Knight, and Carol's handling the vocals. Should be pretty cool.'

'Cool.'

'Yeah, we're all set up, so I've just got to get up on stage and hit the strings. Usual stuff, but Carol's on good form these days.'

'Looking forward to it.' Dean waits as the barman goes off to change the barrel. Once he's out of earshot, Dean leans into Jack. 'On another matter, what are you two up to this weekend?'

'Not sure. Ania's up in London until Monday and I guess I've got nothing planned.'

Dean glances over at the table where the two girls sit. 'Things cool with you guys?'

'Yeah, sure.'

'Good,' says Dean. He leans forward for dramatic effect. 'Well, you might be interested to know that I've got some acid.'

'Acid? Far out.' Jack has taken LSD a few times, and right now a full-blown trip could be just what he needs.

'Yeah. Black microdot. A thousand mikes in a tab the size of a pinhead. Should blow our heads off. Pauline and I are going for it tomorrow with a few of the others – probably Carol and Dillon. It's a quid a shot.'

'Count me in.'

'Cool. We're meeting at the Rose and Crown up in town at midday. Probably go into the park from there.' The barman has finished pouring so Dean picks up the drinks and joins the girls at the table. Jack wanders over to the jukebox, puts a coin into the slot and selects a couple of tracks. The self-assured chords that open Free's *All Right Now* ring out as Jack approaches the table. Dean nods his appreciation and turns back to the conversation he's having with Ania. Pauline shifts over to make a space for Jack.

'So, how are you feeling about the gig tonight?' she asks.

Jack grins back in a self-depreciating manner. 'Oh, you know, a bit fired up, but it should be pretty cool.'

'You were sounding pretty good last time you played.'

'Well, it helps having Carol up front, and Chris and Phil keep it all together at the back.'

'Don't knock it. You were serving up some pretty hot riffs yourself, you know.'

Jack can feel himself reddening under Pauline's gaze. Searching around for something else to talk about, he spots the book that is peeking out of Pauline's tasselled shoulder bag.

'Is that Carlos Castaneda?'

'Yeah,' she replies, taking it out of the bag. '*The Teachings of Don Juan.* I've just finished reading it. It's pretty far out. Have you read it?'

'I finished it a few weeks back. It's the one where he meets the old Mexican guy? Who teaches him all this cool stuff? It is pretty far out. Those are strong drugs they're taking, though.'

'Yeah, although Dean says he can get hold of mescalin, which is what's in peyote cactus. And those mushrooms, the psilocybin mushrooms that Don Juan calls "the little smoke"? You can find those in the fields round here. You've got to be careful to pick the right ones, but all you need to do is dry them out, and Dean knows how to recognise them.'

Jack glances over, but Dean is deep in conversation with Ania and looks like he's building up to a punchline.

'That datura though, what he calls "devil's weed", that sounds quite something. It's what we call mandrake or deadly nightshade, and it'll kill you if you're not careful.'

'Cool, though, when he uses it to fly like a bird.' says Pauline. 'That must have been amazing.'

'Yeah, but did he actually do it? That bit's really cool, where he's questioning Don Juan about whether he actually, really like, flew, or was it all in his mind. He says something like, "But if I chained myself to a heavy rock, so I couldn't move, would I still have flown?" and Don Juan says, "If you chained yourself to a heavy rock, then you'd just have to fly carrying a heavy rock." That's far out.'

'Makes you think, though,' says Pauline, 'what's actually real and what's just in your head? It's like with acid: there's the world you see normally, and there's the world you see when you're tripping. But which one's real? Or are they both just distorted views of what's actually out there?'

'You mean like "through a glass darkly", or however that goes?' says Jack. 'Yeah, when you're tripping, you really start to wonder. I guess it's what Castaneda calls a "special consensus", as in "it's real because there's a bunch of us that agree it's real". It's like we're conditioned right from the start to see just the parts of the world we need to see in order to survive, and we need something like LSD to see beyond that.'

'So, are you coming tomorrow?'

'Yeah. Ania's in London but I'm up for it. Dean said we're meeting lunchtime at the Rose and Crown.'

'That's right. Should be great. My parents are away this weekend, up at my grandfather's, so you guys can come back to my house after and chill out; listen to music and stuff. You can even stay the night if you want. There's plenty of space.'

'Sounds great.' Jack realises the others have already finished and drains his glass.

'I guess we might as well get off to the gig,' says Dean, and the four of them pile out onto the street, now lit only by the sodium orange of the streetlights.

o0o

Dean produces a joint of yet more Moroccan, which they share as they walk a half mile or so in the direction of the Scout Hut, finishing it just before they enter the off-licence opposite the railway station. Jack starts to order a six-pack of Carlsberg when Dean interrupts.

'Excuse me, but is that a bottle of Polish spirit I see perched on your top shelf?'

The shop assistant looks at him derisively, obviously not impressed by their appearance: 'I take it you're eighteen?'

'Yup,' says Dean. 'You're on the button and I've got a driving licence to prove it.'

'I'm nineteen,' adds Ania, helpfully.

'OK, OK,' says the assistant. He reaches up for the half-bottle of clear liquid with the strange label, and places it on the counter.

Jack looks quizzically at Dean, but Dean continues.

'That'll do nicely. I'll take that, and four bottles of Coke, please.' He turns to Jack and the others. 'This is on me. Trust me, it'll be worth it, wait and see.'

Once they're back on the street, Dean explains: 'Polish spirit. Like vodka, but twice as strong. Around 140 proof. It's almost pure alcohol, but it's a really nice high. Just don't mix it with anything else or it'll knock you out completely.' He grins at Ania: 'Perhaps you're already familiar with it? What with being Polish and all?'

Ania grins back: 'Actually, no. I'm a good girl, me.'

The Scout Hut is a few hundred yards further on, past the railway bridge, but it is apparent that proceedings have already commenced with the energetic rhythms of Creedence Clearwater Revival's *Bad Moon Rising* clearly audible across the dark expanse of the playing field. The hut itself is a corrugated iron construction with room for a stage and a decent-sized dance floor inside, tucked away just off the far corner of the playing field and sufficiently isolated not to raise too many complaints from the nearby estate. It's a mild September night so people are lounging about on the benches outside, lit by two glaring white lights mounted above the door that cast stark black shadows. The doors are open to let in the cool air, and inside the place is jumping.

Jack's mate Dillon is behind the two-deck console, leafing through a box of singles for the next tracks to spin. The wall behind him is dimly lit with the lurid bubbling shapes cast by an oil wheel that is the main source of light once you're inside. The floor is crowded with dancers while others lounge around the cheap formica tables that line the walls, keeping an eye on the talent and shouting snippets of conversation into each other's ears. There's a group of sixth-formers from the Grammar, smoking cigarettes nervously and casting surreptitious glances at a group of girls from the corresponding girls' school who are all PVC miniskirts and Mary Quant eyelashes, giggling and pretending not to notice. There's a number of older guys from the estate, posing in the jeans and black leather jackets that mark them out as greasers, and there's loon pants and tie-dye T-shirts in enough colours to fill a rainbow. On stage sits Phil's drum kit with the bass drum displaying their signature Black Knight helmet, and next to it the squat shapes of Jack's precious AC30 and Chris's B-15.

'Hold on a sec.' Dean shouts into Jack's ear. They grab a space by the wall while Dean makes his way over to a table at the far end of the hut that is standing in as a makeshift bar, returning a few moments later with four plastic cups that he puts on the ledge behind them. He fills the cups with Coke, leaving a half-inch which he tops up with Polish spirit, and then hands them round.

Jack takes a sip, feeling the spirit burning on its way down. 'Nice one!' he shouts into Dean's ear. Before he can offer a cigarette, Dean's off with Pauline into the gyrating bodies while Ania's chatting with Carol, who has just come over. Across the floor he can see Paul and Chris, and there's his friend Martin in animated conversation with an attractive blond in a brightly coloured mini dress. Martin says something in her ear to which she responds by slapping him hard across the face and walking off to join a group of girls on the other side of the hut who flutter like a kaleidoscope of butterflies. Martin once told Jack that his trick for pulling chicks was to come straight out with, 'Fancy a fuck?' Nine times out of ten he gets his face slapped, or worse if the boyfriend's around, but occasionally it actually works, or so he claims. Not this time, though, by the looks of it.

Martin wanders across, looking a little dejected. He leans in towards Jack and shouts over the music, 'Oops!' Then he spies Jack's drink. 'So what you got there then?'

Before Jack can reply, Martin's taken a sip. 'Wow, powerful stuff.'

Jack smiles: 'Yeah, it's not just Coke.' But Martin's already downed most of what's left and gone back to scanning the dance floor for his next target. He spies Ania and elbows Jack. 'How about her, what do you reckon?'

'Don't you dare.' Jack replies.

Martin grins and moves off in a different direction, towards a willowy brunette. Jack helps himself to another drink and settles down to watch the outcome, but then Dillon puts on Jefferson Airplane's *Somebody to Love*, his favourite of all time, and Ania grabs his hand and pulls him onto the dance floor to join Dean and Pauline, who are already whirling like spaced-out dervishes. As the last notes of Kaukonen's effortlessly flawless solo scream out, Jack feels a tap on his shoulder. Chris is holding up the key to the store cupboard. It's time to get set up. They're on after the next track.

Ania gives Jack's hand a quick squeeze and then he's off, following Chris round the back of the stage to where Carol and Phil are waiting. They exchange nervous grins. They've got a minute or two yet. Jack unlocks the cupboard and retrieves the Ibanez bass that Chris's parents bought him for his 18th, and his own six-string Strat copy that he put together from the neck of a Hofner Galaxy, a couple of Fender pickups he'd found cheap in a shop off Charing Cross Road and a solid block of mahogany that he carved into shape and stained a deep purple. It's his most precious possession.

The last few bars of Arthur Brown's *Fire* sound out as Jack, Chris and Phil make their way onto the stage. There's a few bangs and dissonant chords as they check their instruments, and a few whistles from the audience as Dillon turns down the disco. They look at each other to check they're ready and then launch into their signature *Black Night* standard, the Deep Purple version, followed immediately by *Born to be Wild*, with Chris making a robust effort at the vocals before giving up and letting Jack take over with an extended solo that soars above the driving beat hammered out by Phil and Chris. This is the bit Jack loves. Something deep inside him takes over, sweeping away any thought of the audience and guiding his fingers across the fretboard without him having to think about it. Even if he were to stop, Chris and Phil are so into the momentum of it all that no one would notice. But he doesn't; he just keeps going, sweeping riffs across the audience like he's holding a fire hose, until he hears the subtle change in emphasis that signals the last few bars, and he brings it to a close. Job done – he's in the groove.

Everyone's attention is now on Carol as she takes up position centre stage, microphone in hand, butterfly T-shirt stretched across her magnificent breasts and knee-length black leather boots pulled over skin-tight jeans. She nods in Phil and Chris's direction and they launch into their own version of *Somebody to Love*, followed by The Who's *I Can See for Miles* with Carol, big brown eyes and blond hair flying, howling into the microphone like a demented mix of Janis Joplin and Grace Slick, while Jack's guitar soars closer and closer to the edge until it feels like he's fucking every note as it snarls out from his fingertips. They come into the last stretch and Jack spots Dean and Pauline just a few rows into the crowd. Dean's shouting something into Pauline's ear and she's gesticulating angrily, obviously upset. As Jack watches, his fingers on automatic, Pauline turns and stomps off. Dean shouts after her, but it's inaudible and she's gone so he turns back to the stage and takes a big swig from his drink. Sensing Jack's eyes on him, he shrugs and smiles back.

But then, before Jack can react, the crowd parts and four guys stride out: big and mean and dressed in black. These are dangerous dudes: greasers with Hells Angel aspirations, outlaws in full regalia with sawn-off leathers and heavy chains, most likely high on speed and carrying knives. Not to be messed with, but here they are, the four of them lined up in a row facing the band. The crowd tenses and Jack instinctively searches for Ania, although it's him with his long hair and hippy paraphernalia that they've got in their sights.

As if on signal Phil and Chris launch into some rock 'n' roll, Phil pounding a punishing pace and Chris accompanying with a driving bass. Carol stands defiant to one side. Jack is alone and exposed in the light that shines up from the floor in front of him.

He grips the guitar like it's a defensive shield, with nothing but the pounding rhythm holding back the silence and the growing tension. He holds the gaze of the first greaser, as though he's facing a bull in an open field. His opponent sneers and beckons him on, daring him to try. Jack crouches down, points the neck of the guitar towards his enemy like it's an AK-47 and fires off a riff that comes back at him like the bark of a bull terrier: low, hard and loud. His target reels back as though dodging a bullet, and then resumes the pose. Jack ignores him and, as the note dies away, swings his guitar towards the second greaser and follows it up with another bark that ends on a harsh howl of feedback that he sweeps across the remaining greasers before launching into a break-neck solo like it's the only thing between him and death.

The four greasers glare back for a long moment and then squat down into the greaser dance: fists on waists, swinging their torsos left and right and up and down in perfect unison. This is their music as much as it's Jack's and his hippy friends' and, just for the moment, they're willing to share. As the tension subsides others tentatively join in, uncertain of the moves but giving it a go, until Phil brings it to an end in a cascade of drumbeats. The greasers salute the band and turn to leave. The crowd parts to let them through.

Jack scans the crowd, trying to spot Ania in the dim light, but before he can find her someone calls out *Street Fighting Man* so they finish the set with the Stones classic, Carol doing the vocals. The crowd roars, and Carol stands beside him, hands around his shoulder, the hero of the hour. Dazed, and somewhat amazed he's survived, Jack takes a bow, and then it's back to the disco. Phil claps him on the shoulder and Chris gives him a thumbs up as they leave the stage.

By the time Jack makes it back to the dance floor they're playing the Doors' *Light My Fire*, the full album version with the seven-minute solo. Somebody turns on a strobe and the world shatters into frozen moments, linked only by the electronic whine of Ray Manzarek's organ, driving relentlessly onward like Bach on acid, and the rush of alcohol, adrenalin and hash running through his veins. FLASH! an outstretched hand. FLASH! tightly stretched silk. FLASH! Ania's face and she's saying something but he can't make out what it is, so she takes him by the hand

and leads him outside and round to the back of the hut where it's cool and dark, and she turns to face him.

Then she's kissing him and her tongue is in his mouth and he's kissing her back and she's thrusting against him and his hands are under her skirt and behind her thighs and she is fumbling with the zip of his jeans, and then she releases him and cocks her leg and leans back against the wall so she can guide him in and he's inside her and they're breathing hard and she's wet and slick and moving against him and he grabs her buttocks and she cries out and then it's over.

'Hold me, just hold me for a bit longer,' she whispers and leans into him, and he holds her until she pulls away, kisses him gently and murmurs into his ear: 'So, what's it like being a fucking guitar hero?'

'So, what's it like fucking a fucking guitar hero?' he stutters back. She laughs her low laugh and bites his ear before pulling away.

He remembers to zip his fly as they make their way round to the front of the hut, past some guy throwing up on the corner, and there waiting in the road is Dean in his car with the passenger door open. Ania turns to Jack and says: 'It's OK, Dean said he'd give me a lift. I'll see you Monday, after the weekend. Don't worry. I'll see you Monday.' And she walks towards the car and gets in, and Dean waves as they drive off.

It makes sense. Ania's place is on the way to Dean's and Jack lives in the other direction. He knows it makes sense, but he can't help wondering what happened to Pauline. Dazed, stoned and confused, but relaxed in the afterglow of orgasm, Jack starts the short walk back to his mother's flat.

# Two

Jack has only taken lysergic acid diethylamide, or 'acid', three or four times in his life, but that's enough to know the effect it can have. He knows, for example, that LSD is so powerful that doses are measured in millionths of a gram, or 'mikes' as they're popularly known. Take fifty mikes and the world becomes brighter and you feel nicely euphoric, like you've smoked some rarefied form of marijuana. But swallow anything more than a couple of hundred mikes, which amounts to a tiny fraction of a single drop of a diluted crystal, and you're going on a trip that will propel you into eternity for at least eight hours, whether you like it or not. You can spend those hours desperately trying to hold onto the wheel of time as it spirals around you in a schizophrenic hell, or you can let go and let it happen. You will come down eventually, hopefully somewhere near where you started, but until then you, quite literally, are gone.

So it's with some trepidation that Jack contemplates the tiny black dot on his fingertip. The size of a pinhead, it contains a thousand mikes of the stuff. He's never taken acid that strong, but he has taken enough to have an inkling of the hell it can create if you approach it in the wrong frame of mind. But hell, he's among friends, the sun is shining and he's not going to be seeing Ania until Monday. He pops it into his mouth and washes it down with a slug of beer.

Jack had arrived at the Rose and Crown just before noon to find Dean and Pauline sitting on one of the wooden tables on the grass outside in the comfortably warm autumn sun, any tension from the previous night apparently behind them. Carol joined them shortly after, followed by Dillon. Once they'd got their drinks, Dean ceremoniously distributed the acid and everyone except Pauline handed over a quid in payment.

Now that the point of no return is past they fall silent, slowly finishing their drinks and their cigarettes and feeling nervous. It normally takes about half an hour for the drug to make its presence felt, so after a short while, sufficient for the acid to hit them at just the right time, Dean gets to his feet and suggests they make a move. The five of them saunter across the road and down the short gravel path through the wood to the old stone wall and quaint wooden gate that gives access to the park itself.

Bordered by the river to the north and the town to the west, Abbey Park has taken on numerous roles through its long history. A little way into the park is a lake fed by a stream from the river, and above that are the remains of an iron-age fort, which in medieval times actually became the site of an abbey, with the lake serving as a source of fish. By the 18th century it had become a deer park and the abbey transformed into a family home, but at some point that was consumed by fire so now only a few broken walls and sections of Gothic arch remain. Part of the park has been turned into a golf course, which gives the wealthier residents of Westerford reason to keep it maintained, but it extends over nearly five hundred acres so there is plenty of room for everyone, whether they be families with children that need to let off steam, or the likes of Jack and his friends looking for somewhere to turn on, tune in and drop out without attracting attention.

The gate opens onto a shallow valley that curves away to the left down towards the lake, and to the right peters out into the distance. The far side is wooded with oak, beech, ash and yew in their autumnal colours but the floor of the valley is grass, broken only by a few solitary trees and fallen logs, and a well-worn path. As they walk on down towards the valley floor the sounds of the town recede, shielded by the trees behind them, and Jack becomes aware of the soft rustling of leaves in response to a light gust of wind, the occasional burst of birdsong and the low drumming of hooves as a small group of fallow deer take fright and run a short distance into the trees before settling once again. The sky is devoid of clouds and the bright sun casts sharp black shadows. It seems too soon for the drug to be taking effect, but Jack is acutely aware of the beauty of the moment.

He is also aware that Carol has started giggling. She catches his gaze and her eyes open wide, and she laughs out loud and dances down the slope and across the path at the bottom, gyrating as she goes and then falling flat on her back in the grass on the opposite slope. Jack looks at his remaining companions, but becomes distracted by the trees that stand behind them. The sharp point of his attention relaxes and widens and deepens, as though he's only now becoming aware of the three-dimensional reality in which he exists. He is acutely conscious of the precise location of each leaf on each tree, its unique relationship with every other and its particular shade of colour. The wind has dropped and the world is still and the leaves appear to delineate a significant geometry, although exactly what it might mean slips his mind as the drug takes hold and drives him into eternity with the force of a Saturn rocket. For a moment he tries to hold on to whatever sanity he has left, but there's really no point. All he can do is go with the flow, and he joins the others as they gyrate down the slope and end up lying in the grass alongside Carol, whooping and laughing out loud.

Sometime later the booster rockets fall away and the five of them reach the perpetual present of high orbit. One by one they get to their feet and wander slowly in the general direction of the lake, gesticulating at various wonders as they go. The filters of their everyday existence have evaporated and everywhere they look is ebbing and flowing with life and colour. They are seeing it as it is, in all its glory, no longer classified, labelled and partitioned according to function or utility.

'Will you look at that!' says Dean, waving at the surroundings in a manner that suggests he has just created them.

'Check out the colours,' exclaims Pauline as she waves her hands in the air, and yes, Jack can see rainbows trailing behind her slim pale arms like flames in the wind.

Carol and Dillon are dancing some sort of jig, going 'Wow! Wow! Wow!' on each beat of the music that evidently accompanies them. The full primal power of the initial rush dies away but Jack can see and feel his own life force, flowing from the core of his being, unrestricted by the boundary that normally defines the extent of his body and out into the wide wondrous world.

But that's not right, because it implies an observer observing the observed, and Jack's no longer sitting safe inside his personal, private bubble like a spaceman peering through his helmet at the 'real world' out there. Instead his bubble's been blown wide open and there's nothing but this wonderful, glorious world. He is not outside it. He's not even part of it. He is it, and there's nothing to separate him from it. It all just is, in this wondrous timeless moment, and there is nothing to be afraid of.

oOo

As they get closer to the lake, Jack falls behind his companions. To the right ferns and nettles cloak the lower slopes, broken only by a narrow path that winds up into a wood of beech trees. The trail has been made by deer seeking shelter from unwanted attention and it seems only natural to take it.

The undergrowth becomes higher and more dense as he climbs the gentle slope, until it meets the trees and a curtain of leaves that extend almost to the ground, presenting a natural barrier that would discourage the casual visitor. However, the path continues through the curtain and Jack's current state of mind could hardly be described as casual, so he pushes on. The ferns and nettles abruptly disappear and he is in a rather different place. Gone is the bright sunlight, stolen by the canopy; gone is the grass, losing out to the roots of the trees that absorb all the nutrients. Instead there is brown earth, dry, dead leaves and shade, broken only by occasional shafts of sunlight that sparkle with hovering insects and dancing particles of dust.

It is a secret place of peace and quiet, and Jack is tempted by the natural seat of a rotting tree trunk that lies across the centre of the grove, until he notices the bulging ridges of fungi that pulsate and swell with obscene enthusiasm. He continues further into the wood, following a path that curves upwards for a while through the uncluttered spaces beneath the leaves and then curves down towards a shallow depression to his left. Jack hesitates and, as he stands there, he becomes aware of a faint sound. Somewhere, at the edge of hearing, someone is singing. It is a pure, clear voice, high in register, and it seems to be coming from the hollow below. He moves slowly forward, careful not to make a sound for fear of scaring the singer or interrupting the hauntingly beautiful melody. Ahead of him is another curtain of leaves, and beyond bright sunlight.

The singing is now loud enough for him to make out three voices, the lower two a counterpoint to the higher central voice, creating an intricate weave that lifts his soul in a fashion only hinted at by the most beautiful of ballads. He creeps forward, parts the curtain and peers through.

In front is a clearing of long grass, perhaps thirty feet across. Without the cover of the trees the sunlight slants down like a spotlight onto a stage. At the lowest part of the depression, half-hidden, lies a slab of stone covered in moss and lichen and too rectangular to be anything but man-made. It lies on top of what can only be a stone coffin.

He can see no obvious source for the singing, but the volume of space immediately above the slab appears to be swirling and the trees behind have lost their focus. A shape is coalescing in the curling air, something that has human form. As it grows more distinct it becomes opaque until eventually it crystallises into the appearance of a young girl with red hair, barefoot and dressed in a plain white dress, but tiny, as though seen through the wrong end of a telescope. As Jack watches, the volume of distorted space expands until it is big enough to accommodate two further figures, both boys. They too appear to be just a foot or so high, clad in baggy trousers and dark brown waistcoats worn over loose white shirts, and self-absorbed as they dance in their bubble above the tomb. Slowly the bubble expands and as they grow taller their voices grow fuller, taking on rich undertones that swirl around the high soprano of the girl. It is hauntingly beautiful and it swells Jack's heart until it feels fit to burst.

Without thinking, Jack stands up and steps forward through the curtain of leaves and into the clearing. The three figures are almost life-size now and clearly teenagers, perhaps fourteen or fifteen years of age. The girl spots him first, her voice changing to express delight at his presence without breaking the flow of their song. She prances towards him, prompting her companions to follow, until the three of them are dancing around him, welcoming him into their world with a song that evokes waves of joy such as he has never experienced before. His voice is too crude for him to join in, but he can't help but dance along with his new companions.

As he does so the song changes, taking on new notes that hint at something darker. Their expressions shift from youthful delight to something more purposeful. The song takes on a new power and a new direction, towards somewhere he is fearful to go. The three teenagers are dancing closer now, surrounding him and almost touching. There is a feeling of entrapment and repression in the melody, and he is finding it hard to breathe. He tries to step away but his feet won't obey, and the music forces him onto his knees. He watches in horror as the dead twigs that lie around his legs turn into snakes, writhing and hissing with malign intent. Before he has time to react, the snakes burst into flame and there's a smell of burning wood and something else he fears might be flesh. Then there's the buzz of bees, loud and close.

He feels like he's about to be consumed when suddenly, without warning, the vision collapses and he's left kneeling alone in front of the coffin. He looks around, confused, but slowly the colours and the sounds and the smells of the sunny afternoon coalesce into the peace and tranquillity of the clearing, with the moss and lichen-covered tomb in front of him. The tension dissolves and his consciousness tentatively expands to once more embrace the seamless reality of his world. He tries to hold on to the fading memory of the tune he has just heard, but what fragments remain drift tantalisingly out of reach.

After a moment he gets to his feet and wanders along a path that winds out of the hollow and up the hill. At the top of the ridge another path runs along its crest. He turns left and after a few minutes the way opens out into a clearing at the end of the ridge. In the centre is a stone bench. Below, the trees give way to fern and bracken and then the grass of the valley floor, where he can see Dean and Pauline and Carol and Dillon cavorting by the lakeside.

The stone bench is obviously very old and has strange symbols carved into the centre of its low backrest. He looks back into the trees, but there is no hint of any danger lurking beneath. The bench looks inviting and Jack is becoming aware his body is fatigued, so he sits down. The bench commands an exceptional view. To the left, the spires of Westerford poke above the trees. Below is the lake, its mirror-like surface ruffled occasionally by the breeze. Beyond, the wooded sides of the Downs rise above the river, broken only by white chalk outcrops. To his right, a stream flows down another valley, and beyond that the woods rise sharply to the flat top of the iron-age fort and the jagged ruins of Abbey House just visible above the trees.

As he relaxes the full force of the drug returns. His body melts into the bench and once again he becomes the life force that surrounds him, only this time it emanates from the landscape itself in an intricate pattern of eddies and currents that tell of interwoven stories played out against an endless cycle of sunlight and water, growth and decay. Any conventional sense of past and future may have disappeared, but there is a strong sense of the moment as eternity, stretching into deep time; of layers of history imposed upon the soil and the rock that makes up this land, going back thousands of years. Mankind may only have been here for a heartbeat in the life of this earth, but has left its mark on everything Jack can see.

Sometime later, but still within the same timeless and eternal present, Jack makes his way down through the trees and the defensive ring of ferns and nettles to the others beside the lake.

'Hey! Wow, where've you been?' asks Dean.

'Flying with the angels!' shouts Carol, before Jack can reply.

'Dancing with the demons!' responds Dillon. 'Buzzing with the bees! Flying with the ... flies!' The two of them dissolve into giggles.

'Yeah, where have you been?' Pauline looks at Jack with a quizzical smile on her face.

'Wow, it was so far out.' But beyond uttering a few disconnected words like 'tomb' and 'singing', he finds it impossible to answer with any coherence.

The hour hands on their watches move on several notches and the landscape adopts a decidedly golden hue before the full force of the drug begins to wane and they start their re-entry through the layers of reality towards so-called normality. There is a chill in the air and they haven't eaten since breakfast, with the exception of the packets of crisps and peanuts that they'd bought in the pub. The boring practicalities of ordinary life are beginning to intrude.

'I'm starving,' says Pauline. 'Let's go – there's food at home.'

Pauline lives with her parents in one of the new houses on the edge of Riverdale, a small village that borders the park on the eastern side of Westerford. Getting there involves a walk around the lake and then along a path through the steadily darkening wood that eventually borders the gardens of the little estate.

The sun has almost set by the time they reach Pauline's back gate and she lets them in to the empty house. They collapse onto the sofas and chairs in the living room, all very modern with French doors that open out onto the patio and the garden and the park beyond. Pauline puts an album on the stereo, a state-of-the-art affair discreetly hidden behind wooden panels, and the familiar harmonies of Crosby, Stills and Nash fill the room. She disappears into the kitchen with Dean while Carol and Dillon snuggle up on the sofa and Jack loses himself to the music. They are all feeling decidedly mellow as the drug continues to wear off and their comfortable everyday selves slowly reconstruct around them.

Jack mulls over what he remembers of his encounter in the park. He wants to put it down to the acid, but it feels too complete – too whole – not to have had some sort of external reality. That said, much of what happened has already faded from memory: the tune, in particular, remains tantalisingly out of reach.

Just as the second track starts, Jack becomes aware that Dean is handing him a can of Carling Black Label and that Pauline has placed a large bowl of crisps and a plate overflowing with sandwiches on the low table in front of him. Both are quickly emptied and they settle back, hunger pangs forgotten for the moment, while Dillon rolls a joint.

'So what happened to you, back in the park?' Pauline asks. 'You disappeared for quite a while.'

The others look expectantly at Jack.

'I'm not really sure,' he hesitates. Perhaps the telling will bring it back. 'I saw this path winding up into the woods, and something made me follow it. I'm not sure what – just a hunch, I guess – and then I heard this singing. It was really beautiful and there was something haunting about it, like you get with the Stones' *Wild Horses*, or *California Dreamin'*, or Joni Mitchell, but just so much more, well, intense.'

He stops, grasping at the memory, but it remains just out of reach.

'And then these three teenagers appeared out of nowhere, two boys and a girl. It was like they came out of a hole in space, or something. There was this tomb, and it was them singing. They seemed really happy to see me, but then something changed and it was like they wanted something from me, something I couldn't give. It got quite intense, and then … well, then they just vanished, like nothing had happened. All that remained was the tombstone.'

Carol is looking at him wide-eyed.

'Yeah, it's really strange. It's like it was some weird fantasy dream that either never happened at all, or happened a long time ago to someone else entirely,' Jack glances around. He feels uncertain.

Dillon breaks the moment, handing him what remains of the joint. Jack takes it, and Dean laughs: 'Yeah, it was really strong acid, that.'

Jack looks at Dean. He wants to shrug it off, but he knows it meant something. Here and now's not the place to work it out, though, so he smiles: 'Yeah, it certainly was.'

Pauline gets up to change the record, putting on some sultry jazz: a soft syncopated rhythm punctuated by long drawn-out trumpet notes.

'Who's this?' Jack asks.

'Miles Davis,' Pauline replies. 'One of my Dad's.'

'It's really cool,' says Jack, settling back.

Carol and Dillon turn their attention back to each other until eventually, looking a little sheepish, they retreat upstairs. Dean takes the opportunity to grab the sofa and promptly falls asleep. It's now totally black outside, with just an occasional light breeze coming through the half-open patio doors.

Pauline looks over at Jack. 'That vision you had. Those teenagers.'

'Yeah?'

'Well, I'm not sure it means anything, but do you know anything about the history of Abbey House?'

'Not really. I mean, I know there was a fire, a couple of centuries back, but that's all. I guess it must have been pretty serious because there's hardly anything left. It's just bits of ruined walls.'

'Yeah, but I think there's more to it than that. I can't remember the details – I'm not sure I ever knew them – but I think there might have been some sort of scandal. Something got hushed up.'

'Wow. And the tomb that I saw. I mean, it's just across the valley from the ruins. I guess there could be some sort of connection. Might be worth a trip to the library, perhaps. But what are we talking about here? Are we talking about ghosts? Or some kind of resurrection? That would be pretty weird.'

Pauline grins. 'Yeah, I guess it would. But you know, I can't help wondering whether I would have seen them too, and heard the singing, if I'd been there with you. That would have been really freaky.'

'Yeah. I guess it's like Carlos Castaneda and his "special consensus", you know?' Jack smiles. 'It sure felt real, although that's not saying much. We're coming down now, but you know what it was like. That was pretty strong acid.'

'Yeah,' replied Pauline, 'but it would be freaky if there was something to it. Something that really happened, way back when.'

'Or maybe it was a manifestation of something inside me – something I can't face up to directly, for some reason, so I have to conjure up a vision to handle it. But it really did seem like they'd come into our world through some sort of hole in space, like a bubble, expanding until it burst.'

'Maybe it's not as clear cut as that.'

'How do you mean?'

'Well, it's like …' She looks at him, not sure how to put it. 'You know my dad's a psychologist?'

Jack nods.

'Yeah, well, he goes over to America sometimes, to these conferences. He went to one a few months back at Princeton University. It's in New Jersey, just south of New York.'

'Sounds cool.'

'Yeah, from what he says the campus is pretty amazing. Einstein had an office there. Anyway, he was telling me about this guy he got chatting with over drinks. They were talking about consciousness: like, what it is, and how it might have come about in the first place. This guy works with schizophrenics and people who hear voices in their heads telling them what to do. You know what I mean?'

'Yeah, I guess so.'

'It's all to do with what they call multiple personality disorder, which is like when there's more than one personality – more than one "me" – inside someone's head.'

'Wow. How does that happen?'

'It's thought that it happens after someone's been severely abused or traumatised during childhood, but they don't really know. The idea is that these people spin off a personality that experiences the trauma and pain directly, but allows them to spend the rest of their time safely isolated in another personality. There's usually two or three main personalities, but sometimes there are other less developed ones alongside. My dad's a bit of a specialist in the subject.'

She picks up the remains of a joint from the ashtray and lights it. 'Anyway, what's interesting is the relationship between these personalities. Usually there's no communication because, after all, that's the point. Each personality simply experiences gaps in their memory that they can't explain. But sometimes they do communicate with each other, which is where hearing voices in their heads comes in. Each personality experiences the other as being outside their head, like the voice of a demon or an angel.'

'Or the voice of God.'

'Quite.' Pauline takes a drag from the joint then, realising there's nothing left, stubs it out and continues: 'Sometimes the relationship can get quite complicated, like they're friends or siblings or something, even though it's all going on inside just the one head. Anyway, this guy my dad got chatting with, he has this idea that, well, that was what it was like for early man. You know, when they thought they were communicating with the gods or with spirits, in fact they were talking to themselves. Nowadays we recognise those "voices" in our head as our thoughts – or at least most of us do – but in those days it felt like they were coming from outside.'

'Wow. Yeah, it's like those teenagers I saw, dancing around the tomb and singing; what you're saying is that they might have come from some other part of my own head?'

'Yeah, and you said they kind of "popped in", like they came from another universe or something.'

'That's what it seemed like.'

'Yeah, and of course the acid would have made it all so much more real.'

'Wow. So has your dad ever taken acid?'

Pauline snorts. 'Don't think so! I'll have to ask him …'

Their laughter awakens Dean, who sits up and looks around quizzically as he stretches his limbs.

'God, this sofa is killing me.' He glances quizzically at Jack in the armchair opposite, and then over at Pauline with a grin. 'Perhaps we can find somewhere more comfortable?'

Pauline rolls her eyes at Jack as she helps Dean to his feet. 'Don't say that – Jack's got to sleep on it!' She looks sheepishly across. 'Don't believe what he says – it's actually really comfortable. There's a blanket in the drawer underneath. Just take off your shoes before you settle down.'

'That's great. Don't worry, I'll be fine.'

Pauline smiles and leans forward to plant a quick kiss on Jack's forehead. 'Thanks for being here. It was a pretty magical day.'

'Yes it was, wasn't it?' He looks at Dean, slightly embarrassed, but Dean smiles back and replies, 'Yes, it was something special.'

Alone in the living room, Jack mulls over the conversation with

Pauline. Something significant happened in that hollow, he's sure of it, but what's really nagging him is the vestiges of the melody still echoing in his mind, hauntingly beautiful but just out of reach and impossible to pin down. In the corner of the room stands an acoustic guitar, but by the time he's got it onto his lap what little he does remember has gone, leaving him pointlessly fumbling at the strings.

He puts the guitar down and settles back. He can feel the last remnants of the acid washing across his mind like waves on a receding tide, bringing the occasional tantalising fragment of music that disappears as soon as he realises it's there. This is the strongest acid he's ever taken. He's experienced the heightened sense of reality, the crystal-clear immediacy and the timeless moment before, but what happened in that hollow feels very different. He may be mistaken, but it really doesn't feel like it came from his inner being at all; it feels like it strayed fully formed into his world from somewhere else entirely.

# Three

Jack wakes the next morning to the sound of Pauline moving about in the kitchen. She waves at him when she realises he's awake and brings over a cup of tea before disappearing upstairs. He quickly gets up and then they're all downstairs tucking into a breakfast of bacon, eggs and toast. There's even mushrooms and fried tomato to spice it up, and freshly squeezed orange juice to wash it down. Once finished they settle back on the sofas.

'That was really great, Pauline, just what I needed.' says Jack, offering round his cigarettes.

'Too right.' says Carol. She leans forward and grabs two, one for herself and the other for Dillon.

'So, what are you going to get up to today?' asks Pauline.

Jack looks at Carol and Dillon, snuggled up on the sofa; and there's Pauline, perched on Dean's lap in the armchair, barefoot and dressed in not much more than a T-shirt. It's fairly obvious they're not going anywhere soon and he can't really blame them; after all, he'd be doing the same if Ania was here. It's not often you get uninterrupted use of a king-sized bed with a sumptuous mattress and crisp, clean sheets, and he is feeling very relaxed and even a little horny himself, despite a fitful sleep punctuated by snippets of music and fleeting visions of teenage faces. Even as he remembers his dreams the last remnants of the tune slips out of reach, leaving him with a faint yearning.

'I thought I might wander back through the park. Check out that tomb again. See if there's anything I missed.'

'Yeah,' says Dean. 'That was pretty weird.'

'Might drop in on Alex, too. I mean, he always seems to know about these kind of things.'

'Good idea.'

It's past midday by the time Jack gets his act together and steps through the French doors and into the park. He looks back wistfully at the house. If Ania had been here they would have spent the afternoon exploring each other in intimate detail before collapsing in a post-coital haze, but that is not to be. He starts down the narrow path through the trees. It's not a dense wood and it doesn't take him long to relax into the sunlight slanting through the leaves.

It takes him about twenty minutes to get to the lake. He walks around the edge with the hill rising sharply to his left up to the ruins of the abbey, hidden behind the trees. Eventually he turns onto the path that leads up the valley towards the park gate where they had entered just twenty-four hours earlier. He keeps his eye on the treeline to his left and it's not long before he spots the path that he must have taken, through the bracken and up beneath the branches. It looks quite ordinary now, with none of the magic it promised before, but it's definitely the right path so he follows it into the quiet, barren spaces beneath the boughs and up the hill until with a start he realises he is looking down into the exact same hollow, and there in a clearing at the bottom is what indeed looks like a tomb. Everything is calmer without the acid coursing through his brain, but there is still an air of anticipation as he approaches the lichen-covered block of stone.

It's much as he remembers it, except now he can examine it with a clear head he can see it has an ornately carved rim. He makes his way around to the other side, which he hasn't seen before. He moves the ivy aside and discovers a raised panel in the centre with a carved inscription. He pulls the lichen away until he can read the words, 'In loving memory of Daniel, Gabriel and Lucy'. His heart pumps loudly in his chest. Not only were they real, they had names. He stares at the inscription for some time, wondering what this could mean, and then slowly makes his way back down to the valley and up into the town. He needs to talk to Alex.

o0o

Alex and his family live at the end of a cul-de-sac just behind the High Street in the old part of town. Indeed, the compact three-storey building with its red brick walls and ancient wooden beams is one of the oldest in Westerford. Their house is filled with the trappings of their lifestyle: hookahs, candles, posters of Hindu deities, tiny silver spoons, rugs from Africa and India, ornate wooden carvings, tapestries, Japanese dragon kites, an expensive German hi-fi, a collection of tiny brass boxes, and lots and lots of books. In the attic room a dormer window looks out over the rooftops; on summer evenings Alex likes to sit cross-legged on the deep oak window seat like a dishevelled elven king surveying his kingdom. From here he can watch the sun set over the town and take in the day's goings on. He has studied the philosophies of the East and watches them unfold in the lives of his neighbours.

Jack was in his second year of sixth form when Dean introduced him to Alex and he instantly took to this well-travelled freak who seemed to know so much about so many things. He's not quite sure how Dean got to know Alex, although he suspects it's either that Dean supplies Alex with exotic substances, or the other way around. Either way, Jack soon established his own relationship and would drop round after school to share a joint and discuss ideas or listen to the latest rock or jazz.

The post-box red door to the little house opens on Jack's third knock to reveal Alex's familiar face, albeit a little more suntanned and weather-beaten than usual following a recent trip to Nepal. They walk through to the kitchen where Alex's wife Moira and their daughter Becky are busy baking biscuits.

Just as the attic is Alex's study and workshop, so the kitchen is Moira's domain. A solid oak work top, covered in cuts and stains and nearly two inches thick, runs the length of the outside wall, supported by a ramshackle row of assorted cabinets and broken only by a cast iron range and two large porcelain sinks. The section beneath the leaded window is clearly a kitchen in the conventional sense, scattered about with saucepans, plates and other implements for the preparation of food. The other end more resembles a laboratory with a pestle and mortar, precision scales, pipettes, a Bunsen burner and shelves laden with bottles of herbs and liquids of various shades. It is here Moira experiments with teas, perfumes and ointments, some of which she sells to specialist shops on the King's Road and in Kensington Market. As always, the smell is of wholesome cooking overlaid with something altogether more exotic.

'Uncool Jack, Uncool Jack! Hello, Uncool Jack,' shouts Becky, jumping up and down with the energy only a four-year-old can muster.

Jack squats down to bring his face to the same level as hers. 'That's right, it's Uncle Jack, but Uncool feels about right just now. How's my favourite young lady?'

Becky blushes and buries her face in her mother's dress. Moira smiles down at him, although her expression betrays concern. 'She's doing fine, aren't you Becky?' Becky responds with giggles. 'But what about you, Jack? You look a little out of sorts. Perhaps I should brew you something. I'll bring it up with a couple of Becky's biscuits.' She turns her attention to her daughter. 'How does that sound, Becky? Shall we give Uncool Jack some biscuits to cool him down?' Becky beams up at Jack and nods vigorously.

'Sounds perfect!' says Alex. He turns to Jack. 'Shall we go up?'

Jack smiles gratefully at Moira and winks at Becky before following Alex up the narrow wooden staircase into the attic. Alex takes his usual seat on one side of the low circular wooden table.

'Make yourself at home,' he says, indicating the armchair opposite. He nods towards the tin that lies open on a small mahogany side table, revealing a packet of Rizla papers and a small plastic bag. 'Feel free.'

Taking in Jack's expression for the first time, he asks: 'Are you OK? You look like you've seen a ghost.'

Jack laughs ruefully. 'Well, I guess that's not so far from the truth.'

Alex settles back as Jack gives him a brief description of his acid-fuelled encounter in the park, and his recent discovery. 'I don't have a clue what it all means, but it sure feels like it means something. I mean, there's got to be some link between what I saw and what's inscribed on that tomb.'

Alex sits silently for a moment and then leans forward. 'Well, it certainly sounds a bit more than your usual acid trip. It does sound like you made a connection with something, and that park's got real history going way back, before even the Romans.'

'Yeah, I know. Wasn't there a hill fort, or something like that?'

'That's right, long before the house was built, and that's pretty old in itself. If memory serves me right Abbey House was originally a monastery, but then it was shut down during the Reformation and ended up as a home for some prominent family. There was a fire around the middle of the 18th century which is why it's just ruins now.' He gets to his feet. 'Look, I think I might have a book about it – local history, you know the sort of thing. Give me a moment and I'll dig it out.'

He rummages through a bookcase, and after a few moments holds up a slim volume.

'Yes, here it is. It's even got a picture of Abbey House on the cover.'

He flips through the pages until he finds what he is looking for.

'OK, well, we're talking about 1720 or thereabouts. Westerford was a small village deep in the Kent countryside, about an eight-hour journey from London by horse-drawn carriage, which was the fastest way of getting around those days. What it says here is that Abbey House and the surrounding land was owned by the Walverton family. Randolph Walverton made a great deal of money working for the East India Company and is now busy cosying up to the aristocracy. He and his wife Georgina pretty well rule the roost, as far as the villagers are concerned. According to this they had three children: two boys, and the youngest a girl. Their names were Daniel, Gabriel and Lucy.'

'The names on the tombstone.'

'That's right. Anyway, it looks like Randolph wasn't much liked in the village. Apparently he was over-familiar with the younger daughters of the villagers; and he liked to appropriate sections of land for his own purposes and increase the rent on what remained.'

'I guess he could do pretty well what he liked.'

'That's right, but there was also talk of witchcraft. Anyway, some of the villagers decided they'd had enough and marched up the hill to Abbey House with torches and razed it to the ground. Turned out Randolph and Georgina were not at home, but the three teenagers were burnt alive. Probably not the intention, but that's what appears to have happened.'

'Sounds pretty nasty.'

'Yeah, it does seem a bit extreme, but we don't know what the book means by "witchcraft". I mean, they were still burning witches in those days. Anyway, afterwards it was all covered up. There wasn't a formal police service in those days, just a few watchmen who would have been villagers themselves. Might even have been involved. It doesn't say what happened to Randolph or his wife after, but the house was left in ruins and nature took over, leaving us with what's up there now.'

Alex holds the book out. 'Take a look. There's even a painting of Randolph and Georgina. She's a bit of a looker.'

Jack takes the book. The illustration is in black and white and shows a stern-looking, middle-aged gentleman with greying curled hair, with his arm around the waist of a younger woman wearing a floppy white bonnet and a white blouse low enough to show a hint of cleavage. They are posed in front of a wooded scene with a large house in the background.

'Abbey House, I assume?'

'I guess. That would make sense.'

'Not someone you'd want to mess with.'

'No, he does look a bit severe.'

Jack flips through the pages and then hands the book back to Alex. 'It doesn't say anything about the singing, though.'

There's a tap on the door and Moira enters bearing two cups of tea and a plate of biscuits, which she places on the table between them. The room is suffused with a heady aroma of cinnamon and fresh baking.

'Thanks, Moira, they smell delicious.' She smiles back at Jack and silently retreats. Alex continues to study the book. Jack picks up a biscuit, smells it and then pops it into his mouth.

'Mmm, that's pretty tasty.'

Alex smiles. 'Yeah, she does bake a mean biscuit. No, it doesn't say anything about singing, but it does say that Randolph might have been involved in a Hellfire Club, which is interesting.'

'A Hellfire Club? What's that?'

'They're something I've been researching recently. They were a bit like hippy gatherings, but restricted to the landed gentry and the people they trusted. I mean, the Georgians were fairly promiscuous, at least in comparison to the Victorians, but they still had to be careful. There was lots of speculation and scandal and the people involved had a lot to lose so it's difficult to find accurate reports, but they held these parties, usually in manor houses hidden discreetly in the countryside. There was sex and drugs, and they performed weird rituals. The only women invited were girls who took the role of "nuns" and were expected to run around in short white shifts and bare feet. It all got a bit kinky, as you can imagine. Like a medieval love-in.'

'Amazing to think they were doing such stuff back then.'

'Yeah, but if you think about it, Bacchanalian orgies go back into pre-history. And there's a lot of similarities between the libertines of the 18th century and flower power today. There's parallels with things like the Thursday Club with Prince Philip and friends: Christine Keeler and all that. Or Aleister Crowley and his Order of the Golden Dawn.'

'So what was going on?'

'Well, Francis Dashwood was a big name in Hellfire Clubs. They started around 1720 and carried on until the 1760s when they died out. Dashwood held some meetings at his home in West Wycombe, calling themselves the Order of the Friars of St Francis of Wycombe, and then he bought Medmenham Abbey, which is this really cool place down on the banks of the Thames. There's also the caves, which are known as the Hellfire Caves, and there's even an underground river called the Styx. You can visit them today – they're a tourist attraction.'

'And this is the right time for our Randolph to be involved?'

'Oh yes.'

Jack sits back and stares at Alex. 'God, this is really freaky. I mean, even the names are the same: Daniel, Gabriel and Lucy. That's what I saw: two boys and a girl, and the girl was wearing a white dress.'

'Yeah.' Alex looks appraisingly at Jack. 'Look, is it possible you might have already known about them? Maybe something you read years ago, or something somebody told you and it's been stuck in your subconscious all this time?'

Jack takes a sip of his tea. 'I don't think so. I mean, I guess it's possible, but I don't remember anything like that. And there's the singing. That was the most important bit.'

'What makes that so important? Tell me about it.'

'I can't get it out of my head – that's what so important. It was quite amazing, really. It was like a kind of intricate dance, the voices of the two boys weaving in and out below the voice of the girl. Her voice was so pure and clear, and the music got right into my head. At first it was just them singing to themselves, but then they noticed me and started weaving their voices around me like they were playing directly with my emotions, plucking them like harp strings. To start off with it was just astonishingly beautiful – the most beautiful music I've ever heard – but then it got edgy and dark. Frightening, like they wanted me to do something I didn't want to do.'

'But you can't remember the tunes?'

'No, and that's what's really weird. It's like they're on the tip of my tongue. I've tried working them out on the guitar. Sometimes I feel like I'm getting close, but then they just slip away.'

'There's nothing in the book about such things, except that vague mention of witchcraft.' Alex takes a sip of his tea. 'You know, while we were in India we did quite a bit with music. Are you familiar with Indian music?'

'I know Ravi Shankar. I've got one of his albums.'

'So you know how it goes. The ragas, and the way the instruments weave around each other, challenging and responding like they're in conversation. They call it *jugalbandi*, but it sounds like it's what your teenagers were doing in the park.'

'Yeah. Sometimes when I'm playing, and the band's really together, I feel like we're feeding lines back and forth. Like we're inspiring each other and challenging each other to take it further. It's like a conversation.'

'Exactly.' Alex places his cup on the table and relaxes back into his chair. 'You know, that mention of witchcraft must have come from somewhere.' He picks up the book and checks out the back cover. 'Yeah, the author is local. Might be worth you popping down to the library and seeing if they've got anything. Trevor, the chief librarian, he's always collecting stuff and he's very accommodating. I mean, you never know.'

'Yeah, that's a good idea. I remember Trevor from when I was a kid. I'll check it out tomorrow.'

'Good.' He looks across at Jack. 'You know the way you describe the teenagers appearing out of the space above the tomb? That's interesting too.'

'Yeah, it was like there was a bubble of "new space" immediately above the tomb, and they were in it. They kind of grew in size as the bubble expanded.'

'Mmm ... Are you familiar with the idea of the multiverse, of multiple universes that exist alongside this one, right here but invisible and inaccessible?'

'Sort of, I suppose.'

'Yeah, there's quite a few ideas out there. One idea is that everything you do, every choice you make, spawns a new universe, and which universe you inhabit depends on the choice you make, which means there's another universe that contains a version of you that made a different choice. In the bigger scheme of things your choices are irrelevant, because everything that is possible happens somewhere, in one universe or another. So there are universes where you never met Ania, or me. There are universes where you don't exist, and universes where you're a big pink rabbit surrounded by lots of lady rabbits.'

Jack laughs. 'Yeah, I think I know what you mean.' He leans forward, struck by an idea. 'In fact, it's a bit like that when I'm playing a guitar solo, particularly when there's an audience and I've got decent amps and a solid backing. It's like we're all flowing down a track. I'm in control, in that it's my fingers that are choosing the notes, but it's almost like they're preordained.'

'Well, in a sense they are, in that they're coming from a deeper part of your mind. Part of the reason you're such a shit-hot guitarist is that you don't get in the way – you let the riffs flow through from somewhere deep within you. Your conscious mind is almost a spectator.'

'Yeah, but sometimes it feels like I can sense a fork up ahead and I can choose which path to take, which direction to take the riff.'

'And at that point, according to the theory, the universe splits: both riffs get played, but which you hear depends on which universe you're in.'

'Wow. It's a pretty way-out theory.'

'Yes indeed.' Alex leans forward to finish his tea and then continues: 'There's also the stuff Carlos Castaneda writes about – the idea of a "special consensus", as in a special space you share with others because at some level you all agree it's real.'

'Yeah, and it did feel like I was being invited to share their own special space. I was talking about that with Pauline – you know, Dean's girlfriend. She was there – well, she wasn't with me when I saw the vision, but we were all tripping together and we talked about it later. She was wondering whether she would have seen the same thing if she had been there, with me. Whether it would have been a "special consensus" that we would have shared.'

'Good question.'

'Yeah.' Jack drinks down his tea. 'The thing is, I don't know what to do about it. All I've got is a sense of anticipation – like something's coming, or something's going to happen. And in some weird way it's all tied up with that riff.'

oOo

Westerford Library is in a large Victorian building that doubles as a museum. It sits on its own plot close to the river and the park, looking grandiose and surrounded by manicured lawn. Jack hasn't entered the place for many years, but he remembers with fondness the childhood ritual of Saturday afternoon visits with his parents. He continued to drop in after school well into his teens, until he became more interested in hanging out with his mates and talking about girls.

Jack gets to the library around eleven the following morning and is looking at the young woman behind the desk, wondering why he didn't think to bring his library card, when he hears a familiar voice.

'It's Jack, isn't it? Well, it's been quite a time since we've seen you in here.'

He turns to discover an elderly-looking gentleman, slightly dishevelled in a beige corduroy suit that is long past its prime.

'Oh, hi. Trevor, isn't it?'

'That's right, lad. Well remembered. Linda, this is Jack. He used to visit regularly when he was younger. So how are you doing these days, Jack? Found something more interesting to occupy your time?'

'Ah, well, yeah. Actually, I'm getting into the guitar. Playing in a band. Hope to make it up to London one day.'

'Well, good for you. And how are your parents?' Trevor turns to Linda: 'They used to bring him in every week, you know, when he was a kid.'

'Yeah, well, that was a long time ago. They're separated now. I'm living with my mother at the moment, but I'm hoping to move out soon.'

'Oh, I'm sorry to hear that. Anyway, what brings you in here again, after all this time?'

'Well, actually, I'm trying to find out about Abbey House; you know, the ruins in the park. I'm trying to find out what happened to it. It's for a … project.'

Thankfully Trevor doesn't enquire further. 'Interesting subject. Not sure what you'll find here, but I guess Local History is a good place to start.'

With a nod to Linda he leads Jack towards the appropriate shelf and leaves him to it. Scanning the titles Jack can see about six books that might be useful, including the volume that Alex had shown him. He takes them over to a nearby desk and starts leafing through. They all contain something about the house, and most contain a reference to the fire and the death of the three siblings. There are some interesting illustrations, including a colour print of that portrait of Randolph and his wife, but nothing he doesn't know already.

He puts the books back on the shelf and is about to give up when Trevor reappears carrying a tattered cardboard box that he dumps on the desk in front of Jack. Somebody has scribbled 'The Vicarage, April 1971' in pencil on the side.

'I probably shouldn't do this, but you might find something in here. There's a new vicar at Saint Catherine's and they were doing a spring-clean. They thought we might be interested in these, but I haven't had a chance to check them through yet.'

'Wow, thanks.'

Jack lifts the lid to reveal a muddled assortment of papers, notebooks and faded newspaper cuttings. He starts sifting through, examining each item and then putting it aside. Most of the cuttings cover events from the First or Second World War, but some are older. Eventually he finds a front page torn from something called the *Kentish Post*. Across the top is an elaborate banner showing what looks to be Canterbury Cathedral, and below that the text of the main story, set in two columns of type. With rising excitement Jack realises it is dated July 1721 and is illustrated by what looks like a woodcut of a burning mansion house. The story describes in detail the fire at Abbey House and the death of the three siblings. Randolph and his 'young wife' are described as 'distraught'. The fire was clearly arson and the arrest of the culprits is 'imminent'. There are calls for the 'harshest' of penalties, but what sends a shiver down his spine is a passing reference to the 'wondrous voices' of the victims who would on occasion sing to the local congregation during Sunday service.

With some trepidation Jack searches through the remaining items. Near the bottom he finds a number of tattered notebooks that look like diaries. They're labelled by year and progress from 1719 through to 1725. He takes out the one marked 1721 and starts leafing through the pages. Most of the entries are of baptisms, marriages and funerals, marked simply with the name and a brief comment, but some are more detailed. In March there is reference to a suggestion from Randolph Walverton that his children sing at the next Sunday service, a suggestion that the vicar clearly takes to be an instruction. However his expectations are exceeded, with a description of voices 'clear as the finest of bells ... their tones winding around each other in a manner that would transform us all to heaven ... we returned to the world of men in a state of bliss, having been borne high by their wondrous voices'. Later Jack finds mention of a 'swarthy gentleman' who acted as a guide or mentor to the teenage protégés. He thinks back to his conversation with Alex. Perhaps the 'swarthy gentleman' is Indian, someone Randolph met during his time with the East India Company.

As Jack works his way through the diary the story unfolds. Initially the vicar is delighted by their appearance every Sunday, but later entries describe a darker side to their singing, a suggestion of something that the vicar finds disturbing: 'I do fear the power of their voices. Usually it is a delight, opening the heart and the mind, but on occasion it hints at a darkness, nay even a devilry or a witchcraft.' It is evident that the villagers share his fears. One villager in particular, named Bartholomew, has already accused Randolph of stealing his land and of 'inappropriate' behaviour towards Elizabeth, his 'precocious' 12-year-old daughter. Eventually Bartholomew incites the villagers into a mob and leads them into the park bearing torches. They set fire to the house, believing it to be empty (at least that is how the vicar portrays it). Randolph and Georgina are indeed away, but the siblings die in the flames.

Jack checks through the remaining contents of the box but there is nothing else. In a daze he packs everything away and returns it to Trevor with a perfunctory 'Thanks'. Had he really seen their ghosts yesterday afternoon, dancing around their tomb in the sunlight? When he was younger he'd shared ghost stories with his friends, huddled together around a candle in a darkened room. He remembers Carol telling them how she'd seen her grandmother wandering around in the shadows at the foot of the staircase, only to discover next morning that she'd died that night peacefully at her home, over two hundred miles away. He'd gone along with it just for the fun of it, but he'd never really believed it. On the other hand, could his vision really be nothing more than an extraordinary coincidence?

He stumbles out into the sunlight, feeling as though he has just traversed two hundred and fifty years into an unfamiliar future.

# Four

It's Monday lunchtime and the college refectory is full of students eagerly queuing and trying to find vacant seats where they can catch up with the latest gossip before heading off to their afternoon sessions. The walls are bare and the floor uncarpeted so their shrieks, the clatter of their trays and the scraping of their chairs on the hard lino floor create an echoing cacophony. David takes a tray off the stack and joins the queue. He accepts the plate of sausage, beans and mash proffered by a bored-looking woman in a white apron and moves along. He gazes out over the crowd and eventually spots what he is looking for.

The clumsy fumbling of the woman at the till, the number of people ahead of him and the fact that Ania is sitting opposite one of the few remaining empty seats prompts him to grab a cup of tea, duck out of the queue and head over without paying. He has no doubt that it will work out just fine, as it always seems to, but his need is greater and all that.

'Excuse me, but is this seat free?'

Ania looks up from the book she is reading while dipping into her salad. A man is standing over her with a quizzical expression on his face. For a moment she feels annoyed at having to share, having just secured a window seat in a relatively quiet corner, but he does look a little forlorn so she puts down her book and flashes him a smile.

'Yeah, sure.'

He pulls out the chair opposite and sits down, taking the plate off the tray, which he props up against a table leg so it doesn't take up space on the table top. It promptly slides to the floor with a bang.

'Sorry.'

'That's all right. These tables are far too small, anyway.'

'So, what do you do here? I'm David, by the way.'

Resigned that she won't be catching up with her reading this lunchtime, Ania slips the book into her bag and holds out her hand.

'Ania. Pleased to meet you.'

'Ania? That's an unusual name,' David replies, as he limply shakes her hand.

She is annoyed at being interrupted, but it's in her nature to be friendly, and there's something about this guy that engenders sympathy. He looks harmless and seems somehow lost.

'Yes. My parents were both Polish. I'm studying art here. We're doing life drawing at the moment. What about you?'

'Life drawing – must be fascinating.' He indicates the pad poking out of the top of her bag: 'Is that your work? I'd love to see them.'

Ania shuffles on her seat. She very rarely shows her drawings to anyone outside the class itself, and particularly not random strangers she's just met. Even Jack's only seen them a few times, and knows not to look without asking. She studies David. He's thin and pale, and his hair is thin and blonde with a ginger tint. Looking more closely she notices scarring on the lower part of his neck, just visible above the collar of his polo neck sweater when he leans forward. She realises there is something familiar about him, as though she's seen him before, but only in passing. She wonders if he's coming on to her, but somehow that doesn't feel right.

Before she can think about it any further, she hands David the pad. He slowly leafs through.

'These are good.'

'Thanks, that's very kind.'

'No, I mean it. You've definitely got something.' He turns a few more pages and then twists the pad to face her. The drawing shows a portrait lightly sketched in pencil. 'This one in particular, it really captures something special.'

'That's Jack, my boyfriend.' It'd been early in their relationship and they'd sat long into the night, chatting as she sketched.

'Yes, I can see that it's been done with a lot of care – with a lot of love.' He examines the sketch carefully, angling it to catch the light from the window. He indicates the few pencil strokes that define the neck: 'Here, for example, you clearly demonstrate an understanding that less is more – that what you leave out is as important as what you put in. Have you studied any of the Chinese landscape artists yet?'

'Yes, we started on them this term.' She shifts in her seat. 'You seem to know quite a lot about this stuff. Do you draw yourself?'

He laughs in a depreciating manner and hands back the sketchpad: 'A long time ago. My father arranged tuition but I had no obvious talent.'

He holds her gaze and she finds herself relaxing. There's something about his eyes that fascinate her. She has an urge to grab a pencil and start sketching there and then, wanting to capture the intimate detail while she can. He breaks the spell before she can regain control.

"So … were you born in Poland?'

It takes her a moment to gather her wits. 'No. I was brought up in London. My family moved to Westerford a few weeks back so my brother could go to the grammar school.'

'Westerford? Well, that's a coincidence. A friend of mine has a place there, too. I spend a lot of time in London, just near Ladbroke Grove, but I'm visiting her later.'

'Ladbroke Grove?' Ania smiles. 'Lucky you. We used to have a place in Kensington, overlooked the Gardens. Westerford's a bit tame after that.'

'Yeah, I know what you mean. It's not quite the same as popping into Kensington Market for lunch, or spending an afternoon in the V&A, is it? But Westerford suits her for the time being.'

Ania laughs, relaxing into the conversation. Once again he holds her gaze in a fashion that should be disconcerting, but somehow reassures her.

'Look, I'm driving back there after this. Could I give you a lift?'

Ania hesitates. She's got work to do later and she hardly knows this guy, but somehow it seems right.

'Yes sure – in fact, why don't you come for tea. Jack usually calls round after I get back from college, so you could meet him, too.'

David sits back and smiles as they finish their lunch. She is indeed quite lovely and will make a worthy addition to his collection.

o0o

As is his custom, Jack arrives at Ania's house around five, which gives her time to sort herself out after a day at college. He's spent much of the afternoon wandering around town pondering the implications of his discoveries, and wondering what he should tell her. However, when she appears at the door she gives him a quick kiss and then drags him into the front room where he finds a tall, pale, fair-haired stranger smiling at him.

'Hi, you must be Jack. Ania's told me about you.'

Jack shakes the stranger's proffered hand. 'Yes, I guess I must be.'

'And this is David,' Ania says in response to Jack's quizzical glance. 'I met him at college today, while I was having lunch. He gave me a lift home.'

'Oh, right.' Jack turns towards David: 'So you live around here?'

'Sort of. My girlfriend has a place here with her sister. It's just a couple of rooms, but it's sufficient for our purposes.'

The front room is quite ordinary in comparison with the main living room with its expanse of south-facing windows looking out over the lawn. This room is smaller and darker with a large bay window obscured by the tall hedge that runs down the drive. It's not often used, so by unspoken consent it has become a living room for Ania where she can be with her friends with more privacy than she would get elsewhere in the house, but without the intimacy of her bedroom. The three of them sit on the comfortable brown corduroy sofas that take up the bulk of the room. Jack examines David more closely.

'You know, you look vaguely familiar.'

'Actually,' replies David, 'you might have seen us in the audience when you did that gig at the Scout Hut. We didn't stay long but I really wanted to see you play.'

'I knew it!' says Ania. 'I knew I'd seen you somewhere before. I just couldn't place it.'

'So what did you think of us?'

'I thought you were pretty good.'

'Thanks! It helps having a band like Black Knight behind you, and of course there's Carol.'

'Yeah, she's got quite a voice. I thought it was interesting, too, the way you handled those greasers. It could have got quite nasty, but you used your guitar like it was a weapon.'

'Yeah, I guess so.' Jack sips his beer. 'It does feel like that, at times. You know, when it's plugged into some decent amplification, just the sound of it has some power. And then, when you get into some riffs against a decent backing and a good audience it just takes off, like it's got a life of its own.'

'I know what you mean.'

'Yeah? Do you play yourself?'

'I do, although I'm more of a rhythm guitarist myself. I sing as well. Actually, we're putting together a band of our own, up in London. There's four of us at the moment. We're trying to explore what you can do with music. The extent of its power, like you said.'

'Wow, sounds great. With Black Knight we mostly stick to the old standards, like you heard. Once in a while I can get into a solo and let rip, but it's really about pleasing the crowd. We don't write our own stuff, or anything like that.'

'Well, you got to start somewhere. We're more into generating our own stuff, though; seeing where it takes us and going with the flow. Hit the right notes and it can really open up some energy. It's a powerful buzz.'

Ania looks at her watch. It's beginning to get dark outside. She hesitates, then stands up decisively.

'Look, I've got some work I really need to finish tonight. I should have done it over the weekend, but I was away. Why don't you two take it down the pub?'

'Sounds good?' says David, looking across at Jack.

'Yeah, why not? We can go down to the Griffin. It's not far and shouldn't be busy.'

'I know it, it's just round the corner from our place. In fact, perhaps I could make a call?'

'Yes of course,' says Ania, 'the phone's just in the hall.'

Once David's left the room Ania puts her hand on Jack's arm and leans up to kiss him on the cheek, whispering as she does so: 'Make sure you pop in before you go home. I want to hear all about it.'

oOo

It's dark outside and it's obviously rained at some point earlier: a brief shower, but enough to leave the pavements glinting as though paved with gold and the leaves of the trees sparkling in the light breeze. The amber street lighting brings magic and meaning to the scene, something the town planners failed to factor into their calculations, but it's a cheap, comfortable glow compared to the far older magic of the moon, bright in the clear sky above the dark silhouette of the woods that rise steeply from the opposite bank of the river.

Jack reaches into his jacket and pulls out a joint. 'It's not far but we've got time to smoke this.'

'Thanks, Jack,' David replies, 'but I don't use it myself. I find it gets in the way.'

'No problem, all the more for me.' He lights up, inhaling deeply as they walk along.

'So, how long have you been with Ania?'

'I don't know, just a few weeks I guess.'

'She's a pretty cool chick.'

'Yes, I know.'

'And talented, too. She showed me some of her drawings, when we met.'

'Really?' Jack glances across at David, disconcerted. 'So do you go to the college yourself?'

'Actually, no. I had a meeting with someone there, so it was just a coincidence.'

Jack's is about to ask more when David interrupts. 'Looks like we're here.' He holds open the door for Jack to enter.

The Griffin is one of the oldest buildings in town, constructed in 1621 if the plaque embedded into the lintel above the entrance is to be believed, and much of the original structure remains, evident in the uneven floor, the lack of right angles and the alarmingly warped and heavily woodwormed beams. Just walking from one side of the bar to the other is enough to make you feel drunk, even if you've had nothing stronger than a Babycham. It's relatively early on a Monday night so the place is almost empty, aside from some solitary regulars up by the bar. The soothing sounds of a Beach Boys track come from the jukebox as the two of them head towards the snug, which hosts the most private table in the place.

'So, what's your fancy?' asks Jack.

'I'll have whatever you're having.'

'Worthington it is then.' Jack goes to the bar to order and returns with two pints, which they sip. After a moment, and an appreciative glance over two girls just entering the pub, Jack turns to David: 'So, what about your girlfriend?'

'Faylin? Yeah, you'll meet her later. She said she'd pop in.'

'Surprised I've not seen you around?'

'Well, we don't spend a lot of time here. Our main place is up in town, Ladbroke Grove, just off Portobello Road. We have a fairly open relationship, if you know what I mean.'

'OK ...'

David glances at the girls, now sat at a table on the other side of the room. 'Chicks are like a hobby of mine. I like to keep a few on the go at any one time.'

'Not sure I could handle that. It's all I can do to keep up with Ania.'

'Yeah, it can get complicated, but that's part of the fun.'

Jack takes another sip of his beer as he mulls over what David has said. A couple of lads join the girls and the music changes to something more upbeat. David looks over at the jukebox: 'Moody Blues, I think?'

'Yeah, that's right,' says Jack. 'I like this one. *Ride My See-Saw* from *In Search of the Lost Chord*, if I'm not mistaken. It's a great album.'

'Yeah. Interesting title, too.'

'Yeah. Not sure what it means, though. It's funny but there's no track on the album with that name, and no mention of a lost chord anywhere on the album or on the sleeve.'

'One of those mysteries, then,' David grins. 'Unexplained.' He takes a sip of his beer. 'You know, you really should come up some time. Do some jamming with us, I mean. We've got some great gear and a soundproof room for practising. You'd fit right in, I know you would.'

'Sounds amazing, ' says Jack. 'Truth be told I'd really like to get out of this place; you know, move up to town properly.'

'And leave Ania behind?'

'No, she'd come with me. We've talked about it. She could get a place at one of the London colleges. There was talk about her signing on at the Slade before they moved down here.'

Jack is about to say more, but is distracted by a pale-looking girl with wispy red curls and a diaphanous white dress who has arrived at their table and placed her hand on David's shoulder. David gets up and kisses her proffered cheek lightly.

'Jack, this is Faylin. She sometimes sings with the band.'

Jack can't help but notice Faylin's demure manner, emphasised by the proprietary manner in which David's hand rests on her rump. She looks like a priceless vase, precious and beautiful, but ready to smash into a thousand pieces.

Jack realises he is staring. 'Hi, can I get you a drink?'

David answers for her: 'No, thank you. Actually, we need to go.'

'Oh, OK,' Jack stands.

'Look,' says David, 'if it's OK with you, perhaps I can pop round to Ania's in a few days time. We've got lots to talk about.'

Jack shakes his proffered hand in confirmation and watches them depart, David guiding Faylin through the door, and settles back to finish his pint. He thinks about David's offer and realises how much he wants it to happen: how much he wants to live in London, and in a place of his own. His father moved to Bayswater when his parents separated, and Jack does get up to town to see his dad, and for the odd gig when there's someone worth seeing. He's wandered round the market in Kensington and the music shops off Charing Cross Road, but at the moment he's living with his mother, Alice, in a flat in Westerford and, truth be told, they're driving each other crazy. He needs a place of his own. Knocking back the last few drops, he sets out on the road back to Ania's place.

oOo

He gets back to Ania's at about half past ten. The house looks quiet but there is a light in the hall so he gently taps the heavy brass knocker. After a moment he can see movement through the stained glass, and then Ania lets him in and leads him through to the main living room.

This is the heart of the house, the long room divided into three areas of companionable size, each with a sofa, two chairs and a table, upholstery the colour of a creamy coffee and delineated by ornate Persian rugs in pastel shades. During the day the room basks in the light that streams through the large French windows that run the length of the outside wall, the potted palms giving it a garden feel. But now the curtains are closed and just one of the standard lamps is on, creating a cosy oasis.

They sit together on the sofa, Jack in the centre and Ania at one end, her legs tucked up under a dark blue silk gown. She taps out a cigarette from the packet on the solid oak table, next to an ashtray carved from pale marble. She doesn't light it immediately but twirls it between her fingers. 'So, how did it go?'

'It was pretty cool. We talked about relationships and stuff.' Jack grins. 'He talked about being in an open relationship with Faylin. She's his girlfriend down here, but he's got other girls in London. He said he likes to have a few "on the go" at the same time.'

'And what did you say to that, Jack Weaver?'

'I said it sounded complicated. That I had a hard enough time keeping up with you.'

'Quite right.'

'I did meet her though.'

'What was she like?'

'She didn't say much – seemed shy, in fact. Under the spell of David.'

'Pretty?'

'Yeah, in a wispy sort of way, like a red-haired pixie. Quite sexy.'

Ania gives him a swift kick. 'Really?'

'Not my type,' Jack quickly responds.

'Just so long as you don't get any ideas.'

'Don't worry, I wouldn't dare. But what about you? How did you meet him?'

'He came up to me in the canteen at college, while I was having lunch. It was really crowded so I let him share my table.' She pauses. 'It seems strange when I think about it, but when he offered me a lift back to Westerford it just made sense.'

'You showed him your drawings. That's not like you.'

She lights her cigarette before answering: 'Yeah, well. He really liked them. He made some very perceptive comments.' She takes a drag. 'What about you, though? You haven't told me about your weekend.'

Jack tells her about the trip in the park and his vision of the teenagers.

'Wow.' Ania is looking at him wide-eyed. 'That sounds really scary. My poor dear! You must have been terrified.'

'Yeah, it did get pretty heavy. I didn't tell David about it because I haven't sorted it out in my own head yet, but we did talk about music. He plays guitar himself and he's even got a band of his own in London. He's invited me to come up and play with them, which would be really amazing. Sounds like they're a bit more experimental than Black Knight, which would be fun.'

'Double wow! Oh Jack, you've just got to do it. And in London, too. We could get a flat in Kensington. You might end up doing a gig at the Roundhouse ...'

Jack does some air guitar. '... or the Rainbow. Backing the Grateful Dead!'

'Ha, don't you laugh – you never know, it could come true.'

'Scary, though.'

'Yeah, but it would be like you always say; you just got to let the music flow through you. It's not you they're listening to, it's the music.'

Jack grins. 'Yeah, right. Still a bit scary though.'

Ania stubs her cigarette out and then leans back on the sofa, uncurling her legs and laying them across his lap. Jack absent-mindedly strokes her thigh where her gown has fallen open, but as he leans forward to kiss her his eyes are drawn to a sketchpad lying on the far side of the table, just inside the circle of light that surrounds them. Ania shuffles disconcertingly as he reaches out and picks it up. He examines the delicate pencil sketch of a young man on the open page.

'It's part of my project,' says Ania. 'Life drawing. At college.'

'It's quite something,' Jack says. He examines it closely. 'It does though ... well, it does look a lot like David?'

'What? No, it's not David.'

'Well, I can see a resemblance.'

Ania reaches out for the cigarette pack, changes her mind, and puts it back down.

'Well, it's not intended.'

'OK. It's really good, though. You should get a good grade, even if it does look a bit like David.'

He grins back. Ania remains silent. After a few moments she lowers one foot to the floor, causing her legs to part. Jack lets his fingers explore further.

'You're not wearing any knickers.'

'I was wondering when you'd notice.'

# Five

It's a couple of days later and he has just reached Ania's front door when he hears voices. He turns to see David and Faylin walking up the drive behind him, hand in hand.

'Hi there,' he says. 'That's good timing.'

Jack taps the door knocker loudly. A few moments later Ania appears, raising her eyebrows at the sight of the three of them standing there.

'Look who I met, coming up the drive,' says Jack. 'And this is Faylin – I think I've got that right?'

She glances mischievously at David before saying in a soft voice with a faintly Welsh accent: 'And you must be Ania. David's told me all about you.'

Ania leads them through the house to the living room at the back, and then through the French doors to the patio where there are wicker chairs and a glass-topped table. The sky is cloudless and it's surprisingly warm so the three of them sit and gaze out across the expansive lawn while Ania disappears inside to make some tea. It's quiet and secluded with the high box hedge giving no hint of the neighbouring houses, and three tall poplar trees casting long shadows across the grass.

Ania reappears with a tray which she sets down on the table before handing out the cups and saucers. They sit in silence, taking in the view, and then Faylin leans across to David, takes his hand and whispers into his ear. He listens with an indulgent smile and nods. Faylin giggles and turns to the others.

'Actually, there is something I should tell you, seeing as we're going to be friends. You see, truth is, I'm not Faylin.' She looks at Jack with a slightly sheepish expression. 'Faylin is my sister. My name is Evelyn. We're twins.'

Ania looks nonplussed; Jack is amazed. 'Wow, really? Shit! You look just like Faylin.'

'Almost identical, in fact. There's not many can tell us apart, except for David, of course.' She looks mischievously back at David. 'Or at least he thinks he can.'

'That's just extraordinary. So how are you different?'

'Oh, we have our differences, but you'd need to know us a lot better to find out.'

'That's true,' says David, who is still holding Evelyn's hand. 'It took me quite a time before I could be sure. For a while I thought she was having a joke at my expense – until I saw them both together.'

'That must have been weird,' says Ania.

'Yes,' David replies, 'particularly when I started wondering who had been who beforehand. Was the girl I met first Faylin, or was it Evelyn?'

'… and he still doesn't know for sure.'

'Wow,' says Jack, 'that's quite something.'

He smiles discreetly at Ania, who glares discreetly back, although he can tell she's equally intrigued.

Evelyn claps her hands together and declares: 'Well, now you know our secrets. Friends shouldn't have secrets, don't you agree?'

'One thing's for sure,' says David, 'there's no secrets between them. What one knows, so does the other. It's like they're telepathic.'

They settle back, relaxing into the chairs, Jack snatching an occasional glance at Evelyn. She really does look identical to the girl he met last night, and it's not just down to the wispy red hair and the white dress. He realises David is looking his way and offers a tentative smile. David winks back.

Jack turns David over in his mind, wondering how much he can trust him. He knows very little about him, except that he seems to have two identical girlfriends in Westerford and more up in town. There's something a bit spooky about him, but he is also charming in an eccentric and self-effacing sort of way. He's certainly captured Ania's interest, and he might well be able to help Jack understand what happened in the park.

'So, David, after what we talked about last night, I was just wondering whether you're cool about drugs? You seemed cool with me smoking a joint, but you said you don't use them yourself?'

'No. As I said, I find they get in the way, but I have taken drugs in the past. I don't have anything against them and they can do a lot to open your mind. LSD in particular, or any of the psychedelics like mescalin or magic mushroom, they can really open your "doors of perception" as Aldous Huxley put it so well.'

'So you've taken acid?'

'Oh yes. It was some time ago, but I've been known to turn on, tune in and drop out with the best of them.'

'Right.' Jack pauses for a moment, and then makes his decision. 'It's just that, well, I wonder if you've ever seen anything like I did last weekend.'

'What do you mean?'

'OK. Well, Ania was away and I was with some friends. We dropped a microdot each. Black microdot. Pretty strong stuff – a thousand mikes a time.' David nods, indicating he knows what Jack is talking about. 'Yeah, it was pretty amazing – blew those doors of perception right of their hinges.'

Jack glances at Ania, but she is smiling encouragement.

'However, there was this one bit. We were in the park, and I followed this path up into the trees, leaving the others behind. It was like I had no choice; something was telling me I had to follow this path. It wound up in a hollow, and then everything changed.'

'Go on,' says David. 'What happened in the hollow?'

'There was this slab of stone, like a tombstone, and this swirling space above it. And then out of the space appeared these, well, teenagers. And they were singing the most beautiful song I've ever heard. It was so beautiful, but I just can't remember how it goes. I've tried, but it's just out of reach.'

'And what happened then?'

'It was like they noticed me, and then they started dancing around me, and their singing got more intense, so intense I thought I was going to pass out, but then, at the last minute, it all just disappeared, like it never happened.'

'Sounds quite something.'

'Well, yeah, but what do you think was going on there?'

'Well, you mentioned some sort of tombstone – did you feel drawn to it?'

'Yeah, and it has writing on it, dedicating the tomb to Daniel, Gabriel and Lucy. The thing is … the thing is, I checked the library and it looks like they really existed, a couple of centuries back. And they were known for their singing.'

David exchanges a glance with Evelyn. 'So what was it about the singing?'

'Not sure, really. It was the tune that really got to me. I mean in many ways it was just like any other tune: wistful, dreamy, catchy. But it had some sort of hook that really got under my skin. OK, lots of songs can do that, but this was different. Much more powerful. Irresistible even. And it's right here, right now, in my head, but somehow I just can't quite catch the notes. I can't pin it down.'

'Sounds like the sort of thing we should be exploring with the band up in town. We've been looking to break out of the mould, find something new.' He glances over at Evelyn with a grin. 'Evelyn's in the band as well. She may not look it, but she's a shit-hot drummer.'

'Faylin's in the band, too.' Evelyn grins back at David. 'She's a shit-hot singer, and she does look it.'

'You should definitely come,' says David. 'Sounds like there's a lot of cool stuff we could get into.'

'Sounds good,' Jack says. 'Yeah, sounds really cool. But ...'

Jack really wants to bring the conversation back to the teenagers – who they were and why he saw them – but somehow they've moved on and the moment is lost.

'We'll get something together,' says David, 'next time we're up in town. Perhaps we can give you a ring?'

'Yeah, sure. I'll give you my number. It's my mother's place.' He scribbles it down on a scrap of paper.

'Thanks,' says David. 'We'll arrange something soon.'

'Speaking of cool,' says Ania, 'I heard Dillon's having one of his parties Saturday night? Everyone at college is talking about it. It's out at his parents' place near Riverside. They don't mind him doing pretty much what he wants when they're out of town. You used to need an invite but there were so many gatecrashers that he gave up on that. Nowadays, if you hear about it then you're in. Everyone goes!'

'Well,' says David, placing a hand on Evelyn's knee, 'in that case I guess we'll be there.' He stands up, holding out a hand for Evelyn. 'But I really think it's time for us to get off. You know how it is – things to do, places to be.'

Jack and Ania stand: 'Yeah, sure, but see you at the party?'

'Definitely, we'll be there.'

They watch, lost in thought, as David and Evelyn depart. They both feel like they're on the threshold of something new, but for Jack it's complicated because he can't help thinking there is much more to it than is being said, because it's not just about the music, despite the importance that has: it's also about the ghosts. They may be long dead and buried, but whoever Daniel, Gabriel and Lucy may have been all that time ago, they remain deeply involved in whatever's happening now, and he can't help thinking that David knows more than he's telling.

oOo

David and Faylin settle back into the pillows with a sigh. Once he's caught his breath David props himself up on an elbow and lays his hand in a proprietary fashion across her inner thigh.

'You do understand why this is important?'

She shifts uncertainly in response to his touch, but his hand remains where it is.

'Yes, I guess so …'

'Oh come on, Faylin. You saw him play that gig. You saw what he did with those greaser guys. He's got the power. We need him in the band. We need him on lead guitar, playing those notes in front of his friends. He'll do it right – better than I ever could – and he won't be able to help himself. It's the only way we'll get justice.'

She stays silent, but lets her finger trace the scar from where it starts at the base of his neck across his shoulder and down his chest to where it ends just below his armpit. David flinches. 'They will burn, just as they left us to burn.'

'And how does my seducing Jack help with that?'

'It'll drive a wedge between them and he'll come running because he has to. It's the only way he's going to get release. I mean, for him it's all about the music. There's nothing else.'

'And Ania? What about her? She seems nice. Basically a good person.'

'Yes, she is, and she'll come running to me for comfort once she sees him with you.' He leans towards her and touches her lips with his fingertip. 'Look, all you've got to do is get yourself to the party, get him in the mood and seduce him. Evelyn won't be around until tomorrow, so you can unleash the full Faylin in all her glory. He won't stand a chance.'

He reaches behind his head, fumbling across the surface of the bedside table until he finds what he's looking for. He presents her with a small phial containing a clear liquid tinged with a hint of yellow. She holds it up to the light.

'What's this stuff?'

'It's a mild hallucinogenic. Some guy gave it to me after I fixed him up with some chick from the squat. I thought it might enhance the evening. Make your job easier. I mean, you never know, you might enjoy yourself.'

Faylin looks up at him with a grin as she toys with the vial.

'I'm sure I will. I mean, he's not bad looking.'

'You'll have a great time.' He kisses her hard on the lips. 'And don't worry, you'll always be my favourite.' He bounds to his feet. 'But now it's time for me to get dressed.'

Once he's left she puts down the vial and reaches across the mattress to the ashtray where there's a half-smoked cigarette. She spots a box of matches that she can just about reach without getting up and lights up.

There's a couple of hours before she needs to be at the party so she picks up a back copy of *Oz* that's also just within reach and idly flicks through its pages, her mind on the task ahead. Her attention returns to the magazine when she realises what's on the page: a cartoon of an over-inflated girl with her pert nipples hanging out under the caption 'Jail Bait of the Month'. She laughs. Despite all the talk of free love and 'cunt power', this is what it comes down to: a bunch of sad old men fantasising about screwing a schoolgirl. Well, she'll show them what cunt power is really about.

She kicks aside the bedlinen, gets up and walks barefoot across the carpet to the small bedroom that they use as a dressing room. Her initial instinct is the wispy white dress that has become their signature garb, but she needs to make more of a statement this time. Folded at the bottom of the closet is a halter-neck dress in satin, knee-length, cut on the bias and weighing next to nothing. Emerald green in colour with a subtle flame motif, it was bought for her to fulfil the erotic fantasies of a well-heeled but short-lived boyfriend. She's always felt it too blatantly sexual to wear in public and David is not aware of its existence, but it's just the thing for the job in hand. She pulls it over her head and eases it down her body, the material shifting as it adapts to her shape and feeling delicious against her skin. She checks herself in the full-length mirror opposite, thrusting out her hip to gauge the effect and noting that her red hair is a perfect match.

Next come the shoes and here the pair bought by that same short-lived boyfriend, deep crimson with shiny three-inch heels and patent leather uppers, will do nicely. Then there's the scent, and it really has to be the Wild Musk that she bought from a stall on Portobello Road just a couple of weeks ago. It was ridiculously expensive, but once she'd lifted the stopper and breathed in its sensual animal fragrance she couldn't resist. She applies a couple of drops to the base of her throat, behind her ears, wrists and the backs of her knees. Satisfied by the effect, she grabs a jacket – the black tailored one with the maroon lining that she bought in a boutique in Soho – slings a shiny maroon leather purse over her shoulder and returns to the main room where she slips in David's phial, takes a quick look round to check everything is in order and exits the flat.

At first she totters on the unfamiliar heels, but her new-found confidence means she soon gets into her stride and by the time she reaches the Griffin, a few streets down, her gait feels perfectly natural. Inside she shows enough interest in a group of young dandies to persuade two of them to drive her to the party, only to abandon them as soon as they arrive. Pushing her way through the crowd she passes the kitchen where a huge bowl of punch sits in the centre of a large wooden table, surrounded by glasses for the guests. She discreetly empties the contents of the phial into the liquid, stirring it gently with the large wooden spoon placed there for the purpose, and fills a glass for herself. Taking a sip, and ignoring the surreptitious glances she is attracting from both sexes, she moves off in search of her prey. She's not quite sure who's driving, but right now she's enjoying the ride too much to care.

oOo

Jack hasn't seen Ania for the last few days as she's had a lot of college work to complete. She's phoned him to say she can't afford to be distracted, but is looking forward to seeing him at the party. Despite rising feelings of insecurity, he reasoned this was all part of being in a mature relationship and didn't kick up too much of a fuss. By the time Saturday evening comes round he's feeling pretty good so he throws a bomber jacket over his Black Sabbath T-shirt, pulls on his fake snakeskin boots and a pair of fairly clean jeans and, after checking that the door to the living room where Alice sits is firmly closed and his window is open, rolls a couple of joints from a quarter ounce of Black and White he scored from Dean a few weeks back – a lump of dark, pungent resin that he keeps for special occasions and which he was told is laced with opium. He slides the joints into the inside pocket of his jacket and sits back to await his ride.

Moments later he hears the buzz of the front doorbell and, being careful to close the window first, bounds down the stairs. He pops his head around the living room door for a quick 'See you later, Mum!', closes it before she has a chance to reply and exits the flat. Outside Martin is leaning against his prize possession, a mustard-coloured Cortina that looks considerably older than its years.

A few of Jack's friends have passed their driving test and are on occasion allowed to borrow their parents' car. Fewer still actually own a car, although in Martin's case there is some doubt as to his possession of a driving licence. He drives in a fashion that would be courting disaster without one, and Jack is pretty sure he can recall an occasion when Martin clearly stated he does have one, but he can't recall him ever taking lessons, despite them being friends since primary school. Regardless, as far as Jack knows Martin's never been asked to produce it, and there is a thrill of imminent death in the way Martin handles a winding country road, so he's happy to go along for the ride. As he hops in Martin hands him a half-full miniature of Bells. He swigs down the mouthful of whisky that remains and drops the empty bottle into the pile of rubbish beneath his feet. Reaching into his jacket he takes out a joint, lights it and hands it to Martin once they've pulled out into the road.

It's about a twenty-minute drive out of Westerford, around the park and then through Riverdale and down to Dillon's place. Martin drives at his usual hair-raising speed but by the time they get there night has fallen and the gravel drive at the front of the house is bathed in the warm orange light that is spilling from the downstairs windows. They can hear the music even before they get out of the car, and as they enter the hall they're blasted by the full force of the Kinks at top volume. They push their way through gyrating guests, drop their jackets in the study, which has become the cloakroom for the evening, and go in search of refreshment. The kitchen is quieter, or at least quiet enough to hear the animated chatter that surrounds them, and in the middle of the oak dining table sits a large wooden bowl, at least two feet in diameter and full of Dillon's infamous punch: a complex mix of fruit juice, wine, spirits and spices. They each fill a glass with the ladle provided, lift them to an undefined toast and down the contents in one.

For some minutes they talk inanely, their concentration elsewhere. Jack is wondering whether Ania's arrived yet, how she might be getting here and whether he should go in search of her. Martin is checking out the chicks and relieved to discover that none seem to recognise him. Spotting a potential prospect, he nods apologetically to Jack and moves off to try his luck.

Usually Jack would hang around to see what transpired, but instead he refills his glass and wanders back into the main room to check out the action. At one end is a huge stone fireplace, big enough to sit inside if it wasn't for the huge fire currently blazing there, adding its glow to the light of two chandeliers that hang down from high oak beams. For a while he stands on the sidelines, watching the dancers. He spies Carol and Dillon on the other side of the hall attempting a conversation, and there's Phil sharing a joint with Chris. He recognises many of the other guests but, as always with Dillon's parties, there is a sprinkling of new faces – most likely friends of Dillon down from London, or up from Hastings where he used to live.

Eventually accepting that Ania is not among them, he sets out across the dance floor, ducking and diving and occasionally stopping to exchange a few steps with anyone willing. As he goes he realises he is rather higher than he would expect after just one joint. He takes another swig from his glass, swilling the contents around his mouth before swallowing them down. Perhaps Dillon has added something extra special to the punch this time around. Whatever it may be, it is making him feel surprisingly good, as though the boundaries between himself and the outside world are becoming thinner, and he is becoming lighter. Could it be magic mushrooms? Either that, or some other psychedelic Dillon's got his hands on.

oOo

His first sight of the girl is in the snooker room. As he enters she is about to take a shot that could pot the last remaining ball in the corner hole. It is a tricky shot so she is stretched out across the table with just one patent leather toe in contact with the floor, seemingly oblivious of the attention she is attracting from the three guys she is playing with. He takes in the taut pale flesh of her back, the hem of her dress stretched tight across the top of her thighs and the swell of her breast crushed against the baize of the table.

There is a crack as the cue hits the ball, sending it bouncing off the cushion and back down the table. In one sleek motion she raises her body out of the way, allowing the ball to clip the side and rebound into the waiting pocket. She stands, sending her flaming hair cascading across her shoulders, and turns to face him.

'Hi, Jack,' she says, ignoring the stares of the other players, and he realises with a shock that she's one of the twins, although he has no idea which.

'Wow,' He stutters, 'that's amazing.' It's far from clear whether he means the shot or the transformation.

'Thanks,' she answers softly. 'David taught me how to play.'

She moves over to him, standing close and looking up at him with eyes bigger and softer than he remembers. He still has no idea whether she is Evelyn or Faylin.

'How are you doing?' she asks. 'Are you here with Ania?'

With a start he remembers Ania. 'She doesn't seem to be here yet. I came with Martin. He's got a Cortina so he gave me a lift. He's in the kitchen. Have you tried the punch? It's definitely got something in it ...'

She places a finger across his lips, and he realises he's babbling. 'Shush. Shall we find somewhere quieter?' She reaches into his jacket and extracts the remaining joint. 'Somewhere we can find out where this takes us?'

Without waiting for a reply she glides through the door and up the stairs that lead to the first floor. Jack mutely follows, transfixed by the sway of her hips as she deftly steps around the couples sitting on the steps, some talking, some sharing a joint, and, as they move higher and the light gets dimmer, some making out.

At the top of the stairs is a large, square landing with three doors, two shut and one slightly ajar. Taking his hand, the girl leads him over the threshold and into a room that would not be out of place in a French chateau. The walls are of white panelling, bordered with ornate gold mouldings and decorated in finely drawn tendrils that sprout a profusion of meticulously drawn flowers of every shape and colour. The ceiling is a deep maroon, crossed by wood beams painted with repeating red and white motifs. The floor is of wide oak planks partly covered by Persian rugs that are similarly decorated with intertwining stems and flowers. Against one wall is a king-sized four-poster, while the centre of the room is occupied by an elaborate chaise longue. Both the bed covers and the upholstery of the chaise longue are the same deep maroon as the ceiling, which perfectly complements the dark green of her dress and the red of her hair.

She escorts him across the room and twirls him around so he is standing with his back to the bed. She drops the joint onto the bedside table.

'I don't think we really need that, do you?' she says. 'Or this?'

Before he can answer she pulls his T-shirt out of his jeans and over his head. Her body is once again disturbingly close, her face just inches from his, and her smell intoxicating. He instinctively clasps her buttocks and then her lips are on his and he closes his eyes as she runs her fingers up his spine.

She loosens his belt and slips her fingers into his fly. Then she leans back and pushes him in the chest so that he falls back onto the bed. Before he can react she's clambered on top of him, and then he's inside her and she's riding him like a horse, her dress up around her waist and her body generating sensations far beyond anything he has ever experienced before. He can feel the drug coursing through his body and brain, heightening his perception until it seems the whole room is writhing with them. With a start, he realises that the tendrils of the carpet and the wall panels have worked free and are caressing their flesh like decorated snakes.

Just as Jack realises he's completely lost control of the situation, he becomes aware of a click and a gasp. Looking past her, he sees that the door to the room is now open wide and there, looking in from the outside world, stands Ania. The girl – whoever she may be – twists round to see what has caught his attention, leaving Ania in no doubt as to what is happening.

Jack cannot tell whether the expression on Ania's sweet face is one of disappointment, disgust or pity. But he can see that nothing can ever be the same between them again. He wants to explain, but he can't move, and there is nothing he could say that would change anything. All he can do is watch helplessly as David appears behind her, offering her consolation as she turns away.

'Oops!' says the girl, turning back to face him. She sits stationary for a moment and then she moves her groin in a way that makes it impossible for him not to climax. Once he's spent she leans forward to kiss him full and deep on the lips, and then, before he can react, steps off him and walks through the door without a backward glance. He cries out, but finds himself unable to move.

o0o

For a moment he feels surprisingly normal, considering the situation he appears to be in and the mix of drugs that appear to be coursing through his veins. He tries to rise from the bed but discovers that he really cannot move, although whether that is because he is paralysed or because he is bound to the bed he does not know. Then the moment passes and his brain is filled with the driving pulse of the music coming from the rooms below, the bed on which he is bound starts to rotate, the room fades from view and the mattress opens up, leaving Jack to sink into a rapidly accelerating whirlpool, held in place only by the weakening grip of the remaining tendrils and desperately flaying about for support. But there is nothing and he is losing himself into a whirling world, trying to hold on to what's left of his mind.

He frantically searches his memory for something that defines him and there in front of him, cast upon the wall of whirling white fluff like the flickering image of an old-fashioned movie, is the face of Ania as she was the last time she smiled at him – open and trusting. He tries to hold on to it, hoping it will lead him back to that fragile structure of thoughts and emotions he calls 'himself', but then the scene flips and the image dissolves into the face of Ania as he last saw it – shocked and disgusted as she turns away. He tries to reject what he sees but the more he pushes against it the more defined it becomes, because it is now fixed in time and there is nothing he can do to change that.

In desperation he tries to conjure up another image, another memory that can define him, but his mind is blank. Even memories of early childhood have faded to nothing. He feels as though he is drowning; that if he can't come up with something quick, he will be sucked down into a pit of oblivion. But then the world rotates and the face of Ania is replaced by the image of Faylin, or is it Evelyn, looking back scornfully as she exits the room to join Ania and David out in the real world, a world that he may never again share, and closes the door again behind her.

Now he is alone but outside, in the open air, and the bed is no longer a bed but a tombstone, and he is bound to the tombstone in Abbey Park, and the thumping beat of the music has changed into something more urgent, and around him dance shadowy figures that coalesce into the teenagers, the same three teenagers that were singing in the park, and he's back there but this time they do not vanish but continue to dance around him, singing that same impossible tune that seems so simple but nevertheless pierces his heart to the core with meaning and power, driving him towards some endgame that he cannot discern but is nonetheless terrifying.

The intensity is rising and behind the dancing figures he can see flames, and the flames are rising and the heat is beating on his body and he can't imagine how any of it can become any more intense, and yet it continues and he is trapped in the moment and there is nothing timeless about this moment: this is time, stretching ahead for eternity with each moment endured in the vain hope that the next might be different.

# *Six*

At some point during the nightmare he must have passed out, because the next thing he is aware of is the light of morning filtering through the curtains to reveal a bedroom that, although tastefully decorated, no longer looks like it belongs to a fairy queen. The house is quiet and seemingly empty as he creeps downstairs. On the ground floor he finds a few remaining guests, most slumped asleep or unconscious on various armchairs and sofas, or just lying on the carpet with their head propped up on a cushion, or another guest. Only Dillon shows any sign of life, lackadaisically waving a barely smouldering joint in his direction.

He can't remember how he made it from Dillon's place back home; he can only imagine he somehow walked the three or four miles that separate them. It's now three days later and he has barely left his room. His only human interaction has been discreet, but increasingly concerned, interruptions from his mother offering him cups of tea, plates of cheese on toast or bowls of cornflakes and milk. After his guitar, Jack's second most prized possession is the Decca record player that sits on his desk. When times were better and he had some spare cash he would wander up to Record Shack on the High Street to buy an LP or a couple of singles, and over the years he's built up quite a collection. For the past few days he has been concentrating on the more mournful records, which means Joni Mitchell, the Doors or the unworldly syncopations of Can's double album *Tago Mago*. Somehow the side-long tracks seem appropriate to his mood.

He wants to forget everything about that night. He can't deny the animal response the girl evoked. Just the sight of her bent over the snooker table, just the suggestion of forbidden pleasure, was enough for him to throw away all that mattered with Ania: not just the sex but all that intimacy, that trust, that life shared. So much for free love. Read *International Times*, flick through *Oz* or even check out some of the stories in the Sunday papers and it sounds like everyone's making out with whoever they fancy whenever they feel like it, and it's all OK. But it's not. He's heard nothing from Ania since that night, and he knows she would repulse any effort to contact her. He's disgusted with himself and he's missing her like hell.

The other thing on his mind is the music. Over the past few days he has tried to reproduce those tunes on his guitar, but although he occasionally hits a run that seems somewhere near the mark, he just can't get it right. He can still hear the voices of the three teenagers, the boys singing counterpart around the higher voice of the girl, but the actual notes remain beyond his grasp. It's as though it comes from a tradition that has little to do with the rock 'n' roll or the blues of his world.

The last notes of the final track on the final side of *Tago Mago* die away and he is just about to reach for his guitar once again when he hears the phone ringing in the hall. His mother picks it up, mutters inaudibly into the handset, and then he hears the pitter-patter of her slippers on the stairs. She taps discreetly on his bedroom door.

'I'm sorry to disturb, but Ania's mother is on the phone. I would put her off, but she sounds a bit upset. She'd really like to talk to you.'

Jack's heart sinks. He knew he'd have to deal with something like this eventually.

'OK, Mum, I'm coming.'

He quickly checks he looks presentable and then descends the narrow staircase past his mother, who is looking even more worried than usual. He picks up the phone.

'Hello, Mrs Polanski. It's Jack here.'

'Oh Jack, thank goodness! It's such a relief to get through to you. I found your number in Ania's room. I hope you don't mind me calling. Are you with her?'

Jack takes a deep breath as he tries to work out what he can say without causing further distress.

'Well, no. Last thing she said was that she's getting a bit behind on her college work, so I haven't seen her since the weekend. We were at Dillon's party. I assumed she was at home, working. You, know, working on her college ... work.'

'But that's just it, Jack. She told us she was going to spend some time in London with her sister, but I've just called Magda and she's not seen or heard from Ania since the previous weekend. I know she's an adult now. She has a right to a life of her own, but it's so unlike her to lie like that and then disappear, for three whole days! Do you have any idea where she could be? Has something happened between you? That would be such a shame.'

'Um, no ... everything's fine – well, obviously it's not fine, but really, I haven't seen her.'

'Do you have any idea where she might be?'

'Not really,' he says, but he realises that will only upset her and he has to say more: 'Look, Maria – it is Maria, isn't it?'

'Yes, that's right.'

'Well, it's a bit late now, but I promise I'll find out what's happened tomorrow. I'll start first thing in the morning and I'll get back to you as soon as I find out anything. Is that OK?'

'Oh Jack, that would be so useful. I wouldn't know where to start, and I don't want to go to the police, at least not just yet.'

'I'm sure it won't come to that.' He tries not to think what that could mean.

'Thank you, Jack. I'm sure you'll do your best.'

Jack mumbles something back and then replaces the phone. He looks at his mother for a moment, and then picks up the phone and dials. After a couple of rings someone picks up.

'Hello, is Dean there? It's Jack.'

'Hold on,' says a female voice that Jack recognises as Dean's mother. At least she sounds sober. 'I'll go and get him.'

A few moments later, and it's Dean: 'Hey dude! What's up?'

'Are you with Ania?'

'No. What makes you think that?'

'Nothing. It's just that, well, I've just had a call from her mum and it looks like no one's seen her since Dillon's party.'

'OK …'

'Look, could we meet up tomorrow? It's kinda urgent.'

'OK … How about Rosie's? Around ten?'

'Sounds fine.'

'See you there.'

Jack hangs up and turns to face his mother.

'What's going on, Jack? Is Ania OK? Look, I know something's wrong. You've been stuck in your room for three days, you've hardly had anything to eat and you've hardly said a word. I let you lead your own life, but this is a bit much.'

She looks like she's about to cry.

'I'm sorry, Mum. Look, I'm really sorry. Yeah, Ania and I are going through some problems at the moment, but I'm trying to work them out. You heard what I said to her mum, and I'll see Dean tomorrow. We'll sort it out, I promise.'

oOo

Rosie's Café is on the High Street, about ten minutes' walk from Jack's home. Truth be told, it's a bit of a dump with its cheap varnished pine tables and benches, enlivened only by the bright orange plastic curtains that adorn its windows. However, it is halfway between the girls' grammar school to the north and Westerford Grammar to the south, which makes it a popular place for sixth-formers to while away the afternoon once lessons have finished. Rosie is long gone but the current owners recently installed a jukebox, realising it would make them considerably more money than the cups of tea their young customers nurse for hours on end.

At this time of day the place is empty but for an old guy at the back who looks like a tramp. Dean has yet to arrive, so Jack takes one of the more private tables along the side and orders a cup of tea and a bacon sandwich from the waitress when she approaches. By the time Dean arrives he's polished off the sandwich and is beginning to feel a little more capable of facing the day.

'You look like shit,' says Dean as he takes the seat opposite.

'Can't say I feel that brilliant,' replies Jack with a rueful smile.

'So what's up?'

Jack fills Dean in on the events of the past few days, starting with their meeting David and ending with his seduction by Faylin, or Evelyn – he's still not sure which, and Ania discovering him in flagrante.

'Wow,' says Dean once he's finished, 'sounds like you've really blown it.'

'Yeah, it wasn't my finest hour.'

Dean beckons the waitress and requests a cup of tea. As she leaves, he fumbles a pack of Marlboro from his top pocket, taps out a fag and offers it to Jack, who accepts gratefully.

'Well, that's one way of putting it. What were you thinking? Well, I can imagine what you were thinking. She must have been quite something, but so's Ania and she's not some weird psycho twin chick with a hot line in silk.'

'All I know is that I was pretty drugged up. I don't know what it was, but it must have been a pretty way-out psychedelic. I don't know where it came from either. All I had was a couple of joints with Martin. Maybe it was in the punch, but I can't really see Dillon pulling something like that. After she went it was like a real acid bummer – I couldn't move, and it was like a full-blown rock concert in my head. That music, I don't know where it came from, but it was the same music that I heard in the park.'

'So what've you been doing since?'

'Nothing much. Just at home trying to put my head back together.

I've been trying to work out the music, but that's about all, and I haven't got anywhere with that either.' He takes a drag on his cigarette. 'It's driving my mum crazy.'

'I can imagine.'

'Yeah, and then Ania's mum rang last night to say she's gone missing. Looks like no one's seen her since the party. I told her I'd find out where she is, and I don't know what I'm going to do about that, either.'

'You told her you'd find out where she's gone?'

'Yeah. I had to really. Otherwise she was talking about going to the police, which would be a real bummer.'

'So she doesn't know you and Ania are no longer together?'

'I guess not, from what she said.'

'OK, look, you need to stop stressing out so we can think this through properly.' He takes a long drag on his cigarette and stares blankly in the direction of the waitress. 'So, the last time you saw her she was leaving the room with David. Is that right?'

'Yeah, but that was four days ago.'

'Mmm, but he might be a lead.' Dean takes a fag for himself and lights it from the tip of Jack's. 'OK. Look, can you describe that girl to me, the twin you shagged. What's she look like?'

'Well, she's quite striking, I guess. She's got really pale skin and frizzy ginger hair. Probably the same sort of age as Ania or Pauline.' He pauses for a moment. 'She's sort of wispy. Likes to wear white dresses, when she's not vamping it up in silk.'

'Still on your mind, I see?'

Jack grins ruefully. 'Yeah, I guess, but you should have seen her.'

'Mmm, maybe I have.' Dean gathers his thoughts. 'Yeah, you see there's this place I go to up in town, in Ladbroke Grove. It's where I sometimes score. It's a squat and there's a guy there who gets me some of the more exotic substances, if you know what I mean. Thing is, she sounds like she'd be hard to miss, and I've seen someone a bit like her wandering around. There's a guy that lives on the top floor of the squat with some sort of harem, and I think she might be part of that. What do you think?'

'Sounds possible. And that guy could be David. He's a pretty strange character and he does appear to have something going with both the twins. They've got a pad here in Westerford, but he told me they've got a place in London as well – in fact he told me it's in Ladbroke Grove. He's kind of strung out, with blonde hair.'

'Yeah, something like that.'

'Maybe it is him. He said they've got a band, him and the twins. They saw me play at the Scout Hut and they'd like me to jam with them, up in town, but right now I just need to find Ania. '

'Sounds like we could be in business then. And as it happens, I've got some business at the squat tomorrow night. Perhaps you should come with me?'

'Yeah, because as it happens, I'm meeting my dad in town tomorrow night. He's taking me for dinner at this place in Soho he likes. Perhaps we could meet after?'

'How about Notting Hill tube at ten? Could you make that? It's a bit late, but they usually let me crash at the squat and I'm sure they'd fit you in. How's that sound?'

'Sounds like a plan.'

They sit back, nursing their respective teas. Jack breaks the silence.

'So how are you doing? I was surprised not to see you and Pauline at Dillon's party. Everything OK?'

'We're … well we're kinda having some problems at the moment. You might have noticed. It's become a bit off and on. Truth be told, it's a lot more off than on these days. She's actually not around at the moment: she's with her grandfather who's losing his marbles. Not got long to go, and they were close.'

'Sorry to hear that.' Jack wants to ask more, but Dean changes the subject.

'Sounds like a bit of a weird one though, this David.'

'Yeah, but there's something about him. By the time we got to the pub I felt totally at ease with him, as though I'd known him for years. And I mean, those girls could have anyone they wanted, but they're clearly well into him. He does have a way about him, and he does know lots of interesting stuff. It's weird, you know, but when I got back to Ania's, after the pub, I discovered she'd sketched a kind of portrait of him. She tried to hide it, but it was clearly his face.' He looks down at the table. 'And now she's gone off with him.'

'And there's his band as well. What about that?'

'I don't know, but this music is driving me crazy. If they could help me get my head around it … well, that would be great. But you know there's so much stuff going on, what with that music, and the "ghosts" or whatever I saw in the park, and the twins, and Ania. I can't help feeling that I'm being played: that there's something bigger going on and I'm only seeing a small part of it.'

oOo

If he hadn't met Ania, Jack would have moved to London months ago, probably to share a flat with Dean somewhere cool like Kensington where he could shop in Kensington Market and watch the models going in and out of Biba; or Soho where he could hang out in Virgin Records. Since his parents' separation a couple of years back, Jack has been living with his mother Alice in a poky flat in Westerford, and that's not the most exciting of places: a so-called dormitory town where men don identical suits and leave identical homes just in time to catch the 7.20 cattle train that will herd them into Charing Cross station, leaving their neat little wives to look after their neat little children and make sure dinner is on the table when they walk back through their shiny front doors twelve hours later. It's all so straight and all so boring. Jack's ready for change.

Following the split, Jack's father Tom moved into a trendy flat in Bayswater with his girlfriend Annabelle, a tall, leggy Twiggy wannabe with blonde hair and a penchant for miniskirts. She's only twelve years older than Jack and over a decade younger than Alice, so Jack tries to avoid interaction wherever possible. Tom works in one of the many creative design companies that have sprung up around Soho to cater for the tastes of the nouveau riche. However, he does make a point of taking his son out for a meal, and sometimes even a film, on a regular basis, which is why Jack is idly gazing out of the window of a late afternoon train that is scheduled to pull into Charing Cross in about twenty minutes' time.

He glances around the near-empty carriage, before picking up a newspaper someone has left on the seat opposite. On the front page is a story about the Vietnam War and a map showing a portion of northern Vietnam. Curiosity aroused, he peers at the map; towards the bottom the positions of the American troops are marked, and near the top are dots representing the suspected location of Soviet personnel. According to the scale they are less than fifty miles apart.

A shiver runs down his spine as he realises just how close American soldiers are to directly confronting Russian soldiers, and where that could lead. He flashes back to a time when he was about twelve and he was standing with his mother in the bathroom of their old home. She was drying his hair as they looked out at a spectacular orange sunset. He remembers her explaining it was caused by the French nuclear tests in the Pacific Ocean that had thrown up all this dust high into the atmosphere where the winds had carried it halfway around the world until here it was, in the atmosphere above Westerford, filtering the light into beautiful sunsets.

A few years back, when his parents were still playing happy families and his father had started earning serious money, they had taken a summer holiday in Yugoslavia. They were pretty well the only Europeans at the resort, but there had been a number of Russian families staying in the same hotel. His father had got into a loud and drunken argument with one of the parents in the restaurant, which had been embarrassing, but later Jack got to know some of their sons and daughters, sharing vodka and even the occasional joint around a bonfire on the beach late into the night. They seemed like good people, as fascinated by his life in the west as he was by theirs. They valued freedom and the right to lead decent lives as much as he did. They certainly didn't deserve to be evaporated in a nuclear firestorm.

Of course it isn't his parent's fault, the Cold War and nuclear weapons hidden in bunkers, ready to put an end to it all with just a three-minute warning. But it isn't like they're saying, 'This is the way it is, and this is how you handle it.' All their generation can say is, 'This is the way it is, and you've got to find your own way of handling it.' His parents were brought up in a war where a single bomb could destroy a house, not a whole city. They don't have the answers, any more than he does. But Christ, if you've only got three minutes, what are you supposed to do? Sit around with cups of tea and talk about whose fault it is, or go out in a blaze of sex and drugs and rock 'n' roll?

He thinks about the three-minute warning. Someone once told him the radio stations have tapes ready to play when the warning comes. Three minutes: no time to do anything really. What would they play? Something straight like the national anthem probably, although *Land of Hope and Glory* might be cool if only because so pointless. Or perhaps it should be something apocalyptic, like *The End* by The Doors. The last thing we'll hear, as we scurry about like rats, seeking shelter under a kitchen table or in a toilet, just before we are incinerated, will be Jim Morrison's scream.

o0o

It is the middle of the rush hour by the time Jack exits the station and he's going against the flow of besuited gentlemen intent on catching the 6.15 back to their cosy suburban lives. These are the straights, those who've never experienced a world beyond the materialistic dream they flounder through, whose idea of getting high is a few pints down the pub followed by a half-hearted grope of their bored wives before they slip into unconsciousness. He could escape the worst by catching the tube up to

Leicester Square and walking to the restaurant from there, but he's feeling on edge and could do with something to dispel thoughts of Armageddon.

Crowd-surfing is a sport he and Dean have honed to perfection, and this crowd is just about perfect. He focuses his mind on the here and now and relaxes so his reflexes can operate unhindered. Slipstreaming into the flow he sidesteps a portly gentleman decked out in grey flannel, slips past another in a sharp pinstripe and deftly dodges a young lady in a brightly coloured dress. He is rewarded by a smile but he's already moving on, slipping and sliding across the Strand and along the side of St Martin-in-the-Fields and Trafalgar Square like a salmon up a Highland stream. If his life is going to be cut short by a nuclear holocaust then he might as well live every moment to the full, and fuck the straights around him with their smug faces and frowns of disapproval. He catches the eye of a tall freak striding towards him in high-heeled snakeskins and faded denim, long black hair tied in a red bandana and looking like he's just returned from Woodstock; he fancies a flash of recognition passes between them.

Jack ducks and dives up Charing Cross Road, past the Garrick Theatre and the entrance to Cecil Court, which houses the bookshop where he bought his tarot cards and his copy of the *I Ching*. He resists the urge to duck in for a quick browse and instead continues north until he reaches the side street that houses his father's favourite Italian.

The restaurant is a caricature of what an Italian restaurant should be, complete with red and white checked table clothes, raffia-wrapped flasks of wine and faded pictures of fading film stars on the walls, but there is a large pizza oven in the corner and it is the real thing, producing the best pizzas Jack has ever tasted. His father, already seated at his favourite table by the window, stands as he comes in and insists on giving Jack a somewhat embarrassing hug. To Jack's eyes he looks tired and there is already a half-finished glass of red wine on the table in front of him.

'So, how are you doing? And how's your mother?' Tom pauses, but not long enough for Jack to reply. 'Anyway, sit down, have some wine. This one is really quite decent.'

He pours a glass for Jack. The two of them take their seats and Jack takes a sip while Tom looks on expectantly. Yes, it really is quite decent, and he is relieved to see the bottle is more than half full, suggesting his father is still on his first glass.

'OK, I'm doing OK, and so's Mum.'

'Annabelle sends her love.'

'OK.'

'And what about that girlfriend of yours? Ania, isn't it? When am I going to meet her?'

Despite himself, Jack relaxes. His dad's only trying to be friendly, and he's really not such a bad dad if you ignore his philandering. At least he keeps in touch, unlike Dean's father who disappeared when he was just a toddler, something Dean hasn't talked about for years.

'She's fine, too. Perhaps I'll bring her up to town, one of these days.'

'That would be nice. Alice tells me she's quite lovely.'

Jack wonders how that conversation went. His parents do occasionally manage a civilised interchange, although usually only for a few minutes before the sarcasm and the innuendos start.

What neither of his parents know, and can never know, is what Jack saw back then, while they were still playing happy families. They'd had a cleaner, a pretty girl in her mid twenties with pale skin and long black hair. It had been a hot summer so she'd taken to wearing denim cut-offs and loose cotton singlets. Jack was about twelve and couldn't help but look. And then one day he had peeked through a bedroom door and seen her bent over the bed, cut-offs round her ankles and his father's hands on her buttocks. He's never told anyone what he saw.

Thankfully he's rescued from such thoughts by a waiter refilling their glasses and asking if they're ready to order. They consider the enormous menus that are de rigueur in such restaurants.

'What do you think?' Tom asks. 'I think I'm going to go for the bolognese. It's usually pretty good here.'

'Mmm,' says Jack, contemplating the list. 'I like the sound of the pizza capricciosa, myself.'

'The full Monty, eh? And why not!'

'Yeah,' replies Jack, as the waiter departs with their order. 'So what's a "full Monty" when it's at home?'

'You've never heard the phrase? It comes from the war, I think. Monty as in Field Marshall Montgomery. It means "the whole lot" or "with everything thrown in", although I've got no idea what that's got to do with the Field Marshall.'

They laugh. One thing Jack does share with his dad is his sense of humour. Despite everything, Tom's always been able to make Jack laugh.

'So,' says Tom, 'have you thought any more about what we talked about last time? About university?'

Jack thinks carefully before answering. For the past few years his dad's paid him a monthly allowance. It started as pocket money, but formalised into a regular standing order when his parents separated. The implication is that it will cease once he gets either a 'proper job' or a university grant. The problem is that 'professional musician' doesn't necessarily count as a proper job, or at least not until it's earning him serious money.

That said, both his parents have encouraged him to play from a young age, and both seem to recognise that he does have talent.

'Yes, I have. I thought I might try one of the London universities, but at the moment it really looks like the music side's opening up. I've been approached by a band in Ladbroke Grove that's got some real potential. They're much more experimental, and I'd really like to see where it takes me.'

Tom takes a sip of wine before answering. 'Actually, Alice does tell me that you're doing great things on the guitar, and there certainly does seem to be money to be made. We often watch *Top of the Pops*, and there's that new one just started, *The Old Grey Whistle Test* I think it's called? Annabelle is more of a Beatles person, but I really like what the Stones are doing.' He puts the glass down. 'Perhaps we should come and see you play one of these days? Annabelle and I?'

Jack grins back. It's a small price to pay.

They are interrupted by the waiter, who places two enormous plates in front of them, tops up their glasses and disappears in a faintly obsequious fashion. They contemplate the food.

His father laughs. 'Well, I think you made a pretty good choice.'

'Yeah, it does look good.' says Jack.

Food has always been something of a ritual for Tom so they eat in silence, except for occasional appreciative mumblings. Once finished, they relax into their chairs and Jack's thoughts slip back to the newspaper he was reading on the train.

'While I was on the train I came across an article in a newspaper about the Vietnam War. It seemed quite scary. It had a map showing how close the American troops are to where they think the Russians are. It made me think. I mean, I know it's thousands of miles away, and it's not got much to do with us, but what happens when Americans start actually fighting Russians directly? I mean face to face? Isn't that pretty serious?'

Tom looks at Jack as though working out what he, as a father, should say. 'I guess it would be,' he eventually replies. 'It's a war I don't think the Americans can win. I just hope they realise that sooner rather than later.'

'I just think it's so stupid,' says Jack. 'I mean, we're talking about countries that have got nuclear bombs. And America's actually used theirs.'

'Hiroshima was terrible, but it did end the Second World War. The

Japanese wouldn't have surrendered without it. They would have fought on to the death, and that would have meant even more people dying.' He stops, seeing the expression on Jack's face. 'I'm not saying it's right – I'm just saying it's complicated.'

'I just think it's wrong – all war is wrong, and stupid!' Even Jack is surprised at the strength of his response.

Tom contemplates Jack before replying. 'Not all war is stupid, Jack. I mean, you can say that because you never lived through what your mother and I had to live through when we were your age. Hitler was evil; we had no choice but to fight him. If we hadn't, he would have destroyed everything worth having. I'm sorry, but you don't know how lucky you are.'

Jack looks at his dad for a moment and then relaxes: 'No, I guess not.'

'Anyway, enough of that. Have I told you about our new contract? It just came through on Monday, and it looks good.'

Jack's expressions of interest as his dad enthuses over the details are not entirely feigned. Despite the minefields strewn across its surface, their relationship is still something they both value, and the chocolate sundae that he ordered for dessert is proving to be particularly tasty.

oOo

Jack says goodbye to his father at around half past nine and makes his way to Tottenham Court tube from where he can catch the Central line to Notting Hill. It's six stops so the journey itself will take ten minutes or so, but he could be waiting twenty minutes for a train at this time of night.

Notting Hill is not unknown to Jack, but it's ten by the time he gets there and he's happy to see Dean waiting on the pavement outside, hugging himself against the chill night air and smoking a fag. He offers one to Jack and they set off, across the wide main road and up a number of side streets, near-empty except for the occasional raucous crowd outside a pub. About twenty minutes later they arrive at a set of steps running up to an imposing portico entrance halfway down a quiet street.

'This is it,' says Dean, using the big brass knocker to knock a complicated pattern on the black wooden door. Silence, then muffled footsteps and the sound of bolts being drawn back: not just one or two, but three. The door opens and David is standing there, looking like he's just got out of bed in a white cotton T-shirt and hastily pulled on jeans, neither of which look like they've been washed for some time. For a moment he just stares at Jack, looking confused.

'Hello, Jack, I wasn't expecting to see you.'

'Kingpin's expecting me,' says Dean.

'I guess you'd better come in then,' replies David, his eyes still on Jack.

Inside the whole corridor is painted black, lit dimly by a bare bulb that hangs from an elaborate ceiling rose. Underfoot are wooden floorboards worn grey with age.

David turns his attention to Dean: 'Kingpin's still holding shop. I guess you know where to go.'

Dean says to Jack: 'I'll see you in a bit.' He indicates David: 'Good luck.'

With that he disappears into one of the downstairs rooms, leaving Jack and David alone in the hallway. Jack breaks the silence.

'So where's Ania? Is she here? Is she with you?'

David sighs. 'I guess you'd better come up.'

He leads the way up three flights of stairs and then a final narrow staircase that brings them to a long attic room that stretches the width of the house. There's a couple of Persian carpets covering the floorboards and Indian scarves draped across the dormer windows. Much of the floor is covered in thin mattresses and crumpled sheets. There's at least two bodies lying there, but no sign of Ania. There is a strong smell of grass and stale sweat.

'So where is she? The last time I saw her she was with you. Did she come here?'

At the sound of Jack's voice the bodies stir to reveal two girls, probably in their early twenties and clad in pale T-shirts. David signals the stairs and they scuttle off, leaving Jack to confront David.

'What's going on?'

'Yeah, we did come here, after the party. She was really upset, you know. Distraught. She needed my help to get her through it.'

'Yeah, well.' Jack sighs as his anger turn into guilt. 'Yeah, I was pretty stupid. But that girl – Faylin, or Evelyn, or whatever her name is – she was just, well …'

'Faylin is a unique spirit. If she wants something she usually gets it. But that doesn't really make any difference, does it.'

'No, but look, everyone's really worried. I'm just trying to help. I've got Ania's mother phoning me wondering where she is, and I said I'd find her. So if she's not here now, where is she?'

David sniffs.

'Something happened here, didn't it?' Jack glares at him.

'She's only just left. She left this afternoon.'

'So where is she now?'

'I … Well, I don't know. I did my best. I offered to help, but in the end she turned me down. Some people are like that.'

In Jack's eyes he looks shifty.

'I think you better tell me exactly what happened. Did you hurt her?'

'No. Nothing like that. Come on, you know me better than that.'

'Do I?'

'Look, I really was only trying to help, but in the end …'

'So she left.'

'Yeah.'

'And you don't know where she went.'

'No.'

'Brilliant.'

Jack looks at David for a moment, and then turns away.

'I'm going to find Dean.'

o0o

He takes one last look around the attic before stumbling down the narrow stairs to the second-floor landing. As he looks around for the main staircase, a door opens and one of the girls who had been in the attic appears. Jack is confronted with a pale, elven face framed by a sharp Mary Quant bob of black hair and a beaming smile. She holds out her hand.

'Hi, I'm Gina.'

He takes Gina's hand and gives it a shake.

'And I'm Jack.'

'Don't mind David, he can be a real idiot at times. Are you … looking for someone?'

'Well, yeah. I'm looking for Dean. I came here with Dean.'

'Cool. He's probably downstairs with Kingpin. Follow me.'

She sets off down the stairs, Jack following close behind. Once they reach the hall on the ground floor she indicates Jack should wait and then taps on the door Dean had disappeared through. It opens, there's a muttering of voices and a moment later Dean appears. He nods at Jack.

'I see you've met Gina. How did it go with David?'

'Not good. She's been here, but we've just missed her. He won't say exactly what happened, but she left this afternoon and he doesn't know where she's gone.'

'Shit.'

Gina looks at them both. 'What's going on?'

Dean turns to Gina. 'It's Jack's … well, it's his girlfriend, Ania. He kinda messed things up and David stepped in and brought her back here. Faylin was involved, you know, the twin.'

'Yeah,' says Gina, 'I met Ania. She was here a few nights. Cool chick.' She looks at Jack. 'She was pretty upset, though.'

Jack looks at the floor. 'Yeah, I know, I was stupid, really stupid, but I'm trying to find her; we're both just trying to find her.'

'I'm sure she's OK,' she says, 'But it's pretty late so there's not much we can do about it now. Look, I'm sure it'll be fine if you crash out in the living room, Kingpin will understand, and then we can sort it out in the morning.'

She leads them to another door further down the hall. The room is large with a dishevelled three-piece at one end and a mattress on the floor behind it. It's covered in a blanket and a sheet and Jack is dead tired, so he smiles gratefully. He wonders whether he's going to be sharing, but then Gina takes Dean's hand and leads him away. Jack is too worn out to think about it so he quickly strips to his underwear and pulls the sheet and the threadbare woollen blanket over him. His last thought as he slips into sleep is not of Ania, or David, or Gina, or Dean. It is that, for the first time in his life, he is sleeping on the floor of a squat in Notting Hill. How cool is that?

# *Seven*

The next morning Jack is wakened by someone shaking his shoulder with one hand and holding a teacup in the other. The sun is shining brightly through the lace curtains that cover the large sash window and Gina is wearing the shortest mini dress he has ever seen.

'Come on, wake up sleepy head.'

'Oh, hi. What's the time?' He takes the tea and scrabbles around for his watch.

'It's about ten, I think. Bathroom's upstairs on the next landing. Someone's doing some washing in the bath, but the sink's OK if you don't mind cold water and there was a bar of soap last time I looked. I'm going outside for a fag. I'll be on the doorstep.'

With that she bounces out of the room. Jack stares after her in a daze, shakes himself and pulls on his jeans. Once he's splashed some soap and water under his arms and got his shirt and jacket on he makes his way to the front door. Even the black paint of the corridor looks more inviting thanks to the splashes of red, white and blue light that filter through the stained glass fanlight above the door. There are three bolts on the door: one buried under decades of paint, and the other two looking as if they were installed fairly recently. There's also a three-foot length of scaffolding pole propped up in the corner within easy reach. Jack opens the door.

Gina is sunning herself on the top step, looking out between the two white Grecian-style pillars that flank the portico. The muffled sound of drumming can be heard coming from a window a few doors down. She waves a greeting at an old woman passing on the other side of the road, and then turns to Jack.

'Hello, stranger. Here, have a cigarette. There's nothing better than the first fag of the day.'

'Thanks, and thanks for the tea. So where's Dean?'

'He's just finishing up some stuff with Kingpin. You know what he's like. He'll be out in a minute.'

'Oh, right.'

He takes a light from the cheap plastic lighter she holds out to him.

He's got no idea what Gina's relationship with Dean actually is, or how much she got to know Ania in the few days she stayed here, but she seems like a good person, if a little distracting. He's trying to work out his best approach when the door opens and there stands Dean carrying a rucksack he didn't have the night before. Gina looks up at him with a big grin.

'Hi there, lover boy.'

'Careful now, you'll shock Jack.'

'Oh, I'm sure he's unshockable. So what's happening?'

Dean looks at Jack, indicating the rucksack.

'I've got to get back to Westerford, but you can stick around if you like. Gina will look after you once she's put some clothes on ...'

'Oh, shut up,' says Gina.

Dean grins back: 'Be nice to Jack.'

She drapes an arm across Jack's shoulders.

'Oh, I will.'

Dean looks at Jack. 'You OK with that?'

'Yeah, but what about Ania? I did promise her mother ...'

'Don't worry about Ania. You're the last person she wants to see right now. Tell you what ...' He pats his jacket until he finds a pencil and a scrap of paper. 'Give me her mother's number and I'll call her. She's probably back home by now.'

Jack jots down the number and hands it back to Dean. 'She might have gone to Magda's. She's her sister. She's got a flat in Maida Vale.'

'I can get the number from her mother. Don't worry about it. Have fun with Gina.'

'Yeah, sounds cool. I'll see you back in Westerford.'

Dean winks at Jack, bends down to give Gina a lingering kiss and walks off, hand raised in a laconic salute. Once he's gone Gina removes her arm and jumps to her feet.

'Right. Let's sort out breakfast. You got any cash?'

'Sure, a bit. What are you thinking of?'

'You can treat me. Let's see what Miles has got to offer.'

oOo

The far end of the street opens out onto a busy thoroughfare, bathed in autumn sunlight. There are people everywhere. A wizened old man wearing a stovepipe hat with a rainbow-coloured band has some sort of monkey scarpering around his shoulders and occasionally letting out ear-splitting screeches. On the pavement opposite Jack is a stall selling fruit and vegetables of all shapes and sizes. An Indian lady in a sari that is even more brightly coloured than her produce is serving a tall black guy dressed in an electric blue waistcoat; he takes a toke on something that looks suspiciously like a joint, before continuing their animated conversation. Further up the street a young hippy is busking a half-decent rendition of a Dylan song, accompanying himself on harmonica and acoustic guitar. There's a van that appears to have a rhinoceros stuck to its roof, while the house opposite has naked women painted on its walls, dancing their way up to the sky.

Gina dances backwards in front of him with her arms flung wide: 'Welcome to Portobello Road!'

He grins and she takes his arm as they saunter up the road to a small café sandwiched between two stalls, one selling leather goods and the other antique trinkets. As they enter Jack's stomach rumbles in appreciation of the smell of freshly grilled bacon. Miles turns out to be a huge middle-aged black guy who greets Gina with a bear hug.

'Hello, pretty lady! And is this one of your special friends?'

'This is Jack. He's a mate. He's a friend of Dean's. Be nice to him; he's buying me breakfast.'

'Ah, I see.' He turns to Jack. 'Well take a seat, my friend, and tell me what you fancy.'

They take a window seat and Jack peruses the menu, hand-written on a giant chalkboard above the counter. Everything comes with bacon.

'Wow.' He looks at Gina. 'So what are you having?'

'Oh, I'll have the usual, Miles.'

'Two poached eggs, runny inside, two rashers, sausage, mushroom and tomato, and a cup of tea. And for you?' He looks at Jack.

'That sounds good, I guess I'll have the same.'

'Coming right up. That'll be six bob – sorry, I mean thirty pence. Still can't get used to this funny money.'

'Yeah,' says Gina as Jack hands over the money, 'Reckon it's a scam, myself.'

'You're not wrong there,' says Miles, and he returns to the kitchen. Once he's gone, Jack turns back to Gina.

'So … how do you know Dean, then?'

'Oh, Dean and I go way back,' she grins at Jack, 'but I guess he hasn't mentioned me?'

'No, well …' Jack realises how little he really knows about Dean's life outside their friendship.

'Anyway,' says Gina, 'enough about me. Tell me about yourself.'

'I don't know … What did Ania tell you? Did she talk about me?'

'Well, yeah. She's a really cool chick and she was really into you, you know. She was pretty upset by what you did. You blew it big time, you silly man. And once she realised David was only really interested in adding her to his collection, she got even more upset. That's when she left.'

'I know. I was a fool, and now I can't do anything about it. I ought to try, though ...'

'No. You should trust Dean. Let him get on with it. You'll only make things worse.'

'Yeah, I guess so.'

Miles saves the moment by placing their two cups of tea on the red and white checked tablecloth.

Gina gives him a reassuring smile. 'One thing she did say is that you're pretty shit-hot on the guitar.'

'I guess I'm OK. I'm no Hendrix though.'

'That's not what Ania said. She said it was the one time you really relaxed, really became yourself, when you're playing.'

'Yeah, it's an amazing buzz, particularly when you've got an audience and enough space to let rip. It's like there's some energy from somewhere else that just flows through you.' He grins at Gina. 'Bit like sex, but lasts longer.'

'Yeah, right.'

She dumps two teaspoons of sugar in her cup. 'You know David's got a band, right?'

'Yeah, he told me, when I first met him in Westerford. He said I should come up and play with them. It sounded cool at the time, but now I'm not so sure.'

'I've heard them practising a couple of times, but I'm not sure they've done many gigs yet. Kingpin let them set up a rehearsal room in the basement. They sound pretty good. Evelyn plays the drums, and she can really use those sticks.' She takes a sip of her tea. 'David's a bit, well, strange at times, but you should give him another chance.'

Jack takes a sip, and then drinks down his tea. 'I'm still pissed off with him.'

'He ... well, he's a complicated character. He appeared a few months back with the twins in tow ... ' She hesitates, as though momentarily confused, 'I think there might have been another girl too ... I'm not sure, but I guess she must have disappeared pretty quickly. Anyway, I think he knew Kingpin from way back. You haven't met Kingpin yet, but he kinda runs the squat. He let David set up camp in the attic with his harem, or at least that's what everybody calls it. He probably was trying to recruit Ania, but he didn't get very far. As soon as she realised what he was up to, she got out. I know she stayed a couple of nights. David can be very persuasive but nothing happened, if that's what you're thinking.'

'Tell me about the twins. I mean Faylin, she was really something.'

'Yeah, but that's your dick talking.'

He snorts. 'I guess so.'

Gina's expression softens. 'She is a force of nature, I'll give you that, but you don't see much of her. She's out working most of the time: cafés and pubs and clubs at night. It's like Faylin's the breadwinner. Evelyn's the one that looks after David.'

Miles appears bearing two plates that he places in front of them and they tuck in. Jack thinks over what Gina's said. He's lived in Westerford all his life, and he's got friends there that go back to primary school. Its streets, its park, the river, the cafés and the pubs are built into him, and probably always will be. But he can't spend the rest of his life there and, now he's blown it with Ania, there's not much reason to stay. And then there's the music. What happened in the park opened a door and he needs to find out where it leads, which he's unlikely to do playing standards with Black Knight.

Once they're finished he offers Gina a Marlboro and they sit back.

'You know, I really would like to get out of Westerford.' He gestures at the window and the market outside. 'I mean, this is where it's at. Westerford's dead, and I would like to see what David's band is into. He did make it sound like they're doing some interesting stuff.'

She beams back. 'Well, then. Tell you what, why don't we go back to the squat and see if he's around. He's usually there.'

'Yeah, sounds cool.'

'And if it goes OK, you never know, you might be able to move in. You'd need to clear it with Kingpin, but I'm sure there's somewhere you could sleep.'

'Wow, yeah, that would be really cool!'

She gets to her feet. 'OK. Come on then, let's go.' She blows a kiss at Miles as they leave.

As they get to the turn-off to the squat, Gina stops and looks down the road.

'You know Hendrix died just a few streets away from here?'

'Really? That was such a bummer, that.'

'Yeah.' She takes a drag on her cigarette. 'I saw him once, you know. Not playing, I mean. He was just standing in a doorway. He had such a lovely smile.'

They turn off Portobello Road down a quieter street and, after passing a few houses, arrive at the squat. They walk up the steps together and Gina lets them in.

'Come on, let's see if David's in,' says Gina.

She leads him up the stairs to the attic. It looks totally different now the sun is streaming through the multi-coloured scarves that adorn the windows. David and one of the twins are sitting on a mattress in the corner, David lengthwise and the girl crosswise with her legs lying over his, smoking what smells like a joint.

As they appear David shrugs her off and bounds to his feet with his hand extended in greeting.

'Greetings, Jack. And please accept my profuse apologies for our earlier … misunderstanding. I do hope I haven't caused too much distress.'

Taken aback, Jack shakes his hand. He looks at the twin, uncertain how to react. David laughs and she smiles back, holding out the joint.

'Don't worry, Jack,' she says, 'Faylin's not here.'

'Oh, OK,' says Jack, taking the joint. 'Thanks, Evelyn, and good to see you again!'

He takes a drag before handing it on to Gina. It feels smooth and light, like quality Moroccan hash.

'And it's good to see you, Jack,' David says, 'So have you thought about our proposition? With the band?'

'Yeah, I guess it sounds cool. I'll give it a try.'

'Excellent. You won't regret it.'

Evelyn turns to David. 'Perhaps we should show him the music room?'

'Good idea. Follow me.'

He leads them down the stairs. A couple of flights down, and Gina taps Jack on the shoulder, 'I'll leave you guys here. Things to do, people to see, but I'll be back later. Enjoy yourself.'

She hands the joint back to Evelyn and, with a wave, disappears through one of the doors.

Jack continues down with David and Evelyn to the ground floor, then David keeps on going, down a further flight that ends in a plain wooden padlocked door. He unlocks it, pushes it open and they enter a large windowless room. Any wallpaper that might have existed has been stripped off and the remaining plaster coated with a cream-coloured paint and adorned with hanging rugs to deaden the sound. A large intricate Indian carpet covers the bare floorboards. Along one wall is a huge, overstuffed sofa in a deep purple leather.

Jack wonders for a moment how they got the sofa into the room, but his attention is on the instruments dotted around. There's a fairly comprehensive Premier drum kit in one corner, a Sennheiser microphone on a stand in the middle, and three guitars perched on purpose-built guitar stands and plugged into amplifiers that line the wall.

'Shit, that's a Rickenbacker, and that bass is a Gibson Thunderbird!' He walks over to the remaining guitar. 'And this is a Fender Stratocaster, and it's the real thing by the looks of it. I've always wanted one of these.'

David smiles: 'Well, the Rickenbacker's mine but the Strat's yours if you join the band. Why don't you try it for size?'

In a daze, Jack picks up the guitar. The sunburst finish makes the body look translucent, glowing orange around the pickups and fading out through red to near black around the edge. He puts the strap around his neck and gently strums a couple of chords.

'What's the band called?'

As he looks up another, guy slips into the room.

'We call ourselves Devil Spawn,' says David. 'This is Deek. He doesn't say much, but he plays a mean bass.'

Deek is short and stocky, dressed in black jeans, a black leather waistcoat, and a red and green check shirt. He has a round, open face topped by a tight mop of black curly hair. He raises his hand in greeting.

Jack nods back before returning his attention back to the guitar. He runs off a short riff.

'Man, the action on this is incredible. I've barely got to touch the frets and the sustain is something else.'

'Why don't you turn it on?' Evelyn says. 'In fact, why don't we have a jam, seeing as we're pretty well all here?'

Without waiting for an answer, she walks over to the drum kit and sits astride the stool, one foot on the bass drum pedal and the other on the hi-hat. She picks up the sticks and bashes out a short roll.

'Yeah, why not?' David says, picking up his guitar. Deek makes his way over to the bass while Jack checks out the amp into which the Stratocaster is plugged, a Vox AC30 Reverb. He flicks the power switch and is rewarded by a feedback howl as his guitar swings towards the speakers.

'Woah.' He steps back as he turns to face the band, knocking off another lick as he does so, each note throaty and exact. As the last note fades, Evelyn nods to Deek and they start laying down a slow blues, David coming in on the second bar with strummed chords. Before he even thinks about it Jack is in there too, firing off short runs that soon blend into longer riffs. The Stratocaster feels like an extension to his brain, and by the time they come into the final four he's into a full-blown solo.

The solo extends through the second twelve, but as they come into the third David throws him a look and starts tossing in a few more jazz-based chords. Jack stops playing for a bar or two just to listen as the others push a strong blues that occasionally spins out into something looser. He shuts his eyes and experiments with a few notes. David echoes them back on the next bar, and before he knows it they're throwing licks back and forth, question and answer, until David looks over at Evelyn and Deek and they bring it to a climax and then a close.

'That was fucking amazing,' Jack says. He is grinning from ear to ear, Evelyn is laughing and even Deek has raised a smile.

'And you didn't even touch your pedals,' David says.

Jack looks down and, sure enough, sitting on the floor by his feet is a Super-Fuzz and a Cry Baby wah-wah pedal.

'Well, what do you know.' He taps the button on the fuzz box with his foot, kicks down on the pedal of the wah-wah to turn it on, and then hits a note that screams out like a banshee on a tight leash. He grins at the others. 'Cool!'

Evelyn looks at David. 'Why don't we try something of ours?'

'Yeah, sure. *Into the Night*, perhaps?' David turns to Jack. 'It's something we've been working on. You'll get the hang of it.'

'Sounds cool.'

Deek opens with a short sequence of notes, pauses for a beat and then repeats it. The second time round Evelyn uses the gap to start a slow rhythm on the tom-tom. Jack and David watch as they build it into a slow, wistful backing, and then David comes in with a short sequence of staccato chords. Once Jack's got the hang of it he adds a few notes on top, no tune as yet but simply punctuation. David lets it run for a few bars and then steps up to the microphone and starts singing the main melody in a low throaty voice:

When nothing seems to come out right,
When everything is making you uptight,
Then all you have left to do,
All you really have left to do,
Is go quietly into the night,
Into the night,
Into the night …

As David rises into the last line, Jack follows on guitar so that David's final high note transforms into a sustained scream. Evelyn and Deek respond by picking up the pace while David lays down a solid backing and Jack goes into a series of variations around the melody at the heart of the song, spinning out ever more involved riffs.

Two or three verses in and the riff seems to coalesce into a more direct, concrete expression of the underlying despair and longing of the song in a way Jack has never known before. He's often felt as though something else, some other force, is playing the notes through him and his solos have never truly been a conscious process, but this is different. David is nodding encouragement and coming in with supporting riffs that nudge him further in. He is spinning off into note combinations that feel totally new, and more profoundly express the underlying emotion of the song than anything he's done before.

It is unlike anything he's played before, but something within him does recognise it, and it has something to do with the singing he heard in the park. He doesn't know what, but there is a familiarity there and it's all the more haunting because he doesn't know what it is. However, with rising excitement he realises he can remember at least a few notes of that singing, and it's driving what he's playing now. He can feel himself returning to the park, and that hollow in the wood where the teenagers had sung.

With a start, he realises David is signalling to him and the others that this is to be the last verse. David approaches the microphone and sings a repeat of the first verse, and then they bring it to a close.

For a moment they stand in silence, then Jack looks at David. 'Wow, man, that was quite something.'

'Yeah,' David replies, 'I reckon you really nailed that. Can't wait till Faylin hears it; she'll really go to town on that.'

'Where is she?'

'Oh, don't worry about that. She's not often around, but when she is, she just slots in like she's been here all the time. She'll really click in if you carry on playing like that.'

'Yeah,' says Evelyn, 'that was really cool, Jack. You've definitely got the Devil Spawn vibe.'

Even Deek is smiling from behind his bass guitar.

'Anyway,' says David, 'We must do some more stuff. I'm away for a couple of days but, once I'm back, well, we'll see what else we can cook up. In the meantime, feel free to use the room. You can always get the key off Evelyn.'

With that they leave the basement, Evelyn locking the door behind them. Jack is in a daze as they make their way up the stairs, trying to understand what has just happened. David and Evelyn are going up to the attic, and Jack is unsure whether to follow. As they reach the second floor, where he presumes Gina lives, he spots a telephone mounted on the wall, and he remembers the reason he came here in the first place. He needs to find out what has happened to Ania. He needs to phone her sister, Magda.

'Hey guys, would it be OK if I use the phone?'

David looks back at him. 'Yeah, I think so. Kingpin's had it fixed so you don't get charged, so you should be OK. Go for it.'

'Great, thanks.'

'Are you OK?' Evelyn asks.

'Yeah, I've just got to work out this call.'

'OK. Look, I've got a few things to do, but we could meet up later, if you want?'

'Sure, that would be cool.'

'Great, how about I meet you in KPH? It's only a few streets away, on Ladbroke Grove. See you at six?'

'What's KPH?'

'It's the Kensington Park Hotel, but everyone calls it KPH. Turn right on Portobello towards the flyover, and then turn left. It's just up from the Elgin. You can't miss it.'

'OK, sounds good. See you then.'

She beams back and then disappears up the stairs behind David. Jack fishes in his pockets and pulls out a small scuffed address book, then picks up the telephone receiver, listening for a dial tone. He opens the address book at 'M', stares at the page for a moment, and then dials the number. It rings a couple of times before he hears Magda's voice, similar to Ania's but deeper.

'Hello?'

'Hi, Magda, it's Jack. Ania's ...'

'Hello, Jack. What can I do for you?'

'Well, I was wondering ... Is Ania there?'

'No, she's not. She was here for a couple of days, but she's gone now. She left with Dean.'

'With Dean?'

'Yes, with Dean. They went back to Westerford together.'

'When was this?'

'Well, I'm not sure it's any of your business, really. It was a few hours ago. He came round to see if she was OK. It's good to know she's got such good friends, because she certainly needs them right now.'

Jack is silent. He doesn't know what to say. To his shame all he can think of is Ania with Dean. He flashes back to the time they were in the Blue Lion in Westerford, Ania laughing at something Dean had said while he was talking to Pauline, and letting him call her Annie. It seems like a lifetime ago. She'd been happy then. Yes, Dean would be a good friend to Ania, and knowing Dean he'd soon be something more. Jack's always suspected there was something between them, and now he's been proved right.

'Look, I'm really sorry …'

Magda snorts down the phone: 'Sorry? Well, you should be. She was in a very vulnerable state when she turned up here. I don't know what that man was up to trying it on like that, and I don't know what you were thinking when you did what you did. Quite frankly she's better off with you out of her life, and if Dean can bring her some happiness, then all well and good.'

Jack tries to think of something he can say that would put things right, some explanation that might justify what he did, but there is nothing.

'Yeah, I guess you're right. Goodbye, Magda.'

'Goodbye, Jack. I just hope you get your priorities sorted out.'

She terminates the call and Jack is left listening to the dial tone. He keeps the receiver to his ear for a long moment, and then puts it back on the cradle with a sigh. Magda is right, he knows that, but now he's got to move on. He's got a new life ahead. He's making new friends and he's becoming part of Devil Spawn, wherever that will take him. Ania is better off without him, although he's not sure he can get rid of the feeling that Dean had planned it all along. If anyone is taking advantage of Ania's vulnerable state right now, it is Dean. Part of him knows that's unfair, but for the moment, he really doesn't care.

# Eight

KPH turns out to be a well-worn corner pub with large picture windows on two sides and a horseshoe bar in dark wood. The place is almost empty this early in the evening and he has no trouble spotting Evelyn sitting at a table in her usual white dress. She's nursing what looks like a gin and tonic and shakes her head when Jack gestures an offer to buy her another so he goes straight to the bar, orders a pint for himself, takes it over and sits down opposite her.

'So, how did it go?' Evelyn asks, 'On the phone?'

Jack sighs. 'As well as could be expected, I guess.'

'Sorry. I shouldn't pry. It's none of my business.'

'No, it's alright, although your sister did have something to do with it.'

'Yes, I heard. As I said, I'm sorry.'

Jack smiles back, determined to separate her from the girl who seduced him. 'It's hardly your fault. I mean, it wasn't you – or at least I hope it wasn't you?'

Evelyn laughs, 'No, don't worry, it wasn't me.'

She puts her hand on the table. On her index finger is a slim gold ring mounted with a small green stone.

'Faylin's has an amber stone. It's one way you can tell us apart – that is, if we choose to wear them.' She cups her chin with her hand, causing the stone to catch the light.

'Next time I'll check.' He grins, 'I mean, not that there's going to be a next time.'

Evelyn laughs. 'Yeah, right.'

'So where is Faylin?'

'Right now?' She looks at her watch. 'She's probably starting her shift. I think she's working some club in Soho at the moment.'

They are diverted by raised voices at the bar. A tall black man looking cool in a wide-brimmed fedora and a canary yellow shirt has started a conversation with the guy behind the bar; it has become quite animated, but then they start laughing and the tension is gone, if it was ever there in the first place.

Evelyn turns her attention back to Jack. 'Yeah, we have a strange relationship, Faylin and me. We used to spend all our time together when we were kids, but as we got older it got … difficult.'

'OK …'

'Yeah. It's amazing the games you can play when you've got an identical twin sister. We really screwed with some guys' heads.'

Jack laughs. 'I can imagine.'

'It caused some real heartache, so now we spend a lot less time together. We kinda lead separate lives, although I guess David holds it together for us.'

'How did you meet David?'

'Well, I was supposed to be meeting Faylin in a pub in Soho, but she didn't turn up so I got talking to this guy on the bar stool next to me. He seemed nice and we were getting on pretty well when I saw Faylin come in.'

She grins shyly at Jack. 'David hadn't seen her so I signalled her to meet me in the toilet. I then excused myself and joined her. I told her what was happening, and she persuaded me to play a trick. So it was Faylin who came back from the loo, not me. She let me know later that they'd arranged to meet again the following evening.'

'And it was you he met up with on your second date?'

'Yeah, she grins at Jack. 'Even David doesn't know that story, so you keep it to yourself.'

'OK.'

'Anyway, it started to get serious between David and me, so Faylin agreed we should tell him about us. So I did, and then he met us both together for the first time.'

'Wow! Must have been weird for him.'

'Yeah, but right from the start he was different from other guys. He treated us both with respect. He'd had a pretty hard time, getting into drugs, and I mean heavy drugs like speed and cocaine and heroin. Faylin … well, you've seen what Faylin can be like. They do spend time together, but I'm the more constant, and we're happy with it being like that. She's happy I'm happy.'

'She screwed my life up, good and proper.'

'Yes, maybe, but you could have said "No", couldn't you?'

'I guess so,' Jack sighs. He looks across at Evelyn; there are things he wants to ask, but he's not sure how far to go.

'Don't you find it, well, weird, him being with other girls? I mean it's not just Faylin …'

Evelyn takes a long drink before replying.

'No, it's not just Faylin. But you see, it's the way he is. He likes to ... collect things. It's just the way he is.'

'And you're OK with that?'

She looks at him hard before replying.

'As I said before, the thing about David is that he's not like other men. When he's with you it's like he's really, really with you. For a short time you become the centre of his world, and for a short time he really, really cares ...' she looks away, '... or at least he does a damn good show of listening and caring. It's difficult to explain.'

Jack takes that as his cue to change the subject.

'So ... how did you get into the music? I mean, you're pretty hot on those drums.'

'You've got David to thank for that. Before we met I'd never thought about actually playing music, let alone being a drummer. Faylin's the musical one. She's got an amazing voice.'

'I can't wait to hear it,' says Jack, with just a hint of sarcasm.

'Yeah, well, you will, but all in good time. She's not one for practising, but it doesn't really matter because she can come on anytime and just blend right in with whatever we're doing. Sometimes she doesn't appear until we're actually on stage.'

'Scary.'

'Yeah, right, but you've seen what we can do.'

'So where do all the instruments come from – I mean, you've got some pretty fancy gear there.'

'Yeah, it is pretty cool, isn't it? There's this mate of David's. Rich guy. Lives in this really fancy mansion out in the country, middle of nowhere. I guess we're like a hobby for him. Anyway, he gave David a whole bunch of cash and we had this amazing afternoon round Denmark Street and Charing Cross Road just buying instruments and amps and such like.'

'Wow. And the Strat? Who was that for?'

'Don't know. I guess David fancied it, and we were short of a lead guitar.'

'And here I am, happy to take the job.' He takes another sip of beer. 'What about Deek? What's his story?'

'He's been tagging along with David ever since I've known him. He doesn't say much, but he's cool. It's almost like they're brothers.'

'He plays a pretty cool bass, too.'

'Yeah.'

Jack and Evelyn watch a young couple sitting on a table across the bar for a few moments. They are both dressed in the latest fashion, like they've just shopped at Biba, and their heads are close together in deep conversation. They've both got long straight blond hair that reaches down to their waists, swirling and intermingling as they move their heads. Jack turns to Evelyn.

'Do you remember, when you came round to Ania's place with David? When we first met?'

'Yeah, I remember. I pretended to be Faylin for a short while.'

'That's right. But do you remember what I was talking about? What I saw in the park when I was tripping – the three teenagers dancing in a hollow in the woods, singing this extraordinary music?'

'Yeah. You were trying to remember it, but you couldn't.'

'Yeah, well, when we were practising earlier and it really took off, it was like I could almost get it – like the tune was just there, just out of reach.'

'Towards the end, when we were doing *Into the Night*, it did seem to really come together, more than it's ever done before. We could really go somewhere, you know, with you in Devil Spawn.'

Jack glances back at the couple. They look almost identical, like twins.

'Yeah, but I can't help wondering where that's likely to be.'

o0o

Once they've finished their drinks they wander back to the squat. Evelyn heads up to the attic while Jack stops on the second floor to see if Gina's around. He's about to tap on her door when the phone mounted on the wall starts ringing. He picks it up.

'Hello?'

'Hello,' says a gruff male voice, 'hi, can I … is Adele there?'

'Adele? I don't know. Hold on, I'll check.'

Jack looks around the deserted landing. Who is Adele? He hasn't met any Adele. He's just about to say as much when the door flies open and Gina bursts out, grabs the handset from Jack and composes herself before answering.

'Adele speaking. What can I do for you?' Jack stands there, confused. He can hear the mumbling of the man's reply, but can't make out what he's saying.

She replies: 'Yeah, I can do that.'

Then, 'The usual.'

There's more mumbling.

'That's going to be a bit more … OK, we can talk about that when I

86

get there, lover boy ... Cavendish Hotel, yeah, got that.'

She rolls her eyes at Jack.

'I'll see you at ten.'

She laughs in response to something the man says, slams the phone down and looks furiously at Jack.

'OK, this is my phone and you don't answer it, is that clear?' Jack nods dumbly. 'Unless I'm out, and then you take a message, you got that?'

'Yeah, I've got it. Sorry, Adele.'

'It's Gina to you. Don't be cheeky.'

'Sorry, Gina.'

'That's more like it.' Her expression softens. 'Look, I don't really mind you making a call if you have to. Just be careful about answering it. Could be bad for business.' She smiles. 'Anyway, enough of that. Look, I was just rolling a joint. You fancy some?'

'Yeah, sure.'

'You better come in then.'

She beckons Jack into her domain. At first glance it looks like a suburban teenager's bedroom. The double mattress on the floor is covered in clean linen, and there's an assortment of colourful pillows along the top with pride of place taken by a red satin heart with sparkly trimmings. There's a light grey dressing table against one wall with a mirror surrounded by naked bulbs and a couple of antique dolls sitting among the assorted makeup and lotions, one wearing a rainbow-coloured tutu and the other in doll-sized denim shorts, waistcoat and a tiara. Golden stars have been spray-painted onto the walls, among posters of Hendrix, Jagger and Lennon. The cheap Dansette record player is playing the Beach Boys' *Pet Sounds*, and next to the bed lies the album cover, covered in the trappings of the half-rolled joint.

'Sorry about the mess,' says Gina as she takes a seat on the mattress and lifts the album cover onto her lap so she can finish rolling the joint. 'It's only stuff, but somehow I seem to collect it wherever I go.'

The only chair in the room is at the dressing table, so Jack sits beside her on the mattress. Once she's finished she puts the joint between her lips and looks expectantly at Jack.

'Oh, right. Hold on.' He fishes in his pockets for his lighter and holds out the flame. Gina leans forward to light the joint, takes a deep drag, holds it in and then relaxes back.

'That's better. Boy, I needed that.' She takes another drag before passing it to Jack, who does likewise.

They finish the joint listening to the ethereal harmonies of *Pet Sounds* while Jack wonders whether he should broach the subject of the overheard phone call, or indeed the whole matter of 'Adele'.

'So, how did the session with the band go?' Gina asks.

He decides not to bring up Adele for the time being. 'You mean with Devil Spawn? It was ... well, it was just amazing. They've got all this gear, I mean I was playing a Stratocaster, for Christ's sake – a genuine Strat. We had a jam and it really came together.'

'That's great, Jack. I knew you should give it a try.'

'Yeah, and David said we should do some more. He's gone away for a few days, but when he comes back ...'

'You need to be here, which means you need to see Kingpin. He's not around today, but he'll be here tomorrow. Look, I'm sure it'll be OK for you to crash downstairs again tonight, so we might as well get smashed.' She grins at Jack. 'It makes it easier to sleep on cheap mattresses.'

She reaches over to the small pine cabinet beside the bed and takes out a half-full bottle of whisky and a couple of glasses. She hands one to Jack and splashes it half full of whisky, and then does the same for herself. She holds out her glass.

'Bottoms up!'

Jack taps his glass to hers. 'Bottoms up indeed!'

They both wince as the fiery liquid hits the back of their throats.

'So,' says Gina, once she's recovered, 'did you find out what happened to Ania?'

'Yeah, apparently she went to her sister Magda's place in Maida Vale, and then Dean turned up and they went back to Westerford. Together.'

'So, that's alright then?'

'Well, yeah, I guess it is. Though I can't help thinking it's all turned out well for Dean, as usual.'

'Is that a problem? You make it sound like a problem.'

'Well, you know Dean.'

Gina shrugs. 'Yeah, but only off and on. Only in London. He doesn't talk much about his past, or anything like that. We don't really have that kind of relationship. I don't really know anything about his life in Westerford.'

'So you don't know about Pauline?'

'No.' She takes another sip of her whisky. 'Who's Pauline?'

'Pauline's his girlfriend, in Westerford.'

'OK.' She waits while Jack takes a slug of his drink. 'So does she know anything about what Dean gets up to in London? Does she know about me?'

Jack sighs. 'I don't know. Probably not. I guess she just knows what Dean's like and accepts it.'

'Dean's like me. We know what we want and we usually get it, in the end.'

'I guess.'

'Look. Dean's a nice guy. He is who he is, and he doesn't pretend to be anything else. I mean, you know that, right? I mean, you're friends, aren't you?'

'Yeah. I guess so. I've known him for years.'

'And it's not like you've behaved brilliantly in all this, is it?' She reaches for the album cover and starts to roll another joint. 'I mean, if they're meant to be together, they'll get it together, and there's not much you can do about it except make a couple of people unhappy, so what's the point?' She slurps some more whisky into his glass. 'Come on, have some more.'

oOo

Jack wakes with a splitting headache and Gina standing over him with a big glass of water. He's lying fully clothed on top of the mattress he slept on the night before and sunlight is streaming painfully through a gap in the curtains. He can't remember much about the previous evening, but he must have stumbled down the stairs at some point.

Gina shoves her fingers in the glass and sprinkles some cold water over Jack's face. 'Come on, get this down you and you'll feel much better.'

He pulls himself to his feet and downs the whole glass in one go. He almost chokes, but he does feel a bit more human. He wants a bath and a change of clothes, but that's clearly not an option yet, so he pats his pockets and extracts a packet of Marlborough. At least he's still got cigarettes. He looks enquiringly at Gina, but she shakes her head so he takes one out for himself and lights up. He turns to thank her for the water, but immediately breaks down in a fit of coughing.

'Charming,' Gina says. 'Look, get yourself together and I'll take you to see Kingpin. Then perhaps you can sort things out in your own room. Or sleep it off.'

'OK. Hold on, I'll be back in a minute.'

He disappears upstairs to take a pee and splash water on his face and various other parts of his body. Gina looks at him expectantly when he returns.

'That's better,' she says. 'you don't look quite so much of a wreck.

Ready to see Kingpin?'

'Lead on, Macduff!'

He follows Gina into the hall and she taps on the door opposite.

'It's open,' a gruff voice responds.

Kingpin turns out to be a ginger-haired, bearded guy of perhaps thirty, dressed in black leather trousers and waistcoat. To Jack's eyes he bears a passing resemblance to the Cream drummer Ginger Baker, if you added a couple of pounds and a couple of years. He's sitting on a swivel chair in front of a huge antique desk bearing an expensive-looking set of scales and weights in brass. Next to him stands a dishevelled-looking kid of perhaps eight or nine. He hands the kid a small package of twisted paper; the kid looks up at them with startled eyes and scarpers. Once the kid's gone Kingpin turns his attention to them.

'Hi, Gina, what can I do for you? And who's this fine gentleman? He looks like he's had a hard night.'

'Hiya 'Pin,' says Gina. 'This here's Jack. He's usually a bit more together than this, but he helped me finish a bottle of whisky last night.'

'Is that so? Well, I'm pleased to meet you, Jack.' He extends his hand without leaning forward which means Jack has to lean right across the desk to give it a shake.

'So, what can I do for you?'

Jack tries to formulate a reply, but his brain doesn't appear to be working properly so Gina interrupts.

'Jack's like a shit-hot guitarist. Really cool. He's been doing some stuff with David – you know, with Devil Spawn? David wants him in the band.'

'Is that right?' Kingpin replies, looking at Jack.

Jack finally finds his voice: 'Yeah, but I've got nowhere to stay, and I'd really like to stay. Gina said you might have a room?'

Kingpin looks intently at Jack. The silence drags on and Jack is feeling quite uncomfortable by the time Kingpin responds.

'Yeah, why not?' His face relaxes. 'If you're good enough for Gina, you're good enough for me. You'll need to pull your weight, though. Don't talk about this place to anyone outside and be very careful who you bring back. We don't have much, but we look after what we've got. Isn't that right, Gina?'

'Too right, 'Pin.'

Kingpin grins. 'And only Gina gets to call me 'Pin, you got that?'

'Yeah, of course.'

'OK. Well, there's a room free in the attic, next to David's harem, or whatever you want to call it. It's not much, but it's yours if you want it.'

He reaches into one of the drawers of his desk and pulls out a key, which he presents to Jack. 'This is for the front door. Sometimes we bolt the door, in which case you'll have to knock, but usually you can let yourself in. Don't lose it, and give it back when you leave.'

'Wow, thanks. Sure, I'll look after it.'

'Thanks, 'Pin,' says Gina.

'No problem.'

Kingpin continues: '… and Jack, just one more thing.'

Jack turns to face him. 'OK?'

'Yeah, just so you know, I might need you to run the occasional errand. A delivery or two. Things that need moving from one place to another. You get my drift?'

'Yeah … sure, Kingpin. Just say the word.'

'I will.'

They exit the room, Gina closing the door behind them.

'OK,' She grins, 'let's go and check out your new home.'

His room turns out to be through a small door off David's attic domain. It is quite small, and you have to stoop in some parts to avoid the rafters, but there's a window at one end and a mattress on the floor that looks quite clean. There's even a small, low-backed sofa tucked under the rafters on one side.

'Nice!' Gina says. 'I don't think I've ever been in here before. What do you think?'

'Yeah, it'll do nicely. I need to get some things, though …'

His room back in Westerford is crammed full of stuff – clothes, books, records, record player. And then there's stuff like clothes and towels, toothbrush and toothpaste. He can't bring it all here – he wouldn't want to – but he's going to need a few things.

'I think maybe I'm going to have to go back to Westerford; pick up some gear, you know? I ought to say something to my mum, too …'

'Yeah, makes sense. You do that. I'll see you later.'

Just before she gets to the door Jack says: 'Gina?'

'Yeah?'

'What did Kingpin mean, when he talked about me doing "errands"?'

She looks at him for a moment. 'Well, difficult to say for sure, but you can guess the business he's in.'

'Yeah, I mean, I guess it's much the same business as Dean's.'

'It won't be anything dangerous. I mean, you're an unknown. The fuzz don't know you from Adam, or at least I assume they don't.'

'I guess not. I guess that's part of the attraction.'

'It won't be very often, either. He's a bit rough round the edges, but he's good guy, Kingpin.'

'Yeah, thanks. I'll See you later.'

# Nine

For Jack, the journey back to Westerford is very different from the journey out. As the train moves through the dirty brick and dusty concrete vistas of south London into the leafy suburbs and then the open countryside, he feels as though he is entering a different universe: somewhere familiar, but only from a distant past. Since he last did this journey he's met a whole bunch of new people: David, Deek, Evelyn, Kingpin and, of course, Gina.

And what is it with Gina? She's sexy and smart, and there's definitely a spark between them, but he's not sure what it is. Last night it felt like they could just tumble into bed together, but something stopped it from happening despite his growing desires. She's open and self-assured on the surface and he fancies her like crazy, but underneath she's a lot more complicated than her perky brightness might suggest.

Then there's the music. He's had only one session with Devil Spawn, but something is going on there unlike anything he's experienced with Black Knight. Chris and Phil are good at what they do, and Carol can belt it out like she's Grace Slick when she really gets going, but there is something about the way Deek and Evelyn play that is looser, freer, more creative. Having David on rhythm guitar helps too. It's like they're leading him into new ways of playing, new ways of thinking about music, that really resonate emotionally in a way he's never known before. The only time he's got close that he can remember was that time in the Scout Hut when they were confronted by those greasers. It was like the guitar became a weapon, like it actually could force them to leave.

And somehow it all links back to those teenagers singing in the park, whatever that was about. He feels like he's on the edge of something; like he's standing at a threshold and a door is opening. All he knows is that he wants to get back in there, back in the music room with David and Deek and Evelyn. And then there's the mysterious Faylin. David can sing, but he's nothing special. Apparently it's Faylin who's got the magic voice, but she's never there. Both David and Evelyn have told him she'll just fit in, somehow, and in any case there's plenty to explore, just the four of them, but there could be more. None of them have talked about gigs yet, but so far it's looking like they've got what it takes. A few months' time and they could be on stage at the Marquee or the Roundhouse. Who knows?

He gazes out at the tidy green fields punctuated by small patches of woodland, and then it's into a tunnel and a minute or so later they burst back into the sunlight, cross the river and screech to a halt at Westerford station.

It's only a short walk to his mother's flat, but as he crosses London Road he looks left to where it slopes down to the river. At the bottom, tucked just out of sight, is the Blue Lion. It's almost one o'clock so the pub is open, and it's quite possible Dean and Ania are in there. It's quite warm for October so they could be sitting on the terrace, watching the river, or they could be sitting in the picture window, where they'd all been sitting just a few weeks ago, Ania with her head back and her eyes bright, laughing at something Dean had said. He could walk down there right now, if he wanted, but it's no longer his world and she's no longer his girl. He carries on the short distance to his mother's place, takes out his key and lets himself in.

Alice comes out of the kitchen at the sound of his entrance, wiping her hands on a cloth.

'Hi, Mum.'

'Hello, Jack.' She looks tired or worried. Probably both.

'I'm sorry, Mum.'

She looks at him for a moment in silence.

'You've been away for two nights, and that's after days when you've scarcely left your room. I've been worried. I don't know what's been happening to you. Of course I've been worried. You promised you'd ring me if you were going to be away more than one night, and you didn't.'

Jack can see how much he's hurt her. 'I know, and I'm really sorry. I really am.'

She holds her hands up in despair.

'But it's OK, Mum. I've been through some bad times. I broke up with Ania. But it's OK now, because I'm going to move out. Dean's got some friends in Notting Hill, just off Portobello Road, and they've got a room I can use.'

She looks at him sceptically.

'It's good, Mum. It's a nice room, in the attic. It looks out over the rooftops. And they've got a band, a really good band, and they want me to join.'

She sighs. 'And what are you going to do for money?'

'Well, there's Dad's allowance, and I can get a job. There's lots of work.' He improvises quickly. 'I mean there's warehouses and loads of shops, or I could be a roadie or something ...'

She softens. She can see he's doing his best. 'Well, I suppose I knew this day would come. I guess there's not much to keep you here now. I just didn't think it would be so soon. Just look after yourself. And keep in touch. You don't have to do much, just ring me occasionally. And stay in touch with your dad. He cares about you – we both do.'

'I know, Mum. I will.' He stands there, feeling embarrassed. Alice comes to his rescue.

'I imagine you need to pick up some stuff? You only need to take what you want – you can leave the rest in your room. It'll still be your room, you know. It'll always be your room.'

'I know. Thanks, Mum.'

At first Jack's taken aback by the mess in his room, then he realises it's always been like this, with more clothes on the floor than in the drawers or the wardrobe, the bed unmade, a half-drunk mug of tea perched precariously on the side table and records everywhere. He pulls a black holdall down from the top of the wardrobe – the one he's always used for holidays – and the sleeping bag squashed next to it. Sheets would be nice but for the moment at least the sleeping bag will keep him warm. Jack starts cramming the holdall with underwear. He chooses a few of his favourite T-shirts and a couple of pairs of jeans, and then collects his toothbrush, towel and some toothpaste from the bathroom. His mother's toothbrush now sits in the glass alone and he tries not to think what it might mean to her.

He takes a last look around his room. There's his record player, his guitar and its amplifier: his most valuable possessions. For a moment he thinks about taking his guitar – it would be nice to have something to strum in his own room, away from the others – but then he thinks of the padlock on the basement door and realises it probably wouldn't be safe. Best not to take anything valuable. On impulse he picks up the small brass statue of Buddha that sits on the mantlepiece and his pocket-sized, leather-bound copy of the *I Ching*, which has the three Chinese coins tucked into a flap inside the front cover, and stuffs them into his bag. They're easily replaced – after all, he only bought them a year or so ago from a stall in Kensington Market – but they're precious to him.

His mother stands waiting for him, holdall in tow, in the hall.

'Have you got everything you need?'

'I think so.'

'Clean underwear? Toothbrush? Toothpaste?'

'Check!'

Jack looks at his mother. 'Are you going to be OK?'

She laughs, although Jack suspects she is close to tears.

'Don't worry about me, Jack. I'll survive.'

'Maybe you could get in touch with Ray, again? You never know …'

Ray was someone who had come into their lives about a year after his parents separated. He obviously liked Alice and he'd done his best to get on with Jack, but in the end he couldn't handle it and they'd parted. Jack had probably behaved badly, but it hadn't helped that Ray was a police constable, possibly charged with keeping his eye on Jack and his mates as part of his day job.

She smiles. 'You never know. Now come here and give your mum a hug.'

oOo

Outside, Jack is in a quandary. It's early afternoon so he's got plenty of time. He could head off into Abbey Park for a few hours to see if he can make any more sense of what happened there. He could go and see if Alex is around; perhaps he's discovered something more about Abbey House and its occupants. But it's raining gently and a big part of him just wants to get away. He's said goodbye to his mother and he feels like he's said goodbye to his childhood. His future is in London and he wants to get back there as quickly as possible. Besides, the holdall's heavy and the sleeping bag is cumbersome, and he can't exactly ask his mother to take care of it for a bit while he wanders around Westerford, not now they've gone through the parting. If he'd thought about it earlier he could have checked out the park and Alex first, and then picked up his stuff, but he didn't. He shoulders the bags and sets off for the station.

The nagging mixture of nostalgia and regret stays with him as he waits on the platform then boards the train. It's only after they burst out of the tunnel that runs under the Downs and into the now sunlit countryside of north Kent that the feeling lifts, leaving him bright with anticipation. By the time he climbs the steps out of Notting Hill tube station he feels like a Londoner, confident that he knows his way home. He crosses the road and turns up Pembridge Road, and then left onto Portobello Road. Fifteen minutes later and he's letting himself into the squat, and there's Gina in the hall.

'Well, hi there, and welcome home.' She indicates his baggage: 'Looks like you're ready to move in?'

'Yeah, and I'll be glad to put this lot down. It's heavier than it looks.'

He follows her upstairs, trying not to look up her short leather skirt as she bounds up the steps ahead of him. In the attic they find David lying across a mattress with a girl Jack has not seen before. She looks young, maybe sixteen or even younger despite the eyeliner and the lipstick. David does not introduce her and indeed barely acknowledges their presence so they continue on through the door that leads to Jack's new home.

The first thing he notices is that the room is not as sparse as it was. Someone has put a low wooden table in front of the sofa together with a cut glass vase containing a bunch of what look like daisies surrounding a solitary red tulip, and on the mattress is an acoustic guitar. Jack dumps his bags on the floor, picks up the guitar and strums a few chords on its nylon strings. It's just a cheap guitar, but it's in tune. He looks up to see David at the door.

'I hope you like it. It'll give you something to strum and the Strat's a bit valuable to leave lying around. Gina sorted out the flowers.'

'Wow, thanks, guys,' says Jack.

Gina takes a bow. David turns to leave: 'No problem. Anyway, I better get back to my new friend.'

Once David's gone Gina says, 'I've got something else to show you, too.'

She goes over to the window, pulls the lower sash up and climbs out. For a moment Jack is bewildered, until he realises she is not precariously balancing on the window ledge.

'Come on out.'

He follows her through the window and discovers a small terrace, about ten feet square and bordered by a low wall. She is sitting with her back against the side of the house and her legs stretched out across the felt, gazing over the rooftops of Ladbroke Grove. She is holding a joint.

'Have you got a light?'

'Yeah, sure.' He sits down beside her and they smoke it in silence, bathed in the orange glow of the sun as it sets behind a low-lying bank of cloud.

'Can I join you?' Jack looks around to see David's head sticking out of the window.

'Yeah, of course,' Jack replies.

'And bring the guitar,' adds Gina. 'Jack's going to serenade me with a song.'

'Sounds cool,' says David. His head disappears and then a moment later the guitar appears. Jack grabs it and David joins them, sitting on the low wall in front of them. The joint has burned right down to the roach so Gina stubs it out.

'So, where's Minnie Mouse?' she asks.

'She's resting,' replies David. 'And her name is ... actually, I forget her name.'

Gina looks at Jack with raised eyebrows. David shuffles uncomfortably on the wall.

'OK ... Anyway, Jack's going to play me a song, aren't you Jack?'

'Yeah, sure.' He thinks for a moment. 'OK, I don't know how this will go, but I'll give it a try.'

Jack has spent long evenings in his bedroom back in Westerford trying to get the riffs and chords of his favourite tracks, and one that he thinks he's got fairly well nailed is the Byrds' haunting ballad *Goin' Back*. He starts tentatively with the opening chords, plucking out the melody on the top strings. As he hits the second verse, Gina joins him. She doesn't remember all the words, but she's got a sweet voice.

'Nice one,' says David as they draw it to a close.

Gina beams. Jack continues playing around, until he finds himself playing the opening chords of *Into the Night*, the Devil Spawn composition they'd practised in the music room. David looks up, recognising the chords, and as Jack comes round to the verse, starts singing. Jack improvises around the basic theme. He's not getting the same buzz as he got in the music room, when he was playing solo against David's rhythm, but something is definitely happening. Something in him wants to take it further, but now's not the time so he brings it to a close.

Gina claps enthusiastically. David appraises him, nodding slowly.

'Yeah,' he says, 'You've definitely got something there.' He stands up. 'Look, I better get back. I'm going to be away tomorrow, but we must do some more practising soon.'

'Yeah, sure.'

David disappears through the window. Jack looks at Gina.

'So what is it with Minnie Mouse, or whatever her name is? She seems pretty young.'

'Yeah, maybe,' says Gina. She looks out across the rooftops. 'She's old enough to know what she's doing.'

The sun has disappeared behind the cloud bank and it's beginning to get cold. She stands up.

'Look, I'm going to be busy tomorrow morning, but we can meet up later, if you like. Somewhere in the West End.' She grins. 'We can celebrate. Maybe do some shopping, catch a movie, or something like that. How's that sound?'

'Sounds good to me. Where do you want to meet?'

'How about Oxford Circus? I'll meet you at two, outside the tube entrance on the south side of Oxford Street. You know where I mean? The one that actually opens out onto the street?'

'Yeah, I think so. On the corner with the street that goes down to Liberty?'

'That's the one. I'll see you there.' She disappears through the window, leaving Jack alone on the terrace.

oOo

They don't actually meet up until ten past two, largely because Jack has been standing at the wrong entrance. Thankfully, Gina had anticipated this and gone looking for him. This time she's wearing a denim skirt that barely reaches her thighs, a wide leather belt that sits low on her hips, an ochre-coloured, open-knit halter top and a pair of boots, calf length in pale brown leather with two-inch polished wood heels. A large string bag is slung over her shoulder.

'Cool boots.'

'Treated myself on the way here. I couldn't resist.' She stretches out a leg to show them off, 'Pretty cool, aren't they?'

'They look pretty good to me.'

'OK, let's do some shopping.'

They wander down the north side of Oxford Street. It's Monday afternoon so the pavements aren't crowded, but there's still quite a few people browsing the shops or looking for somewhere to eat. Gina pulls him into one of the open markets that sell everything from clothes and shoes to books, second-hand records, pipes, chillums and hookahs.

'We need to get you some cooler clothes. Do you know your size?'

'Yeah, sure. I'm a 28 waist and medium T-shirt.'

'You should be so lucky. OK, follow me, but not too close – not like you know me, if you know what I mean. I'll meet you down the street.'

She moves towards a stall not far from the entrance that is densely packed with flared jeans and brightly coloured T-shirts. She fingers through the jeans, takes one out and leaves it lying across the hangers. She moves on to the T-shirts, checking the designs, and eventually pulls out a cream-coloured one with a *Keep on Truckin'* logo, and another with a blue and white tie-dye design. She leaves them on top of the rack next to the jeans.

Jack realises what she's up to when he spots the owner of the shop, a middle-aged guy sporting a denim waistcoat over a bulging belly and a tan leather hat that is not as cool as he thinks. He is looking her over with hungry eyes. She moves across to the other side of the stall where a row of assorted shoes and boots line the floor, waits a second and then, making sure her back is to the guy, bends right over to check them out. Without waiting to check the guy's reaction, Jack quickly grabs the clothes she's selected and runs out into the crowd and down the street. Breathless, he pulls into an entrance a few doors down and turns to see Gina strolling towards him, laughing out loud.

'You OK, then?'

He holds out their ill-gotten gains: 'Yeah, and I think the whole street knows the colour of your knickers.'

'Don't knock 'em: they're sorting out your wardrobe. And I've even got you a present.' She opens her hand to reveal a pale-blue badge emblazoned with "Make Love Not War".

'Wow, those are some knickers.'

'Enough of that.'

Jack realises he is shaking. 'Shit, I've never done anything like that before.'

Gina takes the clothes from him and stuffs them in her bag. 'Get used to it. You're going to be doing a lot of things you've never done before.'

'So what's next?'

'Well, I guess you better try them on.' She points to the Marks and Spencer next door. 'This'll do.'

'OK, so how's this going to work?'

'It's quite simple, really. Just choose something off the racks that you might want to buy, go into the changing rooms and put this lot on.' She hands Jack the bag. 'Then put your old clothes back in the bag. I'll distract the assistants and hopefully when you come out they won't notice you're wearing a completely different outfit.'

'Supposing they're women?'

She looks at him like he's stupid. 'I'll just look shifty, like I'm about to lift something. Don't worry. It'll be fine. I mean, they might be gay.'

'Maybe,' says Jack. 'OK, let's give it a go.'

'Fine, and remember, you don't know me from Adam.'

'Or indeed Eve.'

'Go on, then, smart-arse. Here's the bag.'

He wanders into the shop, a wide-open space with well-ordered racks and a few customers dotted here and there. As far as he can see there's just a couple of assistants, easily identified by their black tops and neat little name badges. He drifts over to the men's section and starts flicking half-heartedly through the shirts, picking out something in white that should be his size. After all, it's not like he's actually going to buy it, so it doesn't really matter. But then his eyes alight on a row of leather jackets. He's always wanted a cool leather jacket, and some of these do look pretty cool, even if they are a bit new to have built up any street cred.

He checks the price tag of something in dark brown with a zip down the front that's about his size. Twenty-five pounds. It's way more than he can afford, but it's a really cool jacket. On impulse he adds it to the shirt and heads over to the changing rooms, which are at the back of the shop and a disconcerting distance from the exit. As he does so he notices Gina. She's hanging around the racks outside the changing area, flicking through the blouses and checking out the scarves, taking things off shelves, wandering off and then putting them back. He nods at the assistant as he enters the changing room, but she's keeping a close eye on Gina and barely acknowledges his presence.

He quickly changes into the jeans and the *Keep on Truckin'* T-shirt. They seem a good fit and the jeans sit nice and low on his hips. Then he shrugs his shoulders into the leather jacket and checks himself out in the mirror. The jacket is if anything a bit large, but the sleeves are fine and he looks really cool. It feels like it belongs where it is, around his shoulders.

He stuffs the clothes he was wearing into Gina's bag, leaves the shirt behind and walks out of the changing rooms. The assistant is in conversation with a middle-aged man whom Jack realises with a jolt must be a store detective. They both have their backs to him so he takes a deep breath and walks as calmly as he can manage across the interminable floor and out to the street. He's expecting a tap on his shoulder at any moment, but nothing happens so he turns around once he's a few shops down to see what's happened to Gina.

She's just got out of the shop and is on her way towards him when the store detective appears behind her. Jack turns away before the detective can realise they're together, but he's close enough to hear the conversation.

'Excuse me, Miss, I need a word.'

'Sorry,' says Gina. 'Do you mean me?'

'Yes, Miss. I'm sorry, but I've reason to believe you may have left the shop without paying.'

'What?' Gina puts on her most outraged voice. 'Are you accusing me of … of stealing? What are you going to do, search me?'

Jack takes a surreptitious look. Gina is standing in front of the detective, arms outstretched to make it abundantly obvious that there really is nowhere she could possibly hide anything. A small crowd is gathering, and it's clearly dawning on the detective how ridiculous the situation is becoming. Nobody is paying Jack any attention.

101

'I'm sorry, Miss. Of course not. I do apologise.'

'Well, I just don't know,' says Gina, as the detective melts away. The crowd disperses and Gina puts her arm through Jack's, guiding him down the road.

'Cool jacket. Shall we get something to eat?'

'Shit, yeah, I really need to sit down.'

They pull into a café and Jack collapses into one of the plastic seats by the window. Gina takes the seat opposite. He's hyperventilating and feels close to fainting. He shrugs out of the jacket in an effort to cool down, hanging it on the chair beside him.

'Calm down,' says Gina. 'Take some deep breaths and you'll be fine. You just need some sugar.'

She orders them each a cup of tea and a slice of Bakewell tart from the waitress, who is looking at Jack anxiously.

By the time the waitress returns with their order, he's feeling much better. He takes a bite out of his cake.

'It really is a cool jacket,' says Gina. 'Although it might look better without the price tag.'

'Oops!' says Jack, as he removes the tag from where it hangs down from the collar.

'That's better,' she says, and they both laugh.

Jack takes a sip of his tea and looks at Gina appraisingly.

'So, don't you pay for anything?'

'Well,' she says, 'you're paying for the tea, so I guess not.'

'Seriously, though.'

'Seriously?' She looks at him and then stretches her leg out from beneath the table.

'I paid for these,' she says, indicating the boots.

'OK, so why did you pay for them? They look expensive.'

'Well, I had some cash to spare from this morning, and I really liked the boots. Besides, it was a small shop, not one of these big chains, and the shop assistant was really helpful. She might have lost her job if I'd walked off with them.'

'Fair enough.'

'And you can't really talk. You've just walked off with that jacket.'

'No, I guess not.'

Gina polishes off the last crumbs of her cake and finishes her tea.

'So, are you feeling better?'

'Yeah,' Jack grins, 'feeling pretty good, actually.'

'What do you fancy doing now?'

He gazes out the window at the passers-by browsing the shop

windows or striding purposefully to somewhere important. It's raining gently, and he's trying to ignore his rising desire.

'We could go see a film.' He indicates a small cinema on the other side of the street.

'Yeah, we could do that. What's on?'

He can just about make out the display. 'They're showing *Klute*. You know, the new one with Jane Fonda and Donald Sutherland. It's meant to be pretty good; they're talking about her getting an Oscar for it. Or, look! They're also showing *Barbarella*. They must have re-released it. Did you ever see that?'

'No, I missed it first time around.'

'I don't mind seeing that again. It's got a really zany plot and it's also got Jane Fonda.'

'I hope it's got something for me, too?'

'Well, you do get to see a great deal of Jane Fonda, but there's also David Hemmings, and there's a really sexy angel, who's a guy.'

'OK then, it's a deal.'

Jack settles the bill with the waitress, and they cross the road through the rain to the cinema. Jack buys two tickets at the box office and they wander down seemingly endless red velvet corridors until they get to the auditorium. It's small and dark and appears to be empty. The adverts have just ended and the film is about to start.

'Perfect timing,' says Jack. 'Back row?'

'Of course.'

They work their way to the centre of the back row and sit down. On screen, Jane Fonda is floating weightless in the cockpit of her spacecraft, slowly shedding her spacesuit. A little later she is naked, covered only by carefully positioned titles.

'Looks like we're the only ones here,' says Jack.

'Yeah,' says Gina.

Jack reaches inside his jacket and pulls out a joint.

'Shall we?'

'Where did you get that? I presume it didn't come with the jacket.'

'Well, no. I skinned up earlier and transferred it in the changing room.'

'Good thing the store detective went for me rather than you, then.'

'Well, yeah, I wasn't thinking straight at the time.'

'So you going to light it, or what?'

Jack rummages around the bag and pulls out his lighter. He lights the joint, takes a few drags and passes it to Gina. They settle back to watch the film.

By the time Barbarella has got around to restoring the angel's ability to fly by having sex with him, Jack is feeling decidedly unsettled. He's been intensely aware of Gina's pale slim thighs where they rest next to his ever since they took their seats, and what is happening on screen is not helping. He wants to touch them. He wants to slide his hand up her leg until it disappears beneath the hem of her skirt. Part of him knows Gina would have already made a move herself by now if that's the way their relationship is going to go, but nevertheless, he places his hand upon her knee.

For a moment it just sits there, inert. Then Gina places her hand on top of his. The palm of her hand rests there for an interminable minute or so, and then she raises his hand up to her lips, gently kisses it, and places it back on his own knee. Nothing has passed between them, and there's nothing more to be said. He returns his attention to the screen where Milo O'Shea is attempting to bring Jane Fonda to orgasm beneath the undulating paddles of his Excessive Machine.

oOo

It's pretty late by the time they return to the squat, having stopped for a drink and then a Chinese on the way. Gina's gone back to her room and Jack is lying on his mattress at the edge of sleep when he becomes aware of a tentative tapping on the door.

'Yeah?' He's wearing just his underpants so he pulls up the blanket. 'OK, you can come in.'

There's very little light but he can make out the shadow of the door as it opens, and a figure dressed in a white shift enters the room and stands there shivering. It's Minnie Mouse.

'Hello,' says Jack gently. 'What are you doing here?'

'I ... David sent me in. He thought you might like to ... spend some time with me?'

'OK ...' He pulls himself upright and taps the mattress beside him. 'Look, why don't you close the door and sit down?'

She sits tentatively on the edge of the mattress, modestly clasping the shift to her body. There's enough light filtering through the window for Jack to see her pale face, long, straight hair and shining eyes. Enough light for him to see that she is very pretty, and very young.

'He told me to say that I'm his present to you.' She looks away embarrassed. 'If you want me, that is.'

She sits there sweet and juicy like a newly ripened tomato, succulent and asking to be plucked. David must have seen him returning after his day with Gina and realised he is sleeping alone. How thoughtful of him.

'You could at least tell me your name.'

'It's Valerie.'

He holds out his hand. 'Hello, Valerie.'

She relaxes a little and takes it in her own hand, giving it a little shake: 'Hello Jack.'

'So, how old are you, Valerie?'

'Oh, it's OK, I'm over sixteen. It's OK, really, for us to ...'

'No, really, Valerie. How old are you?'

She averts her eyes. 'I'm ... well I'm going to be sixteen real soon.'

Jack doesn't push the matter further, although he suspects she's barely fifteen. He picks up what remains of a joint from the ashtray, lights it up and offers it to her. She thanks him and inhales. It's obviously not her first time. They sit for a moment, allowing some of the tension to dissipate.

'So, how did you meet David?'

She exhales slowly and then replies: 'Well, I was standing at the bus stop outside King's Cross wondering where I should go when he came up to me and we got chatting. He took me to a café and bought me breakfast, and then asked me where I was staying. I said I didn't know so he said I could stay with him and ... well, it seemed like a good idea.'

She takes another quick drag on the joint and then hands it back to him. Jack can just picture the scene: David gazing at her as she sits forlorn, and her just wanting someone to care.

'I think he's wonderful,' She looks at him defiantly. 'He's so kind, and he knows so much. And he really listens – there's not many that will listen to someone like me, you know, but he listens like he really understands what I'm trying to say ...'

She looks embarrassed, like she's said too much. Jack wonders if she's really that naive.

'Have you met any of his other friends yet?'

'Not really. Only Evelyn, who seems really nice. There was another girl, but I don't know her name ... and then there's you, of course!' She reaches out and strokes his thigh. 'You do want me, don't you?'

He gently picks up her hand and returns it to her. 'You are quite lovely, Valerie, and someday you're going to make someone very, very happy, but I'm afraid it's not going to be me. David shouldn't have offered you to me like that, really. You know this isn't right.'

She looks away. 'You don't want me, do you? You're just like the others.'

Jack holds up his hands: 'No, no. It's not that.'

'But what am I going to say to David?'

'Don't worry. If he says anything I'll thank him for his present and say we had a wonderful time. And I mean that's not wrong because it was good to meet you, even if we didn't ...'

She smiles at him and stands up, straightens her shift and creeps back through the door. Jack lies back on the mattress and eventually manages to find sleep.

# Ten

Over the next couple of weeks Jack's life settles into some sort of routine. His days are taken up with rehearsals in the music room or exploring the local area, either on his own or with Gina or Evelyn. Most evenings he's in one of the many pubs in the Ladbroke Grove area with Gina, Evelyn and sometimes David, when he's not busy with a new addition to his harem. Alternatively, if it's not raining or too cold, they sit on the terrace outside Jack's room: Evelyn, and perhaps David, with Jack in his new jacket and Gina wrapped up in a woollen shawl, whiling away the time getting stoned and consuming the odd bottle of wine or whisky while Jack strums the acoustic guitar.

He and Valerie occasionally exchange a smile that conveys some sort of understanding, but nothing more. He's tried talking to David about his 'present' several times, but each time David neatly sidesteps the conversation and he's left feeling vaguely guilty despite knowing that he's got nothing to feel guilty about.

Rather more on his mind is his relationship with Gina. Whatever happened in the cinema appears to be forgotten, or at least ignored, and he's trying to come to terms with that. He is still stung by the apparent willingness of Gina to have casual sex with almost anyone except himself, but he also values the obvious ease with which she shares at least part of her world with him. The only difference in their relationship now is that on occasion Gina offers to pay when the waitress approaches, or buys a round when they enter the pub.

But what dominates Jack's life during these weeks is what's happening in the music room. Once they've plugged in and checked their tuning they'll get into something familiar like *Into the Night* or, for something a bit more upbeat, another of David's compositions called *Going for Broke*. Faylin has yet to make an appearance, which Jack still finds strange, but everyone else seems to accept this as normal, explaining that she'll turn up sooner or later, and in any case she always seems to know what she's doing when she does appear. Instead David fills in on vocals, but in any case it makes little difference as the vocal line only serves to introduce the melody. And then, after a couple of verses, either David or Deek introduces an unexpected variation and Jack finds himself following their lead into new territory. Afterwards it's difficult to recall the riffs he played, but at the time they take on a power of their own, building up into sheets of pure emotion that pour out from beneath his fingers and leave him physically drained. Deek rarely speaks, communicating only through his bass line, but even David is reluctant to talk about what is happening, emphasising only that Jack's playing is 'really cool' and 'on the nail', and failing to acknowledge that it is usually his own rhythm guitar that is leading Jack in these new directions.

For Jack, one of the wonders of music has always been the countless worlds that can open up behind the twelve frets on the neck of his guitar that separate one octave from another. With just these twelve notes, or the eight notes of a major or minor key, or even just the five notes of a pentatonic scale, Jack can create a heart-rending ballad or a screaming heavy-metal solo. Just these twelve notes are all you need to play jazz or blues, ragtime or raga, sonata or symphony. And yet Devil Spawn seems to have opened up yet another world, a world that seems to summon deep-running emotions in a way Jack has never experienced before.

In the second week David introduces two new songs to their repertoire: *Lust* and *Rage*. These start innocently enough, but by the end they leave Jack so disturbed that the rehearsal breaks up in silence with Jack unable to do anything but climb the stairs to his room and collapse on his mattress. He feels as though these songs in particular are leading him somewhere specific, somewhere he really needs to go but fears to tread. Each riff he plays is a new yearning, a new striving towards perfection, a new attempt to reach some undefined goal.

On the Wednesday, after they've polished off a particularly powerful rendition of *Going for Broke*, David makes an announcement.

'I think we're about ready for an audience. What do you think, Jack?'

Jack looks at Evelyn. He's not at all sure, but she's nodding in agreement. Even Deek has a vaguely positive expression on his face.

'OK, I guess so,' says Jack. 'What do you have in mind?'

'Well, there's a friend of ours. He's having a party on Saturday. He's got this pad, more of a mansion really, in Buckinghamshire. It's in the middle of a wood, miles from anywhere, and he's well known for these "happenings". There'll be loads of booze and drugs, and everyone goes mad. He's even been known to roast a hog. He's heard what we're up to and he'd like us to do a set.'

'Sounds cool,' says Jack. 'What about Faylin? Will she be there?'

David waves his hand in a laissez-faire manner.

'Who knows? She might appear, which would be great, but we'll be fine without her – I mean, you've heard what we've been doing. You're definitely up to it. I can guarantee that.'

Evelyn pitches in with a quick drumroll.

'Don't worry, Jack,' she says, 'we'll be fine. It'll be fun. After all, the guy who's having the party? He's the guy who got us all this gear, so we really ought to return the favour.'

oOo

Saturday morning and David has arranged an old but serviceable Commer van to take them and their equipment to The Manor, as everyone seems to be calling it. Jack helps carry the gear up the stairs, and as he re-enters the squat to collect the final item, his precious Stratocaster, Kingpin calls through the open door of his office.

'Jack. A moment of your time, if I may.'

'Sure.' Jack enters to find Kingpin in his usual position, sitting behind his desk with his feet up on the worktop.

'So, Jack, how's it hanging?'

'Pretty good, thanks, Kingpin.'

'Cool. I understand you're playing a gig at The Manor tonight?'

'Yeah, that's right. With Devil Spawn.'

'Cool. Well, once you get there you'll meet Julian. He owns the place. He's a friend of mine.'

'OK ...'

Kingpin hefts a small leather shoulder bag from behind the desk. It looks well worn but strong.

'When you meet him, I want you to tell him you've got something for "The Chemist". You think you can do that?'

'Sure thing.'

'And then I want you to give The Chemist this bag.' He holds it out. 'You give it directly to The Chemist, not to Julian or anyone else. Got that? Only The Chemist.'

Jack takes the bag. It feels heavy, but not uncomfortably so.

'You've got it, Kingpin. I'll keep it safe.'

'You do that. Have fun at The Manor. It's a cool pad.'

The music room is empty when Jack gets down there, so he gently eases open the bag. Inside are four tightly wrapped brown paper packets. The edge of one has worked loose to reveal the corner of a crisp, new, ten-pound note. Assuming it's the same thing in all the packets, the bag must contain many hundreds of pounds, and possibly several thousand. He quickly presses the edge of the packet back down and closes the bag.

It's none of his business but the sooner he can hand over the bag, the better.

He's in the process of putting the guitar into its case when David appears. 'Is that everything? The Manor's in the middle of nowhere, so we don't want to leave anything behind.'

'I think so,' says Jack. 'I mean, there's nothing left in here.'

He follows David up the stairs, bag over his shoulder. The back of the van is just a metal box with no seats so, once the guitar is safely stowed along with the rest of the gear, the four of them cram onto the front seats with David driving, Evelyn by the window on the passenger side and Deek and Jack in the middle. It's clean, except for an old newspaper that's got trampled underfoot and the odd patch of rust, and it smells faintly of diesel.

'Should take maybe an hour and a half to get there,' says David as he starts the engine.

oOo

It takes a bit of time to get out of the area, mainly thanks to Portobello Market which is always busy on a Saturday morning, but eventually they pull up a slip road and onto the Westway. David tries to rummage through his bag with one hand on the wheel, then gives up and points to the cassette player mounted into the dashboard.

'Have a check in my bag, will you? I brought some cassettes along.'

Jack searches through the bag, which seems to be mainly full of scraps of paper covered in hastily written and largely illegible notes. He pulls out a pre-recorded cassette.

'Are You Experienced. Jimi Hendrix.'

'That'll do nicely,' says David.

Jack slots it in, presses the rewind button and then Play. As the opening chords of *Foxy Lady* ring out, David leans over and turns up the volume. They relax as the rooftops of Notting Hill and Ladbroke Grove drift past.

An hour later and they're into the green fields of Buckinghamshire. Deek lights up a joint, takes a couple of drags and hands it to Evelyn.

'So,' says Jack, 'tell me about this Julian guy.'

'He's, well, he's an interesting fellow,' says David. 'Bit of a dandy, if you know what I mean. A bit eighteenth century, which kind of fits because The Manor is at least a couple of hundred years old. He inherited it about ten years ago, together with an obscene amount of cash. His parents died in a car crash. His father was a bit of an alcoholic and was probably drunk at the time.'

'Sounds heavy.'

'Yeah, but Julian's always been a bit unhinged. He runs the place like it's a never-ending house party. There's always a few people around, and every so often he puts on one of these big bashes.'

'Have you been to one of these things before?'

'A few. Evelyn's been to one as well.'

'Yeah?'

'Yeah,' says Evelyn, passing him the joint. 'David introduced us early on, and then Julian asked us to come. He ... well, he paid for us to come as "hostesses", I guess you'd call it. He described us as his "nuns". He asked us to wear plain white cotton dresses and nothing on our legs except flimsy sandals that made it look like we were barefoot. We also had to wear a white silk ribbon around our necks. It was OK, though. We weren't treated badly. Most of the guests were too far gone to get up to anything. Most of the time we were just making sure everyone had food and drink, smiling a lot and laughing at bad jokes. Faylin was in her element.'

'I can imagine,' says Jack. He takes a drag of the joint. 'You know, it sounds like something I heard about recently. Hellfire Clubs, they were called. Back in Georgian times the aristocracy held these parties out in secluded mansions away from prying eyes. They were rumoured to be more like orgies. Any women invited were referred to as "nuns".'

Jack looks towards David for a response, but suddenly a car pulls out ahead of them and David has to swerve violently to avoid an accident. Jack drops the joint and by the time he's recovered it from all the debris that's accumulated and they've settled back down, David is indicating and they're pulling off the A-road onto a side road.

'Where are we?' Jack asks. The land now looks wilder, the farmland broken up by woodland and scrub. They begin climbing a gentle incline.

'These are the Chiltern Hills,' says David. 'Not far to go, now.'

They enter a more wooded area and a few minutes later David turns onto a dirt track that continues through dense woodland before opening out into a shallow valley. In the centre sits a substantial red-brick country house in the Gothic style, accompanied by a couple of outbuildings and an octagonal turreted tower. The driveway is lined with mature oak trees that give way to long, stone-bordered, rectangular ponds running along each side, flanked by more formal gardens and lawns and all bathed in the bright sunlight that shines down from an unseasonably clear sky.

'Nice little pad,' says Jack.

'Yeah,' says David. 'Nice and discreet, too.'

David honks the horn as they pull up in front of the house. As they climb out of the van, the front door opens to reveal a guy whom Jack presumes to be Julian by his black velvet suit and starch-white frill shirt. Next to him is a girl who must be six feet tall, wearing an elaborate and undoubtedly expensive contraption cut from various shades of blue silk that looks like it's come off a Paris catwalk. She would not look out of place on the cover of Vogue.

'David!' Julian calls out. 'Good to see you.'

'Good to see you too, Julian.' He indicates the others. 'I think you know Deek and Evelyn. This is Jack, our new shit-hot guitarist!'

Embarrassed, Jack can think of nothing better to do than take a bow. Julian laughs and the girl claps her hands.

'Welcome, Jack. I look forward to hearing you play. David tells me great things.' He indicates the girl. 'This here is Air; she's been helping me liven the place up.'

Air takes an elaborate bow.

'Come inside,' says Julian, 'you can unload later. Air can sort out some tea.'

They enter a spacious, double-height hall with elaborate marble staircases leading to the upper floors. Julian leads them into a kitchen that is empty except for a trendy-looking young couple deep in conversation at the far end of the largest table Jack has ever seen – at least twenty foot of solid oak that looks like it's seen centuries of wear. They take their seats. Air has a quick word with a waiter who also looks like he could be on the cover of Vogue, then joins them.

The faint sound of an extended guitar riff filters through from a distant room. Jack identifies it as one of John Cipollina's irresistible solos from the Quicksilver Messenger Service album, *Happy Trails*.

'Things won't really kick off for a couple of hours, yet,' says Julian. 'Quite a few people are already here, though. But you know what it's like. You came to one a few months back, I think?'

'Yeah, that's right,' says David. 'Evelyn and Faylin were here as well.'

Julian turns to Evelyn. 'Identical sisters, right?'

'That's it,' says Evelyn. 'We were here in the role of "nuns", if you recall.'

'Indeed I do. There'll be a few more around tonight. I hope it went OK?'

'It went fine, if a little cold.'

Julian grins. 'Yeah, well, you'll be on stage this time, so that shouldn't be a problem.'

They turn their attention to the tea the waiter has placed before them, a pale brew that smells a little like lapsang souchong.

'OK,' says Julian. 'I guess you'll want to get set up. I'll show you where you're playing, and there's a couple of rooms on the first floor that Air's set aside for you. She'll show you when you're ready – just come and find her if there's anything you need.'

Once they've finished their tea they follow Julian back to the entrance hall and then down a wide corridor to a pair of large, ornate, double doors flanked by luxuriant grapevines carved in solid wood and topped by a pair of trumpeting cherubs. Julian flings open the doors to reveal a ballroom of substantial size. There is plenty of dark wood, but the atmosphere is lightened by clerestory windows running along each side, suggesting the place might once have been a chapel. Facing them is a deep stage, and mounted on the walls are oil portraits of an assortment of dignitaries. With a start, Jack realises that he recognises one of the paintings.

'This is the main ballroom,' says Julian. 'I think last time you were here the band played outside. This time we thought here would be better. What do you think?'

'Well, so long as it's got sockets it'll be OK for us,' says David.

'You should find plenty along the edge of the stage, and there's a box that's got extension leads and the like. Talk to Drey if you need more amplification. He's handling the disco.' He indicates a skinny young man wearing a surplus army jacket and with lank, straight hair that reaches down almost to his waist.

'It'll do just fine.'

'Excellent.'

As Julian turns to go, Jack says: 'Excuse me, sorry, but can you tell me something? It's the paintings. It's just that I've seen one of them before.'

Julian looks quizzical. 'Oh yeah? Which one?'

'It's that one there,' says Jack, pointing at a portrait of Randolph Walverton posing with his pretty wife.

David and Deek glance at the painting and then walk over to join Drey. Evelyn looks at Jack before joining them. Julian studies the picture for a moment.

'Well, I don't know about that one in particular, but I can tell you that they're portraits of the members of what was called the Hellfire Club. Back in the day they used to hold meetings here. Nice and discreet, if you know what I mean.'

'Right. Wow!'

Julian grins. 'Yes, you could say we're carrying on the tradition. Anyway, I'll be in the kitchen area if you need me.'

Jack studies the picture. The associations with the Hellfire Club and the fact of the portrait hanging there can only be a coincidence, but he can't shake the feeling that it must mean something. He wonders what the night ahead might really have in store.

He turns away and joins the others at the side of the stage next to a table bearing a couple of turntables and a Revox tape recorder. He's just in time to catch Drey explaining the setup.

'… yeah, there's a pretty good PA in this place, so I can easily mike up your kit if you think you need it.'

'Sounds cool. So what sort of stuff are you going to be playing?' David asks.

'Oh, the usual – you know, Beach Boys, Stones, Pink Fairies, The Who, but I've also got a few specialities that might be more in tune with you guys. Managed to get hold of a tape of some Hawkwind sessions that are pretty cool – *Masters of The Universe, Paranoia, Hurry on Sundown* – that sort of thing. Also got hold of the *Live Experience* bootleg with Hendrix on the Lulu show and Top Gear. Thought I might lead in with Hawkwind and play out with Hendrix. What do you think?'

'Sounds cool to me.' David looks at Jack. 'What do you think?'

'Can't really go wrong with Hendrix, and Hawkwind sounds cool. Perhaps we could start the set by playing over it and then you fade it out once we get going. You think that might work?'

'Good idea,' says David. 'Means we don't break up the atmosphere, but just get straight in there.'

'Cool with me,' says Drey.

David, Jack, Deek and Evelyn set to ferrying their equipment from the van to the stage. David plugs a mic into the PA while Drey mikes up Evelyn's drums. Eventually they're all set up and Evelyn smashes out a quick roll to test the acoustics.

'Well,' she says, once the echoes have died down, 'I guess it'll be a lot less lively once it's packed full of people.'

'Assuming it will be packed,' says Jack.

'Oh, don't worry,' says Drey. 'Once things get started there'll be quite a crowd.'

David runs through the opening chords of *Into the Night*. Jack switches on his amp, turns up the volume and joins him with a few accompanying riffs. Evelyn brings in the drums and Deek the bass as David sings through the first verse. Drey walks down to the centre of the room to check the sound; once they get it right he gives them a thumbs up and they stop playing.

'OK,' says David, 'that's sounding good. I think we're ready for tonight. Shall we go and check out the rooms?'

They make their way back to the kitchen where they find Air sharing a joint with Julian.

'I guess you're wanting to see where we've put you? I'll take you up now, if you like.'

As the others follow Air out of the room, Jack lingers behind. He's kept Kingpin's bag close since they've arrived, but he's anxious to get rid of it. Realising he's still there, Julian offers him the joint.

'Thanks.' Jack takes a drag and holds up the bag. 'Kingpin asked me to give this to The Chemist?'

'Did he now? Well, leave it with me and I'll make sure it gets into the right hands.'

Jack keeps hold of the bag. 'Kingpin was most insistent I give it directly to The Chemist, and no one else.'

'Was he, now? Well, I guess that sounds like Kingpin.' Julian gets up, goes over to the wall and presses a large red button, incongruous against the wood panelling. 'OK. You need to go through that door ...' he indicates a plain wooden door set into the opposite wall '... and down the stairs. The lower door should be open and you'll find him on the other side. As you'll see he's a bit of a hermit, but he won't bite.'

'Thanks.'

'No problem.'

Jack follows Julian's instructions, pushing open the lower door – a heavy slab of dark metal with no obvious handle – to find himself in a small antechamber. The frosted glass door on the far side is ajar and through the gap he can see a large glass flask containing a pale pink fluid gently bubbling under the heat of a Bunsen burner. In front of him is a middle-aged man with unruly and possibly prematurely greying hair. He wipes his hands on a cloth and then extends one towards Jack.

'Hi.' He has a soft American accent that Jack suspects is Californian. 'You guys seem to find it difficult to pronounce my name so everyone calls me The Chemist.'

Jack shakes his proffered hand, which has a surprisingly strong grip.

'Hi.' He holds out the bag. 'Kingpin sent me. He wanted me to give you this.'

'OK,' says The Chemist, taking the bag. 'I guess you better come in, then.'

The Chemist's domain appears to be a comprehensive chemistry lab. The pink liquid bubbling away proves to be just part of a bewildering complex of glass tubes, filters, valves and flasks. On the benches that run around the edge of the room are high-precision, electronic scales, what appear to be microwave ovens and several large sinks. In one corner hangs a hazard suit, complete with gas mask, and several fire extinguishers of various types are mounted on the walls around the room.

'As you can see,' says The Chemist, indicating the equipment, 'I've been exploring the locale bounded by MDMA, MDA and EDMA.' He looks at Jack with the blind enthusiasm of a fanatic. 'Somewhere in there is the perfect mix. I just know it.'

'OK ...' Jack has very little idea what he is talking about, but The Chemist doesn't seem to care.

'Yeah, something that gets you the highs of the natural psychedelics, but with more control and without the side effects. Damned if I can find it, though. Anyway, let's see what we've got here.' He opens the bag and checks the contents. 'Everything appears to be in order. Now, where did I put it?' He rummages around one of the benches and eventually finds another leather shoulder bag, similar to the one Jack has brought. 'Here it is. Would you be so good as to return this to Kingpin?'

Jack takes the bag and turns to go. 'Of course.'

The Chemist has turned back to his experiment, seemingly oblivious to Jack's continued presence. As Jack gets to the door, The Chemist turns around.

'And Jack? Tonight, take the pink pill, not the blue pill. You need the pink pill if you're going to play tonight. It's important.'

'OK, sure. Thanks.'

Once again he has no idea what The Chemist is talking about. He closes the door and climbs the stairs back to the kitchen.

oOo

He finds the others in a first-floor room at the front of the house, sprawled across the pristine white covers of a king-sized bed, sharing a joint. They've obviously changed for the party, with both David and Deek in tight black trousers and leather jackets, and Evelyn in her signature flouncy white dress and big hair.

'Evelyn and me are in here,' says David. 'You and Deek next door.'

'OK,' says Jack, 'guess I'll go and sort myself out.'

The room next door is smaller, but not wildly so, and Jack is relieved to see two single beds. He drops The Chemist's bag on the nearer bed and goes into the bathroom to splash water on his face. Back in the room, he gazes out of the window. The view is straight up the driveway and a couple of cars are approaching, presumably bringing guests. One appears to be a Rolls Royce and the other a Bentley. Jack shuts the door so no one can see what he's doing and opens the bag. Inside are two securely sealed plastic bags, both packed with small pink pills. There must be nearly a thousand in there – enough to send him down for a very long time if he is caught with them. He closes the bag and puts it under the bed, up against the wall below the headrest.

He hasn't brought much in the way of clothes – just a clean pair of underpants and his tightest pair of jeans – but they look pretty cool with his new leather jacket. He checks his hair in the mirror and returns to the first room, where Evelyn hands him the remains of the joint.

'Everything OK? You look pretty cool.'

'Thanks,' says Jack. 'Yeah, everything's fine – provided Deek doesn't snore, that is.'

'No guarantees,' says Evelyn, winking at Deek. Jack stubs out the joint.

'Right,' says David. 'I guess it's time to get down there – check out the audience, as it were.'

Downstairs the party's already under way. Beautiful people are parading up and down the corridor, all high heels, bright colours, tight fabrics and outrageous hair. The Beach Boys are singing their hearts out in the ballroom and there is a pervasive smell of burning incense, sandalwood and patchouli to complement the cannabis.

'OK,' says David. 'We're on around nine. I'll go and check the gear now, but see you in the ballroom about ten minutes before?'

'Sounds good,' says Jack. The others nod in agreement. David and Deek stride off purposefully, leaving Jack and Evelyn at the bottom of the stairs.

'I think I might check out what's happening in the garden, before it gets too cold,' says Evelyn. 'Fancy coming?'

'Yeah, sure. Sounds cool. I'm just wondering what they're about?'

Jack nods towards the front door. On one side stands a waiter dressed in a white shirt and black tails, on the other a girl in a plain white frock. In their left hands they each hold a bowl filled with pink pills, and in their right a bowl filled with pale blue pills. The pink matches the bow tie of the waiter, and the blue matches the ribbon tied around the girl's neck. As they watch, a guest approaches the waiter, who whispers something in her ear; the guest takes a pill from the left-hand bowl.

'I don't know,' says Evelyn. 'Shall we go and find out?'

Jack follows her down to where the waiter stands.

'So what have you got here?' she asks, indicating the two bowls.

'Well, Madam,' answers the waiter. 'All I can say is that you are courteously invited to sample from the bowl: either a pink pill or a blue pill.'

'Ooh, that's very generous!' She turns to Jack. 'What do you think?'

'I'm not sure!' He asks the waiter: 'So what's the difference between them?'

'To be honest, Sir, I have no idea. All I can say is that they are different, and that girls tend to go for the blue while guys take the pink – although there are plenty of guys who've taken the blue, and vice versa.'

'Perhaps I'll take one of each.' Evelyn says.

'You are, of course, at liberty to do so,' says the waiter, 'but my understanding is that they cancel each other out, so you'd be back where you started.'

'Ah, clever. So which one are you going to take?'

In answer Jack dips his hand into the left-hand bowl and pops a pink pill into his mouth. Evelyn looks at him for a moment, her hand hovering over the right-hand bowl, and then switches to the left and takes the same.

'Well, that's settled,' she says. 'Wherever we're going at least we're headed in the same direction. Shall we see what's happening in the garden?'

They walk down steps and on to the gravel drive. It's already dark. In the middle of the manicured lawn a juggler stands lit only by the four flaming torches that he is juggling. Along the side of the house are small rockeries alternating with benches lit from above by mounted torches. A group of guests are sitting to their right, and one of the guys is holding out a joint.

'Thanks.' Evelyn takes it and he shuffles up so she can sit next to him. Jack takes a seat on the low wall next to the bench. For a moment they watch the juggler and then the guy extends a well-tanned hand.

'Hello there. My name's Troy, or at least that's what people call me.'

Jack shakes the proffered hand. 'I'm Jack.' He can't think of a witty rejoinder, but thankfully Evelyn butts in.

'Jack's our guitarist. You'll hear him play later. He's really hot.'

The girl sitting on the other side of Troy leans over. Her hair is a carefully designed cascade of auburn highlights and curls, and she nearly drops a tall flute of what looks like champagne as she places a bejewelled hand on Jack's knee.

'He's not just hot, sweetie – he's gorgeous!'

'If a little young, Lydia darling,' says Troy, grinning at Jack.

Jack knows it's meant in fun, but he's acutely aware he's the youngest in the group, and that the leather jacket Troy is wearing did not come from M&S and would have cost many times the price of the one he is wearing, even if he had paid for it.

'So you're in the band, huh?'

'Yeah, that's right. Evelyn here's the drummer.'

'Wow, chick drummer – now that sounds cool,' says Lydia.

'Yeah, it's good fun,' says Evelyn. 'Once you get into the groove you can really take it out on those skins.'

'Sounds a bit kinky to me,' says Troy.

'Well, you'd know all about that,' says Lydia with a smirk.

'So,' says Evelyn, 'did you guys take the pink pill or the blue pill?'

'Troy took the pink pill,' says Lydia, 'but I went for the blue. It seemed more appropriate.'

'And is it having any effect?'

Lydia throws her head back and laughs. 'Well, sort of. I do feel very … mellow, and like, ready to take whatever's coming.' She looks at Troy. 'How about you?'

'I'm really buzzin' – ready to dish it out, if you know what I mean.'

'Later, darling, later!'

Jack's having trouble keeping up with the innuendos. 'So do you know where they come from, the pills?' he interrupts, trying to forget the bag that's stashed under his bed, and the major-league chemistry set that's stashed in the basement, complete with mad scientist.

'The pills?' Troy looks at Jack sceptically. 'Not really. I mean, Julian gets hold of this stuff – all kinds of stuff. He's got his sources. Somewhere in London, I would imagine.'

Lydia looks at Jack. 'So which pill did you take, lover boy?'

Jack looks at Evelyn: 'We both took the pink.'

'Did you, darling?' Lydia stands up and holds her hand out to Jack. 'Anyway, enough of that. Shall we find out what's happening?'

Without waiting for an answer she slips her arm around Jack's and leads him back into the house. Troy brings up the rear with Evelyn.

From the ballroom comes the driving beat of the Electric Prunes, and the sedate lighting has been replaced with flashes of red, blue and yellow interspersed with bursts of stroboscopic white. Inside, the music is deafening and Jack can feel an organic excitement rising within him, partly as a result of the pill he has taken, and partly because Lydia is enthusiastically rubbing her body against his. Between the gyrating bodies Jack catches sight of Evelyn for a moment, her buttocks firmly in the grip of Troy's groping hands, and then they whirl away. In each corner of the room stands a podium above the pulsating crowd, topped by a girl cavorting around a metal pole, her bikini iridescent under ultraviolet light and her ankle secured to the pole by a metal chain. The air is thick with the smell of marijuana, sweat and adrenaline. Along the back wall are a couple of metal frames to which muscular men clad in leather are bound. Jack watches a girl pick up a leather flogger that must be three feet long and flick it none too gently across the man's exposed flesh. His body contorts in a display of pain and pleasure.

Now Lydia has disappeared and he is in the possession of a willowy blonde wearing something insubstantial in silk and seemingly intent on full body contact. Before he can react she has passed him on to someone else, and then suddenly Evelyn is shouting in his ear telling him it's time to play. She leads him by hand through the gyrating bodies to the stage.

Deek and David are already in place with their instruments, and Drey has Hawkwind in full flight on the deck. Jack picks up the Strat, puts it around his neck and stands next to David at the front of the stage, looking nervously out at the expectant gaze of the audience. Behind him Evelyn takes her seat, whirls her sticks above her head and starts pounding the drums in unison with the music. At a signal from Drey, Deek brings in a bass line that mirrors Hawkwind's but deviates into their own *Going for Broke* as Drey fades down the tape deck. David brings in the main chord sequence, Jack comes in with the signature riff and they're into the song, feeding off the vibe coming off the crowd and serving it back with an even stronger energy. David comes in on vocals, but it's the little variations he's introducing with his rhythm guitar that are guiding Jack in new directions, spinning off riffs that tweak the waves of emotion as they break over him and driving them all closer and closer to some sort of climax.

Evelyn subtly changes the beat and they're into first *Rage* and then *Lust* with an extended guitar solo. Jack feels as though an uncontrollable force is flowing through him, lashing the crowd with sheets of desire. The girls on the podiums have shed their bikinis and now writhe naked around their poles, deftly avoiding the reaching hands that threaten to drag them down into the crowd. The bound men are being lashed in earnest by masked women clad in tight leather and have lost most of their clothing too. Everywhere Jack looks clothing is being removed and breasts and buttocks are being stroked and groped. The audience is in a frenzy of desire and it is not long before several couples are openly copulating in the corners and up against the walls.

This is raw, uncontrollable want, divorced from any attainable goal. If satisfaction does come it is the short-lived spasm of orgasm, a brief moment of relief that fades all too soon, leaving body and soul unrequited. For Jack it manifests as a relentless drive to find that perfect riff, that combination of notes that will finally bring fulfilment, but he is beginning to suspect it's a desire that can never be sated and it will not stop until it has driven them all mad.

oOo

Eventually it does come to an end, leaving Jack barely conscious by the time Drey fades up the turntable with Hendrix and an extended version of *Purple Haze*. The frenzy of the crowd continues as he staggers off stage and they hardly seem to notice as he pushes his way through the thrusting flesh and flashing lights. It's a little quieter in the corridor. He is breathing heavily, heart pounding and body aching all over, and behind him Hendrix's guitar still screams. Jack's restless and highly charged, like a hosepipe inside him has come loose and is spraying something hot violently but aimlessly in every direction.

He sees Gina coming towards him. She's dressed as a 'nun' but with a white neck band, a symbol of submission that he cannot resist. He grabs her by the waist and pulls her hard against his body.

'Hey, what do you think you're doing?'

She pulls back, trying to break free, but Jack is not listening. All he can feel is the swell of her buttocks through the thin white shift, the heat of her body and the pressure of her pubic mound against his groin. All he can think about is satiating himself on her body. All the energy that he generated in the ballroom is flooding back with irresistible force. He wants her. He's wanted her ever since he set eyes on her and now she's here and he's going to have her. She is screaming at him but he's not listening so she slaps him hard across his cheek – so hard he almost falls. The wave of lust vanishes.

'Oh, my God. I'm so sorry.' He turns away, breathing hard and unable to look her in the eyes.

She grabs him roughly by the arm and screams into his face.

'What the fuck do you think you're doing? God, you men, you're all the same. Just because I wear what I like and do what I like, somehow you think it's all some sort of come-on? You think it's all for your own benefit? You think it gives you some sort of right to … to this?' She sticks out her hips and strikes a pose. 'Well, it doesn't!'

'I'm sorry, Gina …'

'And I'm sorry too, Jack, because there's one thing you've forgotten. Tonight it's not Gina at this party, it's Adele; and Adele decides who she's going to sleep with, not you. It's my choice, not yours.'

'I just thought … what with Dean and …' He can't believe he's just said that.

'What happens between me and Dean has nothing to do with you, Jack. And as for Adele, well, I'm sorry but I don't intend to spend the rest of my life behind the counter of some crap burger bar being groped by some fat fuck who reckons that, just because he pays me barely enough to cover the rent on some crap room in a crap part of town, he's got a right to my body. If it means being Adele for a couple of hours, well, that's just fine with me.'

She stops for a moment, composing herself.

'The thing is, Jack, the girl you know is Gina, not Adele. You wouldn't like Adele, not really. She pretends. She lies. She says she's having a good time when she's not. She's a bit of a bitch, really.'

'But …'

'Sex just gets in the way, Jack. Sex is for Adele. Sex is a quick fumble and a sticky patch on your thigh. It isn't real. Sex with Adele is just …'

'A financial transaction?'

Gina is silent. She looks at Jack for a long moment, then takes a compact out of her purse and dabs her face.

'I think you'd better go.'

oOo

A long time later, having aimlessly wandered around the party for several hours in a daze, punctuated by a pointless fumble with someone in some dark corner, Jack finds himself outside. The flaming torches have gone out, but an autumn moon has risen and is bathing the garden in silver. He collapses on a bench and tries to relax. He is feeling calmer, but he knows he's going to have a hard time coming to terms with what he did in there, with Gina. It's going to take a long time to forgive himself, and he's pretty certain that whatever he had with Gina is finished.

'Well, hello, lover boy. What are you doing out here all on your own?'

Evelyn is walking towards him, which is something he's really not ready for. She sits beside him and puts her hand on his thigh. A hand that bears a ring with an amber stone.

'Faylin?'

She laughs a deep throaty laugh and gently strokes his thigh.

'Could be. Would you like it to be?'

Part of him can't help but respond, but he is exhausted and confused.

He's really got no idea how to react.

'So what are you doing here? Why didn't you join us on stage?'

'Yeah, I guess I could have done. I almost did, but you were doing so well up there without me. I mean, you really got the crowd going, and that's what it's all about, isn't it?'

'Yeah, I guess, but how did you get here?'

'Oh, I've been here for a while. I'm with Julian as a "guest". Julian and I have this thing that's been on and off for ages. Right now it's most definitely on,' she gives Jack's thigh a squeeze, 'but that doesn't mean you and I can't have some fun.'

'OK, but what about Air? I thought Julian was with Air?'

She laughs. 'Yeah, that's the impression he likes to give. I guess he thinks it's good for his image, but the truth is that Air is his sister. She's Julian's little sister.'

As Jack tries to digest this she puts her arm across his shoulder and pulls him closer, nuzzling his neck with her nose. When he fails to respond she rests her head on his shoulder and they gaze together across the lawn, now glistening silver under the crisp moonlight.

'You know,' says Faylin, 'we've played here before, the three of us, but that was a very, very long time ago. We were just innocents then. We didn't understand what we were doing. We didn't know what was going to happen.'

'OK ...'

She laughs, and raises her head to look directly at Jack. 'Don't worry. I'll be there for the final gig. I promise you that.'

'The final gig?'

'Abbey Park. Halloween. Has David not said? Maybe I'm speaking out of turn.'

'Maybe, but final?'

'No, I don't know. Ignore me – I don't know what I'm saying.'

She stands up and kisses him hard, all lips and tongues, and then pulls away.

'Anyway, I think I'd better find out what Julian's up to. Give my love to Evelyn, and I'll see you on Halloween. Don't worry, I'll be there. I'll definitely be there.'

Jack watches her disappear into the shadows around the front door before rising and following her, but by the time he gets to the entrance she's vanished.

# *Eleven*

For most of the return journey the band sit in silence on the front seat of the van. David has put Neil Young's *After the Goldrush* on the stereo and is concentrating on the driving. The others are lost in their private worlds; for Jack, it's not a pleasant place. He'd eventually made his way to bed in the small hours of the morning and spent most of what remained of the night miserably failing to reach some sort of reconciliation with what remains of his self-image: a self-image already in tatters following his betrayal of Ania. And then there are the inevitable comparisons with Dean, his supposed best friend who jumps into bed with Gina whenever he feels like it and could well be screwing Ania right this moment. In the end he was lucky to manage just an hour or so of fitful sleep.

But if he's honest about it, there's also the possibility Gina might actually value her friendship with Jack more highly than a quick fuck with Dean. And, if he can put aside his lust for a moment, maybe that's actually what she was trying to tell him last night, which makes it even worse. He can blame the drugs for what happened, and who knows what was in those pills; he can blame the waves of carnal desire that swept through them as they'd played, and he certainly hadn't felt like it was him in the driving seat even though it had been his fingers on the fretboard; but ultimately it had been his choice to do what he did, and his alone. All of which leaves him wondering how he's going to react when he next comes face to face with her. Or how she's going to react, for that matter.

He can't really blame Dean for sleeping with Gina, given the opportunity. What he's having a harder time accepting is that Dean appears to have ended up with Ania, too. Had he planned it that way? Had he known, when they'd first gone to the squat, that Ania was already at Magda's? He'd always been aware of something between Ania and Dean, but he'd also known Ania would never act on it, or at least not while she was with him. Not while Dean was with Pauline, either. Ania was just too decent for that; she was just too decent for all of them.

It's only as the last strains of *Cripple Creek Ferry* die away and they enter the outskirts of London, that Jack comes to his senses. He shakes his head, catches Evelyn's eye and remembers the other conversation he had the previous night.

'You know I ran into Faylin last night. She was in the garden, after the gig.'

'Yeah, she's been staying there for a few days. She has a thing going with Julian.'

'She said.'

'Yeah,' says David. 'Didn't you see her? She was one of the girls on the podiums. Back left, if I remember right.'

Jack remembers the girls. In particular he remembers getting into a real dialogue – a *jugalbandi* as Alex would called it – with one of the dancers, her body moving in perfect harmony with the notes coming off his guitar, back and forth, as though he were controlling her dance, and her body his music. But she'd been front right.

'Wow, I didn't notice.' He lights up a fag. He's got a joint in his jacket pocket, but right now he needs a clear head. 'Anyway, she mentioned something about a gig in Abbey Park? On Halloween? Which is next weekend?'

'Yeah,' says David. 'Didn't I mention? We thought it would be pretty cool. I've been talking to some people down there. Dean's getting some stuff together. We thought we'd do it actually in the ruins of the abbey, using a generator. It should be far enough from the town not to attract any attention.'

'You haven't said anything.'

'No? Well, I'm sorry about that. Don't worry about it, though. It'll be cool … in fact it'll be really cool! It's such a great setting.'

'Yeah, I guess so. And Faylin said she'd definitely be singing, which should be interesting.'

'Not just "interesting". You wait. You're in for a treat. When she gets going it's out of this world.'

'Sounds cool. She said something else, though. She said it would the final gig. What did she mean by that?'

David glances over at Jack and then returns his eyes to the road.

'Did she say that? I'm not sure what she meant. I mean, you know Faylin. She likes to be provocative. It'll be something really special, though. Out of this world. I can promise you that.'

o0o

A little later they're off the dual carriageway and heading towards Ladbroke Grove. David slows as they come up to the flyover and pulls up just before they go under the bridge. He looks over at Jack.

'We've got something to take care of just around the corner, so you might as well hop out now and make your own way back to the squat. Go straight on under the flyover and you'll get to the Elgin. I guess you know the way from there?'

Jack looks at the three of them. He senses something's up but he can't put his finger on it, so he's got no choice but to comply. 'Sure, no problem,' he says and jumps out.

'Don't forget this.' David leans over, holding out the leather bag The Chemist gave him.

Jack reaches up and grabs it. 'Sure, see you back at the squat.'

'Yeah, see you there.' David slams the door, starts the engine and drives off, leaving Jack to watch as the van passes the tube station and takes the next turning right. Too late he remembers that his other bag – the one with his clothes and stuff – is still in the back. He shoulders the pouch and sets off under the flyover.

It being Sunday, the Elgin has closed after its lunchtime session and won't open again until the evening so the street is fairly quiet. As he reaches the corner he notices a tall, clean-cut guy on the opposite pavement who seems to be ambling along fairly aimlessly. The guy doesn't appear to be taking any interest in him, but Jack is now intensely aware of what's in the pouch he's carrying. The squat is only a few streets away, but now it feels like he's crossing a crocodile-infested swamp. He takes a surreptitious look. He'd read somewhere that you can tell a copper by his shoes, even if he's wearing shabby jeans and a T-shirt. Apparently they're always shiny, polished with military precision. He can't really tell at this distance, but it does look like the guy's shoes might have a good shine. Jack turns the corner and quickens his pace. Maybe this is why David dropped him off early, before they got too close to the squat: he'd got some inkling of what might be in the pouch and didn't want it in the van if they were stopped. Understandable, but it does make Jack the fall guy.

He picks up the pace as he heads towards Portobello Road. About halfway down he stops and bends down, as though to tie his shoelaces. He takes a quick glance behind. The guy has also turned the corner and is still behind him, but he's a long way back and appears to be making no effort to catch him up. Somewhat relieved, Jack continues down the road. Maybe it's just paranoia, but it's probably justified given his circumstances. He's not sure what's actually in the pouch but whatever it is it's almost certainly Class A, and almost certainly too much to count as 'personal use', no matter how good his defence. He'd be looking at a lengthy prison sentence, and he'd rather not think about the consequences of that.

Eventually he reaches the turning to the squat. For an agonising moment he stands on the corner, not daring to look behind, then the guy pulls into view in front of him on the other side of Portobello Road. Jack stands stock still as the guy ambles past, seemingly oblivious to Jack's presence. Either he's extremely good at his job or he really is just a guy with a penchant for shiny shoes out for an afternoon stroll. Either way there's not a lot Jack can do about it so he walks down the street and up the steps. Just as he's reaching for his key the door opens and there stands Gina.

'Oh hi, I'm just on my way out, so good timing. Toodle-oo.'

She pushes past him and struts off on ridiculously high heels, leaving him speechless on the top step. Thankfully he comes to his senses before the door slams shut behind her and stumbles into the hall where he stands breathing heavily, his heart beating at an unhealthy rate.

Eventually he calms down and knocks on the door to Kingpin's office. At first there's no reply and Jack starts wondering what he should do, but a second or two later he hears Kingpin's voice.

'Enter.'

Inside Kingpin is in his usual position seated behind the desk, feet up on its surface, which is covered with the usual paraphernalia.

He looks Jack up and down. 'You look a bit of a mess. I guess the party must have been a success?'

Jack nods dumbly, still trying to catch his breath.

'I'll take that as a yes. And I guess that pouch is for me?'

'Yeah,' says Jack, and he places the pouch on the desk in front of Kingpin. 'The Chemist asked me to give it to you.'

Kingpin picks up the bag and takes a quick look inside. Satisfied, he drops it into a desk drawer and picks up the slim envelope lying in front of him. He taps it slowly on the desktop, scrutinising Jack as he does so.

'Any ... problems on the way?'

Jack thinks back to the guy with the shiny shoes.

'Not really. No, it all went pretty smoothly.'

'Glad to hear it.' Kingpin holds out the envelope. 'This is for you.'

Jack takes it. 'Thanks!'

'OK. Well, I'm sure you've got things to do.'

'Yeah, I guess so,' says Jack, and he turns to go. Outside he opens the envelope to find a couple of crisp twenty-pound notes and a small cube of what looks like top notch Moroccan.

For the next few days, life at the squat is pretty much the same as it had been before the gig at The Manor. Jack spends much of the afternoon in the basement rehearsing with Evelyn, David and Deek. He feels a certain satisfaction as the riffs they're playing around with now seem closer to whatever it was he heard in Abbey Park, but there is still something missing that is leaving him frustrated and drained. Most days they wander round to Miles' place for something to eat at some point, while he spends his evenings either alone in his room with the acoustic guitar, trying to get closer to those evasive tunes, or with the rest of the band in David's attic room getting stoned, usually after a visit to the pub. The only difference is the absence of Gina, who is either making a concerted effort to avoid him or has genuinely disappeared.

On the Wednesday evening, following a particularly strenuous rehearsal, David and Deek disappear on some mysterious errand so Evelyn suggests they wander down to KPH for a drink and perhaps something to eat after. Jack hasn't been out all day so he's pleasantly surprised to find it's a balmy night for the time of the year, and he starts to relax as they walk the short distance to the pub.

'God, that's better,' Evelyn says, waving her arms about and stretching out her fingers. 'It's great practising, but it really makes my arms ache!'

''Yeah, I know what you mean.' Jack flexes his fingers. 'It's like you get locked in one position, and everything seizes up.'

Evelyn feeds her arm through his and gives it a squeeze. 'It's getting really good, though. I mean, you were playing some shit-hot licks back there, and you're really getting it together with David's rhythm.'

'Helps having a solid bass and drums, though.'

Evelyn laughs as they reach the door of the pub. 'Yeah, but perhaps that's enough self-congratulation for a while.'

It's quite early but already there's a small bunch of people up one end of the KPH where a lanky guy is playing acoustic guitar and singing. Evelyn takes a seat at the back of the pub while Jack buys the drinks: a pint of Worthington's for himself, a gin and tonic for Evelyn, and a packet of peanuts to share. He takes a seat next to Evelyn and they listen to the performance for a bit, savouring their drinks and picking at the nuts.

'He's not that bad,' says Evelyn.

'Yeah. Bit Bob Dylan, with that voice.'

As if on cue the guy winds up a ballad that is beginning to outstay its welcome and embarks on a version of *Lay Lady Lay*.

'One for the ladies, I think,' says Evelyn, raising her eyebrows.

Jack laughs as there are indeed a couple of hippy chicks at the front of the guy's audience, gazing up at him with adoring eyes.

'Seriously, though, I think we're pretty much ready for the Abbey Park gig.'

'Yeah, I reckon so.' He looks appraisingly at Evelyn. 'You know, do you remember, back when we first met, I told you about the singing I'd heard in the park, when I was tripping? The three teenagers that I'd – well – hallucinated, singing this amazing music?'

'Yeah, I remember. You said what you're playing with us is somehow similar? But you just can't remember the tune?'

'Yeah, that's right. I don't know what it is, but it's driving me crazy. I feel like I'm playing better than I've ever done before, but it feels like it's not me. It feels like it's some other force that's flowing through me, and that if I just keep playing I will, eventually, hit the right notes.'

'Well, you're playing some pretty shit-hot stuff, you know. I mean, at The Manor gig you had them tearing their clothes off and slobbering all over each other. I'm surprised you weren't mobbed when you came off stage.' She looks at him. 'But you don't let it go to your head, do you? I mean, you're not interested in the fame. You're not like David, who loves being the centre of attention.'

Jack smiles ruefully. 'Truth is, I was a wreck by the time we got to the end of that gig.' He thinks back to his encounters with Gina and Faylin. 'I mean, I had my own stuff to deal with. I just wanted to get away.'

The singer has moved on to another interminable ballad.

'You know the reason David wanted you in the band – the reason he asked you? It's because of what we saw when you were playing in the Scout Hut, in Westerford. He saw what happened with the greasers, the way you faced up to them, and he said, "I want him in the band". It's because he knew you were better than him. He knew he couldn't do that.'

'Yeah, well ...'

'It wasn't just that, though. It's also because he knew you wouldn't upstage him. You aren't in it for the image or the fame. You just want to play guitar.'

'I guess that's true. I mean, I do feel like I'm on a mission.'

'Well, you never know. We'll be playing Abbey Park, where you first heard that tune, and Faylin will be there too. Might jog your memory.'

'Maybe so. It certainly feels like something big's got to happen soon.'

'Anyway,' says Evelyn, draining the last of her drink, 'I'm hungry. Shall we go and get some chips?'

'Sure.'

Jack knocks back his pint and they leave the pub, stopping at the fish and chip shop on the corner. They both choose sausage and chips, eating them from the newspaper as they wander slowly back to the squat. They finish just as they arrive back, so Jack lifts the lid of the dustbin next door to chuck away the greasy paper. His attention is caught by something inside the bin so he reaches inside and pulls out an antique porcelain doll. It is dressed in denim shorts and waistcoat and has a tiara on its head.

'I've seen this before. It belongs to Gina.'

'OK,' says Evelyn. 'Is there anything else in there?'

'Quite a lot of stuff. I think it might all be Gina's.'

Ignoring Evelyn he bounds up the steps to the squat, flings open the front door and continues up to Gina's room. The door is closed, but he pushes it open without knocking. As he feared, the room is empty. The threadbare carpet, the bed, the dressing table and the wardrobe are still there, but the record player, the records, all those dolls, the posters and everything that made it Gina's room has gone, as though she'd never been there.

Without thinking he bounds downstairs and throws open the door to Kingpin's office. Kingpin is sitting behind his desk.

'What do you want? And what's wrong with knocking?'

'Where is she?'

'Who do you mean?'

'Gina ... Look, I'm sorry. I'm really sorry, but her room is empty. Where's she gone? Please?'

Kingpin looks at him sceptically. 'And what's it to you?'

'It's just that I ... well, I might have pissed her off badly. I really care about her. I want to know she's OK.'

Kingpin looks at him like it's a story he's heard before: 'I've got no idea where she is, Jack, but I'm sure she's OK. All I can tell you is that Gina comes and goes. She leads her own life and it's got very little to do with either you or me. If you really want to find her you could try the telephone boxes. That might get you Adele, if she's putting herself out there, but I guess what you're really looking for is Gina, and if Gina wants to be found, she'll find you.'

oOo

'Hi there, stranger!'

Saturday lunchtime and Jack's sitting at his usual table by the window in Miles' café, nursing a cup of tea and staring vacantly at the hustle and bustle of the market outside. They've spent the morning loading up the van so they can drive down to Westerford later in the afternoon, and he's just polished off a bacon and egg sandwich. At the sound of a familiar voice he looks up to see Dean grinning at him. Without waiting for an answer, Dean squeezes between the tables and sits down opposite. He's carrying a small leather shoulder bag.

Jack comes out of his reverie. 'Well, hi there. Yeah, been a long time, I guess.' He nods at the bag. 'You up here to see Kingpin?'

'Yeah, but not just Kingpin. I wanted to see how you're doing, too. I mean, it's been quite a while and I hear good things about the band. You know, Devil Spawn and all.'

'Yeah. It's going good. I mean, you know about the gig we're doing at Abbey House? Inside the ruins? It's tomorrow night.'

'Yeah, Halloween. Should be cool. I've been helping David with that. We're getting a generator sorted. Martin's handling it. I've got something cool to help with the atmosphere, too. Put everyone in a receptive frame of mind, if you know what I mean.'

'Not something dreamt up by The Chemist, by any chance?'

Dean takes a cigarette from Jack's packet, which is lying on the table between them. 'So you've met The Chemist, then?'

'Yeah,' says Jack as he flicks open his lighter and holds it out for Dean to light his cigarette. 'We did a gig at The Manor and Kingpin asked me to do a delivery.'

'Cool.' Dean holds up his hand to bring Miles over and nods at Jack's cup. 'You want anything else?'

'I'm cool.'

'Just a cup of tea for me then, Miles.'

As Miles disappears Dean asks: 'So what's happened to Gina, then? I popped into her room, but it's empty.'

'She's ... well, she's gone.'

'Yeah? That's a shame. She's quite a chick.'

'Yeah, well ... she's just gone, alright?'

Dean looks at Jack appraisingly.

'Yeah, well, she does that from time to time. She leads a complicated life. She usually surfaces eventually.'

All Jack can think about is the expression on her face when he last saw her. The anger and the shame. 'Well, I guess you'd know about that.'

Dean holds up his hands in surrender. 'It's cool, man. None of my business.' He takes a sip of the tea Miles has put in front of him.

Jack looks at him. It's true; it's not Dean's business. Jack needs to sort out his feelings for Gina by himself. Dean's right, and probably does know Gina better than he does.

'So how's Ania?'

'She's doing fine. She's looking forward to the gig, and seeing you play. We both are.'

'So are you together now? Like an "item", as it were?'

'Yeah, I guess you could say that.'

'What about Pauline? Or Gina?'

Dean looks out at the crowd flowing passed the window.

'Well, Pauline's still looking after her grandfather.' He turns back to Jack. 'And Gina's disappeared. As you well know.'

Jack holds his gaze. He's on dangerous territory, but he can't stop.

'So, when you brought me up to the squat, did you know where Ania was already? Did you know she was with Magda? Were you going to get together all along?'

'What, you think I set it up?' says Dean. 'That's a bit rich, coming from you. I mean, it was you she caught screwing Faylin, and that really screwed with her head, as you well know. If anyone else is to blame then it's David for trying to seduce her into his harem. He might even have got Faylin to come on to you, so as to isolate her. But it was you that betrayed her. I just wanted to help because I cared about her. And you. You might not believe it, but I do care about you.'

'Yeah, but …'

'But nothing! Look, when I phoned Magda, I just wanted to make sure she was OK. It was Ania who asked me to come over. I didn't take advantage of her. I really didn't, but things just happened. She chose to be with me of her own free will, and I really, really didn't push it, I promise.'

'OK, OK, I'm sorry. I guess I'm just being an idiot.'

'It's cool, but yes you are. Look, you need to chill. And you need to be careful. David's got something going. He's not a nice person, from what Ania's told me. And the twins are in the band? I mean, are you and Faylin …?'

'Well, yeah, they're in the band. Evelyn's cool – we go out drinking and stuff – but Faylin's never there. I've only seen her once since I've been up here. That was at The Manor when she told me she'd be singing at the Abbey House gig, but she doesn't practise with us. Evelyn says she just fits right in on the night. I guess we'll see what happens tomorrow.'

'So you and Evelyn …?'

'No.' Jack looks at Dean, aware that he's blushing and it probably shows. 'I mean no! We're just friends. She's the most normal of the lot.'

'But you do fancy her? I mean, she is Faylin's identical twin, after

132

all?'

Jack looks out of the window, 'Well, yeah. But at the moment she's just a good friend, and I don't know whether she wants anything more. I don't want to ruin it by pushing it.'

'OK ...'

He looks back at Dean: 'I know what you mean about David, though. He's a strange guy. A bit creepy, too. But he plays a mean rhythm guitar and he wrote most of the material.' He shifts in his seat. 'The thing is, I really need to do this. I can't really explain it, but it's got something to do with what happened in the park when we were tripping. You know – the singing. I don't know what it is, but I'm playing better than I've ever played before and it's David who's helping me do it. When we get into a groove it's like he's steering me towards something really important. You'll see, tomorrow night. It'll be really something, I can tell you that now.'

'Can't wait. As I said, we're really looking forward to it. Just ... well, are you sure it's taking you somewhere you want to go?'

'I'm not, but in truth I'm not sure I've got any choice in the matter. It's just something I've got to do.'

o0o

They finish their tea, Jack settles the bill and they step out into the bustle of Portobello Market. All around are stalls selling leather bags, T-shirts and tie-dyes, intricate antiques in silver and bronze, and tables full of hippy paraphernalia. The crowd thins as they get to the turn-off to the squat, and then Dean comes to a standstill so suddenly they almost collide.

'Don't look now,' says Dean in a harsh whisper from the corner of his mouth, 'but I think we're being followed. You need to back off. They don't necessarily know we're together.'

Without saying a word Jack backs off, just as he would if he'd collided into a complete stranger. Once there's a decent distance between them he stops and looks round. Dean has walked straight past the turn-off to the squat and is heading down Portobello Road towards the next stretch of market stalls, and there are clearly two guys following him. They look quite ordinary: faded jeans and cloth jackets, one of them with a flat leather cap drawn down over lank, shoulder-length hair. Just guys from the crowd, and no sign of shiny shoes, but they're definitely moving in.

Jack scans the street. There are plenty of people about, but no one appears to be paying him any particular attention. He turns back just in time to see one of the guys reach out and put a hand on Dean's shoulder. Dean stops, and the other guy steps in front. He's holding out a badge and saying something, but Jack's too far away to hear. He's also holding Dean's bag. He takes a peek inside and says something else. Dean nods and holds his hands out in front of him, wrists together. With a swift motion the other guy whips out a pair of handcuffs and clamps them on him. Some passers-by have stopped, and a young woman is even remonstrating with the cop, but they ignore her and strong-arm Dean down the street and around a corner to where a car presumably waits. The crowd closes behind them as though nothing has happened, leaving Jack stunned and alone.

There's nothing he can do, and he's probably safe for the moment, but he's got to think quickly if he's going to stay that way. He could hightail it out of town – get the next train back to Westerford and pretend none of it happened – but he knows that's not really an option so he walks slowly back up Portobello Road. He stops outside Miles' place and looks around. The street is crowded with people going about their lives, browsing for a bargain or a memento and wondering where they can get lunch. He could sit in the café for a while in a state of high anxiety, but that's not really an option. The reality of the situation is that he should return to the squat and warn the others. He retraces his steps back to the turn-off to the squat. The street is far from empty, but no one seems to be watching so he climbs the steps and lets himself in.

The first sign of anything untoward is that the door to Kingpin's office, normally only opened on his barked command, is ajar. Jack peeks round to see Kingpin hastily packing the contents of his desk into a rucksack.

'I see you've heard what's happened,' says Jack.

'Yeah,' says Kingpin. 'A little bird just told me. I understand you were there.'

'Yeah. It happened right in front of me.'

'Well, it looks like you're OK for the moment, otherwise they'd have picked you up at the same time. Looks like the fuzz haven't sussed the connection between here and The Manor, and Dean knows his rights. He's not going to make it easy for them, but you still need to get out of here as quick as you can.'

'We were going to drive down to Westerford this afternoon, anyway.'

'Sounds like a plan. As far as I know, David and the others are still upstairs, but I'm out of here right now.' He shoulders his bag.

'OK,' says Jack, 'I guess this is it.'

'Yeah, I guess it is.' Kingpin holds out his hand. 'Good luck.'

Jack takes it and they shake hands. 'Thanks. You too, man.'

Kingpin disappears behind a curtain that hangs discreetly down the back wall of the office. Jack watches him go then bounds upstairs to the attic where he finds David and Evelyn waiting. On the floor between them are two tattered rucksacks.

'Deek's already in the van,' says David. 'Grab your stuff, we need to get going. Just take what you need, but don't count on coming back here any time soon.'

Jack ducks into the room that has been his home for the past few weeks. There's quite a few things he'd like to take as mementos, and in particular of Gina, but in the end he just stuffs his clothes, his statue of Buddha and his copy of the *I Ching* into the holdall and grabs his sleeping bag. At the last minute he spies the "Make Love Not War" badge that Gina had nicked for him and pins it on his T-shirt under his recently acquired leather jacket. He takes a last look around.

The three of them hurry downstairs to the hallway. Jack is bracing himself for arrest the moment they open the front door, but David ushers them through Kingpin's now empty office and sweeps aside the curtain to reveal a nondescript wooden door. Daylight pokes through two small glass panels at the top.

'This takes us through the garden,' says David as he opens the door. 'Should be safer.'

The door appears to open into an impenetrable mass of ivy, but they push through and stumble into what was probably once a manicured lawn surrounded by ornamental border beds. The grass is now knee high and the plants loom over them in an almost threatening fashion. They fight their way through to the rear wall, six feet high in brick black with lichen and with a rotting wooden door. David opens it a crack and looks round. Satisfied, he beckons them through into a narrow alley that takes them out to the street just a few doors down from the squat. Parked opposite is the van, with Deek at the wheel. Nobody seems to notice as they pack themselves into the front seat and drive off, but it's only once they've crossed Bayswater Road that they start to relax, satisfied no one is on their tail.

o0o

It's about an hour and a half's drive down to Westerford, most of it through London suburbs. For much of the journey they sit in silence, lost

135

in their private worlds. Jack's is dominated by Dean. He keeps replaying the arrest in Portobello Road. Why couldn't Dean have got rid of the bag? Maybe he had tried to lose it before they actually caught up with him, but Jack's back had been turned so he didn't see what was happening immediately before the arrest. And why hadn't they arrested him at the same time? Presumably they hadn't made the connection between Dean, Jack and the squat, but they must have followed him, unless it was all some horrendous coincidence. If they'd seen Dean coming out of the squat, why hadn't they arrested Kingpin? And how come Kingpin already knew about the arrest? He remembers the kid who had been in Kingpin's office when they first met. It had seemed a bit Dickensian, like Fagin with his gang of look-outs, but that was probably the answer.

He's also wondering what Dean is going through right now. Jack's only once been inside a police station, and that was in Westerford a year or so ago. He and Martin had been caught smoking a joint and Martin had said something unfortunate, which resulted in them both being hauled in and formally cautioned. It hadn't been much fun. They'd sat in an empty room for nearly an hour not knowing what was going to happen, but then he'd seen his mum's ex Ray having a quiet word in the corridor and next thing they were being released with a stern talking-to and nothing on the record. It wouldn't be the same for Dean. Whatever was in that bag would get Dean a lot worse than that.

'Don't worry too much,' says Evelyn, breaking the silence. 'I'm sure Dean knows how to handle it. He'll get in touch with Release and they'll get him a lawyer. I mean, their office is only round the corner from where he was arrested.'

'Yeah,' says Jack, 'I guess so.'

He looks out the window. They're out of the suburbs now, green fields rolling by on either side. It should feel like he's coming home, but it doesn't. With a pang he realises how much he's going to miss the squat and the life they'd created there: rehearsing in the basement, nights in the pub, smoking a joint on the balcony outside his room with Evelyn and Gina. Gina, who he's unlikely to ever see again.

'Anyone fancy a joint?'

'Yeah, sure,' says Evelyn. 'I think there might be some papers in here.'

She opens the glove compartment, pulls out a packet of green Rizlas and hands them to Jack. He pulls a tattered A to Z from the pocket of the door, sticks it on his lap and starts putting a joint together from what remains of the hash Kingpin had given him.

'Woah, steady on,' Jack says as Deek swerves around a pothole, almost sending his half-made construction on the floor.

'Sorry, man,' says Deek.

'You know, Dean could make a joint in even the most horrendous conditions. I remember one time round at Pauline's place. He was boasting, so Ania challenged him to make a joint blindfold. We put an album cover on his lap and positioned the grass, the papers and the fag packet for him to see, and then Pauline got a scarf and tied it around his eyes so he was totally blind. It took him ages but he did eventually get it made, and it didn't fall apart when we smoked it. It was pretty cool. And hilarious.'

'Perhaps we should blindfold you,' says David.

'No thanks, I'm having a hard enough time with Deek's driving.'

Deek laughs and swerves the van unnecessarily. Jack just about holds on and manages to finish the joint without incident. He lights it, takes a drag and passes it to Evelyn. David passes as usual.

By the time they finish the joint they're winding up the slopes of the North Downs, just a few miles from Westerford.

'So what's the plan?' Jack asks.

'Well,' says David, 'I think we should stay at Evelyn's tonight. It's a bit cramped, but you've got your sleeping bag. Of course that's up to you. I mean, you may want to stay somewhere else.'

Jack thinks about it. Yes, he could go back to his mother's. He could even stay at Alex's, if he's around, and it would be good to see him. But in the end, he just wants to get the job done. He can feel inside that something's building up and he's not sure what it is, but he just wants to get it out of the way. After that, who knows.

'No, that's fine with me.'

And then they're across the bridge and there's the Blue Lion and they turn down Riverside and there's Ania's house, and then the Griffin and into Evelyn's street.

# Twelve

Jack is woken by the sound of Evelyn shuffling around the kitchen. He's had a restless night, not helped by the sofa being too short and, of course, the events of the day before. His mouth feels dry and unpleasant.

'A cup of tea might help with that,' says Evelyn, looking at him sympathetically.

He smiles back although he still feels groggy. 'Yes please!'

She brings the kettle back to the boil, cleans out a cup and pops in a teabag. Jack fumbles around and eventually finds a packet of cigarettes beneath a cushion. He takes one for himself and holds out the pack to Evelyn.

'No thanks. I don't really, unless it's a joint.'

'Sensible policy,' mumbles Jack as he lights up. He turns at the sound of David coming out of the bedroom. 'Hi there! So what's the action today?'

'Well,' says David, looking at his watch, 'Chris and Martin should be around pretty soon. It's their job to sort out a generator, so once you've got your act together you can help them get it up to the park and make sure it works.'

'OK, better get up, then.' Feeling slightly embarrassed he shrugs out of the sleeping bag to reveal his two-day-old underpants. He quickly pulls on his jeans and T-shirt, which are lying in a heap on the floor, and stands up.

'Thanks,' he says, taking the tea from Evelyn. She is looking at him with slightly raised eyebrows. She's also dressed in jeans and T-shirt, but they look a lot cleaner than his, and her hair still manages to tumble effortlessly about her shoulders. 'I guess I could make use of the bathroom.'

'Feel free,' she says. 'You might even find a towel you can use.'

A few minutes later and he is feeling considerably more human. He gratefully takes the slice of buttered toast offered by Evelyn and sits down. He's just finished when David answers a knock on the door to reveal Chris and Martin. Jack stands to greet them.

'Well, hello, stranger.' Chris holds out his arm and they go into a gladiatorial handshake.

Martin puts down the strange-looking box he's carrying and pats him on the back. 'Good to see you, mate!'

'Yeah,' says Jack, 'it's been a while.'

Truth be told, he's surprised at the depth of his feelings. This is where he comes from, and he's only now realising how much he's missed it. 'So, how do you guys know David?'

'Dean put us in touch,' says Chris. 'That's when we first heard about this gig you're doing in the park.'

'Right,' says Jack. 'So have you guys met Evelyn?'

'Not had the pleasure,' Martin says, taking a step towards her and holding out his hand while giving her the once-over. She gives it a firm shake.

'Evelyn's our drummer,' says Jack.

'I bet she is. Cool.' He gives her a wink and she grins back.

'Hey, you guys heard what happened to Dean?'

'Yeah,' says Martin. 'Ania told Carol what happened, or at least what she knows. I gather she's up in town right now.'

'That's right,' says Chris. 'Last I heard he's still being questioned. Ania's talking to Release – you know, the legal people – to see if there's anything they can do.'

Jack sighs. 'You know I was there, when he was busted? He realised he was being followed and told me to back off so they wouldn't get me at the same time. There was nothing he could do – he was caught red-handed.'

'Bummer,' says Chris.

'Yeah,' says David, 'but I guess he wouldn't want it to dampen the ceremonies. So how's it going? You guys sort out a generator?'

Martin indicates the contraption that is sitting on the table. 'Actually, we've done better than that. This here's an inverter a mate of mine put together. He's a bit of a geek but he reckons it should handle a couple of amps for at least six hours and it's a lot quieter than a generator. It runs off a couple of car batteries. I've got all the stuff stashed in the car ...'

'... and it did work when we tried it at home,' says Chris. 'It handled my amp fine, even at high volume, which my mum was none too happy about.'

'Sounds cool to me,' says David. 'Deek's already taken the van up to the park, so you guys can sort out the power side of things.' He turns to Jack. 'Look, we've got a couple of errands to run but I'll meet you back here later. About four, maybe?'

'Sure thing,' says Jack. 'I'll see you later.'

Martin's Cortina is parked outside. Martin puts the inverter on the back seat and the three of them hop in.

'The batteries and the leads are in the boot,' says Martin as he turns the ignition. The engine starts up with its customary roar. 'I've also dug up a small trolley we can use to get it all into the park, and a tarpaulin to cover it up safe. The batteries are fucking heavy and full of acid so probably best not to carry them by hand.' He grins. 'I mean, it's a pretty steep hill.'

They pull in at the Rose and Crown, and park next to the van that brought them down from London. The pub isn't open yet and there's no one about so they start unloading the car. Martin takes out the trolley, a childlike construction involving a shallow wooden tray, small rubber tyre wheels with bright red hubs, and a handle for pulling it along.

'Where did that come from?' Chris asks.

'Don't know, really,' says Martin. 'It's something that's been knocking about the house since forever. Must have had it when I was a kid.'

'Still,' says Jack, 'it should do the job.'

'Yeah, here's hoping,' says Martin. He looks up at the sky. There's a few clouds and there's a definite nip in the air, but the sun is out and it's largely a clear deep blue. 'Looks like the weather's on our side, too.'

o0o

They load up the trolley and Martin pulls it carefully across the road and down the path through the narrow band of woods that separates the park from the town, Chris and Jack following. Everything is still in the park, the peace broken only by the rattle of the trolley's wheels as Martin pulls it over the gravel path. The last time Jack was here he had been with Pauline, Dean, Carol and Dillon, and about to come up on the strongest trip of his life, blissfully unaware of what he was to encounter. He looks across the valley into the woods on the other side. All looks calm and unperturbed.

They carry on down the path that leads to the lake, cross Fern Brook and then clamber up steeply through the woods to where the natural contour of the hill gives way to the grass-covered mounds of the fort. There's a few occasions when the trolley threatens to tip over, but Martin manages to rescue it just in time. Then they hear voices and they're through to the remains of Abbey House.

Anything in the house made of wood was destroyed by the fire some two centuries earlier and much of the stonework has disappeared, mined by the villagers over the passing years for their own constructions. All that remain are misshapen portions of wall broken by empty windows and door frames, all heavily overgrown with ivy, moss and various hues of lichen. The voices are coming from an area further into the ruins, a larger space that most likely had been the ballroom. The ground here is covered in grass cropped close by the deer, with little undergrowth, and one end is slightly raised, making for a natural stage. Most of the walls are fairly intact to a height of four or five feet, with occasional sections going up ten or twelve feet and showing the holes where the beams supporting the upper floor would have been secured. To the east the walls are lower, affording a view across the relatively flat interior of the iron-age fort.

Deek and Phil are sitting next to a small pile of drums, amplifiers and leads, sharing a joint. Phil stands as the others approach and holds out the joint: 'First smoke of the day. We thought we deserved something after hiking that lot up here.'

Deek raises a hand in greeting, but remains silent. Jack takes the joint and smiles at Phil. 'Good to see you, mate! Been a while.'

'Yeah,' says Phil. 'Certainly has. Deek's filled me in on what you guys have been up to, or some of it at least. Sounds interesting – I'm looking forward to the gig.'

'Yeah, it's been quite a trip. Anything could happen.'

'We thought we'd set this lot up later, before it gets properly dark,' says Phil. 'Deek found a small room through there where we can stash it.'

He indicates an area hidden in shadow behind a gap in the ruined wall behind him.

'Sounds like a plan,' says Martin. He pulls the trolley through the gap, which had probably once been a door. Jack picks up his amplifier and follows him through to what remains of some sort of anteroom. Soon they've got all the gear stashed away, and Martin covers it with the tarpaulin.

'Should be safe here, at least for a while. It'll be fairly well hidden and there doesn't seem to be anyone about.' He looks at his watch. 'Time for a pint. Shall we adjourn to the pub?'

The others express their enthusiasm, but Jack holds back. He's still feeling decidedly uncertain about the gig and really wants to spend some time on his own.

'Look, you guys go ahead. I'll see you later. I won't be long. I just …'

'Don't worry about it,' says Chris. He hands Jack what remains of the joint. 'Something to keep you company. We'll see you later.'

They make their way out, leaving Jack alone in the ruins. Their voices fade and Jack stands in the sunlight and the silence, broken only by the occasional bird song. The tomb where he saw the teenagers and first heard that song lies just across the valley, perhaps five hundred yards away. He sets off down the hill, crossing Fern Brook at the bottom, then turning left, following the stream as it winds through the valley. The dense wood on the right rises steeply up the hillside; after a short distance he finds a path that takes him up, winding through the trees, until he reaches the path that runs along the ridge at the top.

He's not quite sure where he's come out, but he knows immediately it's the path he stumbled along after he saw that vision all that time ago. If he were to turn right he would arrive at the stone bench where he sat overlooking the lake, watching Carol and the others dancing below. Instead he turns left, looking for the path that will take him down to the hollow. After just a few steps he's looking at a stony track that angles down through the trees. Something within him has no doubt this is it; that if he walks down this path he will come to a hollow under the trees, and in that hollow he will see a tomb made of stone.

He steps forward to walk down and find that hollow, but something stops him; he can't even place his foot on the ground, as though there is an invisible barrier that won't let him go down that path. He pushes forward until something gives and he feels like he's making progress, but a moment later he realises he has somehow turned around and is now back on top of the ridge. He tries again but this time feels a rising terror, an inexplicable horror so strong he turns back and almost runs along the ridge path until, once again, he comes out to the clearing that overlooks the lake. He collapses on the bench, out of breath and his heart beating far faster than it should.

Sometime later, once his body has returned to normal, he shakes out a fag, smokes it slowly and then, once he's finished, makes his way back into town. He feels unsteady and he's really not sure he's going to make it through the night. He just wants it all to be over.

o0o

Jack gets back to the flat to find David in the kitchen making a cup of tea. The place looks even more dishevelled than usual with clothes and half-open sleeping bags scattered around, and unwashed plates stained with half-congealed food lying on the floor. Not for the first time he is struck by the incongruity of the mess against Evelyn's seemingly orderly personality. It's supposed to be Evelyn's flat, but it's obviously not she who is setting the style.

'Hi,' Jack says, 'what's happening?'

David looks up. 'Deek and Evelyn have headed back to the park. I'm just waiting for you so we can go down together. Do you fancy a cuppa?'

'Yeah, sure. Thanks.'

'No problem.'

There are no clean cups so David rinses one out from the sink and pops in a teabag. The kettle's boiled and there's even some milk in the fridge that smells quite fresh. Jack watches David put it together and then they retire to the living room. David sweeps some clothes off the sofa and they sit down.

'You ready for tonight?' asks David.

'Yeah, I guess so.'

David pulls his jacket out from the pile on the floor, rummages through the pockets and digs out a crumpled sheet of paper.

'Here.' He hands the sheet to Jack. 'We put together a set list. What do you think?'

The list looks much like the gig at The Manor, opening with *Going for Broke*, running through *Lust* and *Rage* and a couple of others, and ending with *Into the Night*. It's a standard set list, but Jack knows in his heart that something's going to be different this time.

'Looks good. Any idea when Faylin's going to appear?'

'Well, no, but you know what she's like.'

Jack faces David. 'Well, no, actually I don't. So what's going to happen? Is she just going to appear? Out of nowhere?'

'No ... I don't know. What I do know is she'll fit right in, like she always does.'

'But she never has, at least not since I've been around.'

'OK, but seriously, don't worry. She's ... unpredictable, I'll grant you that, but it's always worked in the past. I mean, chill, it'll be great whatever happens! Look what we did at The Manor, and that was without Faylin.'

Jack looks long and hard at David. 'Yeah, and it was also pretty weird. I mean, something's going on, isn't it? I mean, even Hendrix didn't get people tearing their clothes off and having sex right there in the auditorium, did he?'

'You were playing really great, that night. We were really together, weren't we? I mean, that's what music's all about, at least good old rock 'n' roll: getting up the vibe and taking it in and throwing it back at them. And it was one hell of a vibe, that night, wasn't it? Look, we're in it together, and if we carry on like this, we're really going places.'

'Yeah, but … David, where are we going? What's really going on?'

David looks down at the table, and then back up at Jack.

'What do you think's going on, Jack?'

David holds Jack's gaze, and Jack feels the silence expand. It's like David is looking into his soul, right down into the depths where the dangerous stuff dwells. Jack wants to talk about the trip in the park and his vision of the tomb and the teenagers and the singing and all that, but somehow he just can't bring it up. He wants to talk about the tune that haunts him and what it all means, but it's like there's a sign up saying 'move along, nothing to see here', and he's just moving along even though, deep down, he knows there's plenty he's not seeing.

'I … I guess I don't know. It's just … well, it's like something else is playing through me, and I'm really not sure where it's taking me.'

'Yeah, but Jack, do you really want to get off the bus? Is that what you're saying? I mean, do you really have a choice?'

For an indeterminate time Jack can do nothing but return David's gaze.

'No, I guess not.'

'OK, that's the ticket.' David breaks his gaze and bounds off the bed. 'Good, 'cos I've got something that'll really blow your mind.'

He disappears into another room and reappears a moment later carrying a battered beige guitar case that he places on the floor in front of Jack.

'What's this?'

'Open it and find out.'

Jack snaps open the fasteners and lifts the lid. Inside, cradled against a red flannelette lining, lies a guitar. To Jack's eyes it's instantly recognisable as a Stratocaster, even without checking out the logo. It looks battered, like it's been extensively repaired, but what really stands out are the vines, roses and hearts that adorn the red body and the white scratch plate, lovingly picked out in black and pale aqua paints.

He lifts it out gingerly and puts it across his knees. He places his fingers on the fretboard and gently strums a chord. Despite the damage, the action is tight and the sustain is really good. It even appears to be in tune.

He looks up at David in wonder. 'So, what is it?'

'Can't you guess? No, perhaps not. It's the Monterey Strat.'

'The Monterey Strat? What, you mean the one Hendrix set alight at the Monterey Festival? From what I read he smashed it up. Shit! Is this for real?'

'Yeah, it's for real. After he set fire to it he smashed it into three pieces which he threw into the crowd. This guy I know managed to round them up and put it back together again, which is what you're holding now. He did a really good job, but if you check it out carefully you can still see some burn marks. He was working at the Festival as a roadie. Hendrix wasn't interested. Once he'd sacrificed the guitar it was gone, as far as he was concerned.'

'Fuck!' says Jack, picking out a riff. It rings out clear. He traces one of the vines that trails around the scratch plate and down to the jack cup, a vine that must have been painted by Hendrix himself. He's touching a sacred object, the rock 'n' roll equivalent of the cross itself.

'So, you want to play it tonight?'

'What, really? Too right!'

'We better get going, then.'

Jack gingerly returns the guitar to its case and snaps it shut. As they stand up to go, David picks up a brown leather pouch that looks very like the pouch he'd brought back from The Manor for Kingpin.

'What's in the bag?'

'Just something Kingpin got together for me. Should spice up the party.' He holds the pouch out to Jack. 'Take a look.'

Inside, Jack sees a plastic bag containing several handfuls of what looks like finely ground sugar, except that it's pink – the same pink as the pills in the bag that The Chemist had given him.

'Cool. What's in it?'

'No idea, really, although I imagine it's something similar to the stuff Julian was dishing out at The Manor: you remember the pink and blue pills? He told me you can smoke it in a joint or snort it up your nose, whatever wets your whistle, so to speak.'

'Cool.'

Jack picks up the guitar case and follows David out of the flat to the Rose and Crown and the entrance to the park.

o0o

At the car park they discover the van is locked and there's no one around so they head down the path and into the park. The sun is just above the horizon and the sky is no longer cloudless. It feels unseasonably warm and strangely unsettled, with clouds scuttling across the sky and sudden rushes of wind. Jack shivers. This is the peace before the storm: balances have been disturbed and forces awakened, and a reckoning is coming soon. Jack stands for a few seconds trying to make sense of it all and then follows David down into the valley, around the lake and up through the woods to the ruins above.

In the abbey some ten or twelve people are already mingling around the stage area. Jack can see Dillon, Chris, Phil, Deek and Evelyn, and he knows most of the others by sight, but it's Carol who spots him first and comes bounding towards him.

'Well, look who it is, at last. Hello, stranger!' Jack just about manages to put the guitar case down by the time she reaches him, grabs him in a bear hug and gives him a big wet smacker right on the lips. She holds him out at arm's length. 'You're looking pretty wired. Ready for the gig?'

'Yeah, feeling good,' Jack grins, and he does indeed feel better for seeing Carol. He picks up the case and they walk back to the group, where the others shake him by the hand or give him a high five.

'How's it going?' David asks.

'Well,' says Chris, indicating the stage. 'We've got most of the gear set up and the inverter seems to be working, so it should be OK.'

'Excellent.'

'And then there's the lighting.' Chris grins. He points to the centre of the clearing where they've piled up dead twigs and branches some three feet high. 'As you can see, we've already got a decent amount of wood together for a bonfire and there's plenty more around. Dillon's also made some torches we can stick into the walls.'

'Yeah,' says Dillon, holding up a length of wood about three feet long and nearly two inches in diameter. One end has a rag wound tightly round, which looks like it's been soaked in wax. 'I've got six of these, which should give out a decent amount of light for quite a few hours. If we stick them in the walls they shouldn't be visible from the town.'

'We'll be lit by flames,' says David. 'That's as it should be.'

'They won't be able to hear us, though? Down there?' Jack says.

'Maybe,' says Dillon, 'but I mean, it's Halloween. There should be plenty else going on in the town to keep them busy. We've just got to keep an eye out.'

'Guess so.'

'Hold on a minute,' says David. He opens up the pouch so Chris and Dillon can check out the contents. 'Here's some stuff that should get us all in the mood. We could rub some into the torches. Help spread the atmosphere!'

'Be my guest!' Dillon says, holding out the torch. David opens the plastic bag and dips in a couple of fingers, collecting a pinch of the powder. Gingerly he rubs it into the wax, spreading it evenly. Phil gets the remaining torches and David applies the powder until they're all coated.

'So what is this stuff?' Chris asks.

Jack looks at David before replying. 'It's something David got hold of, from the guy that supplies Dean.' He looks at Carol. 'Bummer what happened to him. You heard anything more?'

'Not really,' says Carol, looking embarrassed. 'I mean, Ania's still in town. She'll call me if anything happens.'

'Yeah, I guess so.' He looks down at the ground, wanting to say something about him and Ania and Dean but unable to find the words.

Carol lifts his chin with the tip of her finger and looks him in the eyes. 'Look, I know these things happen. You were an idiot and you lost Ania, but that's in the past now and neither her or Dean would want it to spoil the party.'

'Yeah, you're right.'

'And it's certainly not your fault he got busted. I mean, he knew the risks and he chose to take them.'

'That's true,' says Jack, giving her a rueful smile.

The sun has disappeared while they've been talking, replaced by a moon that is almost full and, to Jack's eyes, abnormally large. The light fades from the warm afterglow of sunset to a more silvery tint and the wind dies away. Chris, Phil and Dillon start fixing the torches into suitable cavities in the walls, putting a match to each as they go. Soon they are all burning, the flickering orange light delineating an area thick with the smell of burning wax and an undercurrent of something else that Jack assumes to be the powder. Indeed he can already feel the effects, quite similar to what he'd felt at The Manor: like a mild dose of acid with an edge of something else; something vital and even aggressive.

Someone sets fire to the pile of wood in the centre of the clearing and a cheer goes up as the flames catch hold of the bone-dry logs. More people have arrived and there is now a crowd of perhaps twenty people in front of the stage. Many have brought bottles of beer or wine and have started dancing along to the loose blues Chris and Phil are playing on acoustic guitar and a set of bongos.

Jack's wondering where he can get a drink when he hears more voices coming from just outside the ruined walls. He looks at the gap in the wall that marks the entrance and there's Martin together with a couple of guys and some girls he's not seen before. They're carrying crates of beer.

'Here!' Martin shouts, dumping his crate on the ground. 'Look what we found.'

'Nice one,' Jack says. There's now four crates lying under one of the walls near the entrance. 'Where did these come from?'

'We ... well, we kind of "liberated" them. They were round the back of the Rose and Crown, looking neglected.' He picks out a bottle of Double Diamond, cracks open the top with a bottle opener he's got stashed in his pocket and passes it to Jack. 'Here, I'm sure you need it more than they do.' He opens one for himself.

'Cheers,' says Jack, holding out his bottle.

'Cheers!'

They clink their bottles together before knocking back a swig.

'God, I didn't realise how much I needed that.'

'So, you ready to entertain us with your new band?' He looks over to where David and Evelyn are sorting out a microphone. 'Cool chick, too. Weren't you with her at Dillon's party?'

'No ... yeah, well, actually that's Evelyn. She's Faylin's sister. She's really cool, but no, we're not an item. She's with David. It's a long story ...' Jack hesitates, realising how long it's been since he was last in Westerford.

'I bet it is. You got anything to smoke?'

'Well, as it happens ...' Jack produces another joint, lights it up and hands it to Martin. 'Look, I better go and help with the gear. Not sure when we're going to start, but it should be soon. Catch you later.'

Martin holds up the joint in silent salute and Jack heads to the stage. Evelyn is behind the drum kit, already bashing out a rhythm. Deek plugs in his bass and tries out a couple of notes that come right back at them through the speakers. Satisfied it's all working, the two of them lay down a basic rock 'n' roll beat. Chris and Phil stop playing and soon there's a group dancing around the mounting flames of the fire. Jack hurries over to the side of the stage area where he left the guitar case, snaps it open and gingerly lifts out the precious antique. He puts it around his neck, plugs it into his amplifier and strums a few chords. Then he turns to face the crowd.

The scene that greets him is almost medieval. There are now perhaps thirty people within the confines of the broken walls of the ballroom and the flickering light of the torches. In the centre is the fire, flames now rising six feet or more, and the smoke is getting thicker and the smell of burning wax stronger. As he throws out the odd chord to punctuate Evelyn and Deek's driving beat, he sees David walk over to the fire, open his pouch and fling a handful of powder into its burning heart. The effect is immediate. Bright sparks of iridescent reds, greens and blues flash out of the flames and the air becomes more pungent. He can feel the layers of his rational mind dissolving and relaxing, putting him in contact with something deeper and more primeval.

His attention returns to the music and he starts strumming in earnest, throwing in short riffs that have yet to coalesce into a definite tune. The guitar feels like a living thing under his fingers, filled with a spirit that is fighting to be free. He remembers they're supposed to be opening with *Going for Broke*, so he starts riffing around the underlying melody. Deek and Evelyn pick up what he's doing while they wait for David to get to the stage, sling his guitar around his neck and grab the microphone.

'Hello, Westerford!' David's voice is loud and clear and elicits a cheer from the audience. 'We're Devil Spawn and we've been waiting to play this gig for a very, very long time. We do our own stuff, and this is *Going for Broke*. We hope you like it.'

He breaks straight into the opening chord sequence, Jack doubling him for a couple of bars, and then he starts belting out the lyrics. As far as Jack can tell the invertor is working well and they're making a decent noise. He starts to relax; after all, he knows the stuff off by heart and David's on good form. The Monterey Strat feels like it's playing itself and there's that familiar energy flowing through him and out into the audience. David finishes the verse and Jack's into his first solo. As always, David feeds him flourishes that send him in new directions, and the guitar feels like a wild animal under his fingers. They move into the next verse and then an extended solo, David and Jack trading short runs back and forth, punctuated by longer riffs from Jack supported by snatched chords from David. They finally pull back to the signature riff and David steps back to the microphone and sings the final verse. As they close Jack can see Dillon in the audience grinning ear to ear and giving him a double-barrelled thumbs up.

'Well, thank you Westerford, and thank you Jack for a great solo.' David graciously gestures towards Jack before turning back to the audience. 'Now, some of you may have noticed Jack is playing a rather special guitar. Well, let me tell you, that is no ordinary guitar, or even an ordinary Stratocaster. No, that is the Monterey Strat!' A few in the audience are clapping and whooping, but most look baffled. 'Yes, ladies and gentlemen, that is the Strat Hendrix himself set on fire live on stage at the Monterey Festival back in 1965. Some guys I know put it back together and now here it is at the Westerford Festival. So, are you going to set fire to it, Jack?'

Jack clutches the guitar and shakes his head in an exaggerated fashion.

'Glad to hear it. Anyway, here's another one you've never heard before. We call it *End of Time* and it goes something like this ...'

David and Jack simultaneously hit the anthemic chords that open the song. Jack's never quite understood how it works, but they always manage to hit the opening chord at the same moment. Evelyn and Deek come in on the third bar, Evelyn hitting the tom-toms like some African witchdoctor and Deek rolling out the slippery bassline. By the time they get into the extended bridge, the guitar feels like a bucking Bronco and Jack is holding on for dear life, the notes spinning out from under his fingers like wild snakes. Someone has thrown more wood onto the fire and the crowd is going wild. They go straight from *End of Time* into *Rage* and the audience is ducking and diving as Jack lashes them with fire and fury. The glowing pit that surrounds them is shrouded in an orange smoke that occasionally sparkles brightly with what remains of the powder David rubbed into the torches. The flames are now towering some eight feet over the audience, whose faces peer up from the shrinking space left to them.

Next comes *Lust* and Jack can feel that familiar desire swelling up inside him, crying out for release. He has an insatiable need to play that riff, that tune he first heard all those weeks ago in the woods just across the valley from where he's standing now, but he also feels a mounting sense of dread. He's within touching distance of the sequence; he just has to reach out a little more and it'll all come flooding back and he'll be free of the beast that's gnawing away at his mind.

o0o

They bring *Lust* to a close and then it's *Road to Oblivion* and finally *Into the Night*, which is to be the last song of the set. As he plays the opening notes David steps up to the microphone and yells, 'As someone once said, do unto others as you were done by. So here it is, Westerford, coming right back at you.'

The initial sequence goes well, but as they get into the main part of the song Jack senses a shift, a change that's gone almost before he notices it. For a moment he's not sure it's anything more than a passing gust of wind, but then he realises that everything has changed, as though they've moved into some parallel world. The music is louder, the fire is burning with a greater ferocity and there's a new voice in the air: a female voice winding tightly around the notes coming from his guitar, a voice that is driving him in a direction that offers both hope and dread. He glances over at David, but he has stepped back and is crouching over his guitar, spinning out the doom-laden chords that follow the intro. Standing in his place, holding the microphone and belting her heart out in a language that doesn't even sound like English, is Faylin.

He instinctively looks at Evelyn but she is still there, head down, pounding out the rhythm. Faylin is now facing him, taunting him with her eyes and lashing him with her voice. He cannot help but respond, firing back notes that serve as some sort of answer. She snakes across the gap that separates them until they stand face to face, her lips just inches from his. Jack's fingers take on a life of their own, twisting around the fretboard. The guitar is a living thing in his hands, squirming with energy. All he can see are her eyes. All he can hear are their voices: hers winding around the howl of his guitar, the spiral of sound they are throwing out into the night.

With a wrench he tears his eyes away and looks out over the crowd. At first all he can see are flames, but in the gaps he makes out the cavorting shadows of his friends, lost to the driving beat and the lashes of sound. His fingers are on automatic but he can feel David and Faylin driving him in a particular direction, down a path that will inevitably end in that deadly sequence of notes. He tries to counter but his fingers won't stop moving towards that tune, hauntingly familiar but still just out of reach.

David senses that Jack is almost there and lashes him with increasingly intense riffs that push him further and further towards the fateful tune. With a sinking feeling, Jack realises he is just not strong enough to resist. Whatever happens, he is going to play those notes: he cannot help it. But he also senses a fork in the road up ahead that, if he can just force a switch, could take them out of this world and into another. He starts making the subtle changes to his fretwork necessary to drive them in that direction.

At first David doesn't seem to notice, but then he looks at Jack, sensing that something has changed but not sure what. He starts pushing back, trying to undo what Jack has done with increasingly frenetic licks, but Jack overcomes him with a series of intense variations that drive them inexorably onward. David is fighting him with all his strength, but then they reach the fork and, with a last desperate twist of the guitar, Jack throws the switch.

The effect is immediate. It's still Evelyn bashing out a driving rhythm but the other three have metamorphosed into the three teenagers that he saw in the park dancing around the tombstone. In place of David stands Daniel, in place of Faylin stands Lucy, and in place of Deek stands Gabriel. Jack has become part of their reality, their 'special consensus', and now they are unveiled he cannot understand why he did not see the resemblance earlier. This was always their plan: revenge on the good people of Westerford for what happened all those centuries ago.

Before anyone has time to react, Faylin feeds him a certain sequence of notes and it all comes flooding back. He can do nothing now but respond with the riff that he heard in the park all those weeks ago. The circle is closed; the question is answered. Just as with any other tune, one note follows another, but this time it's different because this particular tune resonates with something very deadly buried deep within each one of us.

As the last note cries out the universe shrinks to the space framed by the flames, and now there are other ghostly figures prancing around the edges and carrying torches of their own. What little is left between the fire and the torches is also on fire and he realises that what he is seeing are bodies writhing in agony. The last thing he hears are their silent screams. The last thing he feels is the intense heat of the flames. The last thing he smells is burning flesh. And then there's a snap, like a rubber band giving out at full stretch, and consciousness ends.

# Thirteen

The first thing he hears is a 'beep'. He lies still, aware there is a world out there but for the moment happy to remain huddled behind his eyelids. There's another beep and then another, and then a voice that can't be ignored.

'Come on, young man, it's time to wake up.'

He opens his eyes to a kindly-looking face, concerned at first but now smiling at him in reassurance. Her crisp, pale-blue uniform and white apron suggest she is a nurse, and her name badge suggests she is Edith. He starts to smile back and tries to sit up, but seems to be restrained. He starts to panic, then falls back, too weak to struggle.

'Now, now, you just relax, my dear. You've had a nasty shock and you need to take it easy.'

He lets her ease him back down into the soft pillows.

'What happened? Where am I? I just remember ... I don't know what I remember.'

'You mustn't worry. You're in Pembury Hospital. All I can say is that you were brought in late a couple of nights back, out cold and in a bit of a state. But you had no injuries to speak of and you're much better now.'

'But where are the others? Where's everybody else? Are they here?'

'I don't know about anybody else. As far as I know you were brought here by ambulance. Someone said they found you out in Abbey Park, the police, I mean, but it was just you. And that is really all I know.' She pats his hand. 'Just sit back. You've missed breakfast, but lunch will be along in an hour or so and I'm sure the doctor will want to see you soon. Rest is what you need: peace and quiet and plenty of it.'

She disappears from view and he hears the soft click of a door closing, and then just the calm of the hospital broken only by the 'beep' of the machine. He cautiously probes his memory, not wanting to know but knowing that he has to know what happened. He can remember standing on the stage in the ruins of Abbey House. He can remember the strange shift and then Faylin standing next to him, and the force of her voice and the energy flowing through his guitar winding round it and out into the crowd. He can remember the fire and the flames and the heat.

He can remember the screams and the shadows, writhing and falling. It has the reality of a nightmare, but if it were real would he really be lying here, alone, unguarded? Surely there'd be police at the door, and the nurse would be rather more circumspect? He gives up and drifts back into an uneasy sleep.

The next thing he sees is his mother's face. She looks worried, but smiles when she sees he's awake.

'What are you doing in here, Jack? You haven't even eaten your lunch.'

With a start he notices the table slotted over his bed and a tray bearing a ham sandwich cut into quarters and a glass of orange juice. He realises he is very hungry so he pulls himself up on his pillows and tucks in. Alice waits patiently until he's finished.

'So what happened? Ray told me they found you out in the park, lying unconscious in one of the rooms of that old ruined house, up on the hill above the lake. What were you doing out there? Ray said there'd obviously been some sort of party, but everyone had run off into the woods, leaving you lying next to a fire that was burning out of control. Eventually they got you onto a stretcher and into an ambulance.' She sighs. 'The doctor tells me you're alright. They've X-rayed you and there's no injuries to speak of, but you've obviously had some sort of shock. What is it? I mean, what did happen up there?'

'I don't remember any policemen. Was Ray there?'

'He said it was a raid. He said they had reason to believe there'd be drugs, but someone was obviously on lookout so everyone scattered as soon as they realised the police were coming. The park is huge and they needed to get you to safety, so they didn't manage to catch anyone. "A lot of evidence but no one to pin it on", that was how Ray put it.'

'They didn't find anyone?'

Alice sighs. 'Just you, Jack, and I don't suppose you're going to tell us what was going on.' She smiles. 'But at least you're OK, and you can come home as soon as you're ready, although I think you'll be in here for another night so they can keep an eye on you.'

'Thanks, Mum. To be honest, I'm not sure what was going on myself. It's been a long, strange trip. It's going to take me a while to sort it out in my own head, let alone anyone else's.'

'Yes, well. Anyway, I've brought you some fruit, although the food here doesn't look too bad.'

'Thanks, Mum. Yeah, it's pretty cool, the food.'

He lies back while Alice goes in search of a bowl.

After his mother leaves, Jack drifts into a state of semi-consciousness. He's more relaxed now he knows he wasn't actually discovered surrounded by burnt-out bodies, and that much of what he remembers can't have actually happened, at least not in this world. He was pretty spaced out on whatever was in David's powder; in fact the smoke was so dense they must have all been well out of it, so it's unlikely anyone knows how it really played out with any certainty. His memories of the flames and the screaming and the charred bodies are still there, but they're fading into a parallel world that is slowly diverging from this one.

Sometime later he opens his eyes to find Dillon's dishevelled face hovering over him.

'Well, hi there, dude. Fancy a joint?'

Jack grins back, partly because Dillon has indeed produced a joint from his inside pocket. 'Yeah, sure. Perhaps Nurse would like some too?'

'Perhaps not.' Dillon tucks the joint away and picks up an apple from the bowl. 'So, what are you doing in here, then?' He takes a bite and chews noisily.

'To be honest, I'm not sure.' Jack gingerly probes his memories of that night, which include a clear impression of Dillon's burning body. 'What do you remember of that night, in the park?'

Dillon frowns. 'Well, we were all pretty spaced out on that stuff your mate was dishing out, and it was all getting a bit out of control. There were these guys who kept throwing stuff on the fire, and there were the torches that were throwing off a lot of smoke.' He grins at Jack. 'And there was you playing some pretty shit-hot stuff on that guitar. Did it really belong to Hendrix?'

'I don't know. That's what David told me, and it was pretty shit-hot to play. I've no idea where it is now, though – in fact, I've got no idea what's happened to any of the gear.'

'Me neither. Anyway, you guys were really belting it out, particularly you and that singer. She was really cool and the two of you were really in the groove.'

'So you saw Faylin? She was really there?'

'Yeah, sure. Hot-looking chick with red hair. You really took off when she joined you on stage.'

'So what happened then?'

'Well, I think someone was coming up the path, late to the party or something like that, and they spotted the fuzz coming up behind. Anyway, someone shouted a warning and we all just dropped everything and scattered. I grabbed Carol and we ran down through the woods and then up to the top of the valley to the kids' playground. Some other guys were already there so we shared a joint and a couple of bottles on the merry-go-round. No idea where anyone else got to, or what happened to you, and no sign of the fuzz either. We just assumed everyone made it out of the park, one way or another.'

'Shit! Yeah, my mum was in earlier and she was telling me there was a bust but no one got caught. She used to go out with this guy who's with the pigs – although it was them that found me in the park and got me in here, so I suppose I should be grateful.'

'I guess so. Hey, I guess you haven't heard what's happened to Dean yet?'

'No. Last I heard he was being held for questioning. Ania was trying to sort things out, up in London. Talking to Release, I think.'

'Yeah, well, he got up in front of a judge and got sent down. Seven years is what I heard. They decided to make an example of him, the bastards, so they gave him the maximum. They've already transferred him to Borstal, that juvenile place out near Rochester.'

'Oh my God, that's a real bummer. Jesus!' Jack struggles to pull himself up into a sitting position.

'Yeah, it's pretty shit. Ania's taking it real bad. I think she's been trying to visit him, but it's not easy.'

'Shit, that's really tough on her. She's had a pretty bum time of it, recently.' He collapses back on the pillow. 'I guess I should go and see him, when I get out of here. I mean, if it wasn't for him I'd have been busted as well.'

'Yeah, you should go. I know you two had problems, with Ania and all, but he'd want to see you.'

oOo

It's night by the time Evelyn comes to visit, at least as far as Jack can tell from the window at the end of the ward. It's outside visiting hours, but here she is, pulling him out of a disturbing dream as she places her hand over his where it lies on the bedspread.

'Hi there,' he says, blearily opening his eyes. Somehow he knows it's Evelyn without having to check for a ring.

'Hi there,' she smiles. 'I told them I'm your girlfriend so they let me in, but I can't stay long.'

'It's good to see you.'

'You too, especially after all that happened.'

156

'Yeah, but I'm not sure what did actually happen. How's David? And how's Faylin?'

Evelyn shuffles awkwardly. 'I don't know, really. After we all scattered, I eventually made it back to the flat. David and Deek were there, stuffing stuff into bags like they were about to go. David was in a right strop, blaming you for something but he wouldn't say what. You know what he's like; he's not happy if he doesn't get what he wants. He had the Monterey Strat with him, but he'd smashed it up so it was in pieces again. Then they just left, and I haven't seen them since. I've no idea what happened to the rest of the gear. I guess the fuzz are holding it, hoping someone's stupid enough to claim it.'

'What about the gig itself? What do you remember of that?'

'Well, I remember we started on *Into the Night*, which was going to be the last song in the set. We'd just finished *Road to Oblivion* and we were really tight. You were playing some shit-hot guitar, and the party was going wild – everyone screaming and dancing around. The fire and the torches were burning bright so there was a lot of smoke and everything was glowing orange. We were a couple of bars in when Faylin appeared, grabbed the microphone and started singing. I mean, she's usually pretty hot but this time she was really smoking, and it was like you two were feeding off each other, getting wilder and wilder. And then ... well, I'm not really sure what happened then. It felt like it was really getting out of hand, but then we seemed to shift into another place entirely.'

'Yeah, I remember that. It's one of the last things I do remember. I think I might have had something to do with that. While I was playing, just before the end, it was like there was a fork up ahead, and if I played just the right notes I could switch us into, well, into another reality. I can remember David trying to force us back, but he hadn't realised what I'd done until it was too late. Faylin fed me the tune and I can remember seeing everything burn, but I don't think it happened in this world. I think it happened in their world.'

He props himself up so he's facing her. 'I saw, them, Evelyn: I saw them as Daniel, Gabriel and Lucy, not David, Deek and Faylin. Three teenagers that have been dead for two hundred and fifty years. It's like we switched into their world.'

'Maybe we did. It certainly felt like something had changed, something pretty fundamental.'

'Yeah.' He drops back onto the bed. 'And what about Faylin? Where is Faylin, after all this?'

'I don't know ... she's gone away. She came back to the flat, after David and Deek had gone. We didn't know what had happened to you but it was obviously the end of Devil Spawn, so we sat and talked for ages, just like we used to do when we were young. In the end we decided it would be good for us to spend some time apart. We don't always work well together, these days. We need our own space. I need time to be myself – really be myself for a change.'

'So she's disappeared as well?'

'Yeah … well, no. She's gone travelling. She got hold of one of those Eurorail cards – you know, the ones that let you travel cheap around Europe? She took the train down to Dover last night so she'll be somewhere in France by now.'

'Yeah, right.'

'Look, it's not been easy, her and me. When I was a kid she was my only friend. The only one I could turn to. She was always there for me, no matter what. But when we got older it was like she changed. She'd disappear for days on end and do reckless things that caused me a lot of problems.' She smiles ruefully. 'Well, you know what I mean. You've seen her in action.'

'Right little heartbreaker!'

'Don't be too harsh. We've both had a hard time, over the years. I couldn't have made it without her. But the band, well … I really wasn't sure about the band, towards the end. After that gig at The Manor I just wanted out, but Faylin insisted.'

Jack thinks back over all the time he's spent with Evelyn, since they first met. They've been good times, but there's never been a moment when he's actually seen her alongside Faylin, ever, except for that last gig in the park, and it seems highly unlikely that actually happened, at least not in this world. He remembers his conversation with Pauline, right at the beginning of all this. Evelyn and Faylin clearly have very different personalities and even lead different lives, but that doesn't preclude them being splintered fragments sharing a single body. And if that is the case, then the only way Evelyn can handle her life day-to-day is by presenting Faylin as a distinct, separate person. Everyone at the squat went along with the fiction, even Gina, but that was probably down to David's manipulative scheming as much as anything else. Certainly, it suited David to have everyone believing he's screwing identical twins. It gave him a sense of power. It created a "special consensus" that they could inhabit together.

He thinks back to a time when he was younger and he'd been with a girl who'd decided she didn't want to go to a party. In the end he'd persuaded her to spice it up by pretending to be her own identical sister, recently returned from abroad. They'd all been pretty stoned but he'd been struck by how many of their friends – people who'd known her for years – just went along with it. When it comes down to it, most of us believe what we're told, if only because it's easier that way. And then of course there's the powder that David rubbed into the torches. Was anyone capable of reporting what actually happened?

'Evelyn, tell me the truth. She doesn't really exist, does she? Faylin, I mean. Out in the real world.'

Evelyn stares at Jack intently, and then looks away. 'Of course she exists. She's just ... well, she's just not here, at the moment.'

Jack looks at her intently. He is fairly certain that if Faylin ever did return it would be in the body of this young woman, sitting in front of him right now, looking vulnerable, but he says nothing.

After an uncomfortable pause she looks at him again: 'Look, I know it all seems pretty weird now, but there was something about David that just kept us coming back for more. There was me and Faylin, but there were others too. Even Gina, when she wanted something. He created this world in which you could be whoever you wanted to be. He didn't judge. He had this way of looking at things that just made sense.'

'And Minnie Mouse.'

'Yeah, but don't laugh. Minnie Mouse, whoever she is, she's me not that many years ago.'

'Her name is Valerie.'

'OK, but there's something about him that just pulls in the vulnerable. I don't know what it is – I mean, it's not like he's particularly great shakes between the sheets. A bit childish, really; like there's always something wrong, and it's always your fault. God knows why but we kept coming back for more. I guess we thought he could give us something we needed, in the end, and to give him his due, there aren't many guys who can handle both Faylin and me together. Even Ania fell for it for a little while, until she realised he's a fake. She saw through him pretty quickly.'

Jack turns away. He still finds the idea of them together disturbing.

Evelyn sighs. 'Look, I guess it's all over now, the squat and even Devil Spawn. I certainly don't ever want to see David again, but it would be a shame to lose everything, wouldn't it? I mean, we're still friends, aren't we? It doesn't all have to end, does it?'

Jack smiles back as he realises that he really does care for her. 'No, of course it doesn't, Evelyn. Of course we're friends. We always will be. We've been through a lot together, you and I.'

She leans over, pulls him into her arms and hugs him tightly. Taken aback, Jack returns the gesture, holding her to him as he tries to think of the right thing to say, but then somehow the words don't matter and he becomes acutely aware that he is holding a warm and beautiful woman, and that he really does want her in his life.

There is a tension in the air when they eventually pull apart and she rises to leave, a tension that has not been there before. When she reaches the door she turns back and smiles awkwardly. 'Actually, I've still got your bag, what you grabbed from the squat, so I guess you're going to have to come round to the flat and collect it.'

'Sure thing,' he grins. 'I look forward to it.'

'So do I,' she says as she closes the door behind her.

# Fourteen

The doctor finishes with Jack around noon. In the absence of any discernible trauma he's at a loss to explain exactly why Jack remained unconscious for nearly two days but suspects it's the result of some sort of psychological shock in combination with an 'unusual' cocktail of drugs.

'I'm not going to say anything to the police, but I do suggest you think very carefully before putting any more dubious substances into your body.'

Jack assures him he will be more careful next time, and then grins when he recognises the inherent contradiction in his reply. The doctor shakes his head and wishes him well.

Jack's already put some thought into his next step and quickly realises he has little choice but to move back into his mother's place, at least for a while. If nothing else, he's not sure he's got the energy to counter her protests if he chooses to stay elsewhere. He's still got some money in the pocket of his jeans so he calls her from the payphone in the corridor to tell her he's on his way, and her response confirms he's made the right decision. He manages to dissuade her from picking him up, which would be a good hour's round trip on her part, and instead takes the train back to Westerford, grateful for some time to himself.

As the suburbs of Pembury slip past the window, replaced by green fields hazy in the pale light of the overcast sky, he feels as though he's coming out of a long, strange dream. Something took possession of his life when he encountered those teenagers in the park, and it set him on a catastrophic course driven by a ruinous obsession that came to a head with those visions of death and destruction. Even now he finds it hard to dismiss it all as unreal.

Whatever happened was driven by his burning desire to recreate that riff, that tune he'd heard them singing in the park. That desire has now been satiated by the playing of it. He's not even sure he can remember the riff, although it'll be interesting to see what happens when he gets behind his old guitar once again, which is presumably still sitting in his old bedroom. Whatever, it no longer consumes his mind.

The more he thinks about it the more he realises the obsession was also driven, or at least steered, by David. David, who somehow popped into his life just a day or so after that trip. David and his 'harem'. He remembers the articles about Charles Manson from when he was convicted a few months back, and he has to admit there are similarities. There is something about David that suspends your judgement; stops you asking questions about what he is doing and what he is asking of you. Something about him that puts girls in the palm of his hand, even though he isn't much to look at or even – at least from Evelyn's testimony – much between the sheets. And, if he is honest, it isn't just girls, because he too has gone along with whatever David suggests with hardly a second thought.

There's also those scars. From what he's seen they're pretty extensive, running from the base of David's neck right across his chest. They're the sort of thing you would get if you were caught in a fire. They may be separated by centuries, but there was definitely some sort of connection between David and Daniel. He'd seen that for himself at the gig in the ruins of Abbey House, just before he passed out, just yards from where Daniel himself had burnt to death some two hundred and fifty years earlier.

He sighs, grateful that it does, at last, appear to be over. Except for Dean, of course, who's facing anything up to seven years locked up in that place. He can't imagine what Dean's going through, but maybe in the end you make it through each day holding on to the belief that eventually it will be over and you will have some sort of life to go back to. After all, people made it through the trenches, in the war, and it can't be as bad as that, can it?

And then there's Ania and Gina. He thinks about Gina and the way she reacted when he forced himself on her after the gig at The Manor. He'd been really hyped up after that gig, and just couldn't help himself – or so he wants to believe, hollow as that excuse actually sounds. He'd known even as he was doing it that it was wrong, but he'd gone ahead and done it anyway because he somehow felt he had the right.

Maybe it's just not possible to be friends with someone you fancy. Evelyn is very pretty, there's no doubt about that – it's quite something to see her astride the drum kit, pale, slim arms pounding those skins and tumbling red curls flying about her shoulders – but he's only now realising that he wants her as something more than just a friend. It seems strange considering she's physically identical to Faylin. Maybe in some way Faylin embodied Evelyn's sexual nature? Maybe Evelyn transferred that side of her being to Faylin for some reason, long ago, and that's why

Faylin is so sexual while Evelyn is so, well, down to earth? And maybe, now that Faylin's gone, Evelyn's starting to rediscover her sexuality?

It is with some relief that he realises the train is slowing down and they are pulling in to Westerford. He disembarks and walks the short distance to his mother's flat, a journey so familiar it requires no thought. Alice ushers him in and he sits at the kitchen table while she makes him a 'nice cup of tea'. She fusses around him for a bit, rustling up a plate of digestives and asking him if he wants a sandwich, which he gratefully accepts.

'I hope you're going to take it easy, Jack. I mean, you've had quite a shock.'

'Yeah, sure, Mum. I'm not thinking of doing much, at least not for a day or two.'

She smiles, visibly reassured. 'Good, I'm glad you're going to be sensible, for a change. Your room's just as you left it. I did dust things, while you were away, but I've not moved anything, I promise.'

Jack smiles back. 'Thanks, Mum.' He pauses for a moment, wondering how best to broach the next subject. After all, he's not sure how much his mother already knows. 'I'm going to visit Dean, tomorrow if I can.'

Alice sighs and shakes her head. 'Well, I guess that's inevitable. Ray told me about Dean. After all, it's his jurisdiction; he gets informed if anyone "of interest" is arrested. Or convicted.'

They look at each other across the table. Alice has expressed her concern at Jack's involvement in drugs many times, and is well aware Dean is a source: a 'bad influence', in her books. On the other hand, she knows how important Dean is as a friend to Jack, and also that Dean has had a difficult life at home, living with a mother who is, frankly, an alcoholic. And she was shocked when she heard of Dean's sentence.

'You do whatever you have to.'

'Thanks, Mum. I need to use the phone.'

Out in the hall, Jack picks up the phone. Directory Enquiries gives him the number and then he calls the prison. The phone rings for an interminably long period before a surly male voice answers.

'Name?'

'Jack Weaver.'

There's an interminable silence before the voice comes back.

'We don't have a Jack Weaver here.'

'Oh. Sorry, no, that's my name. His name is Dean ... Dean Stonemartin.'

Another silence, shorter this time, then, 'Yes?'

163

'Yes, well, I want to arrange to come and visit him, tomorrow if possible?'

'Are you a relation?'

'No ... well, we're good friends. He's my best friend.'

There's another pause, and then, as though reading from a leaflet: 'Visiting hours two to three PM tomorrow. You are advised to bring as little as possible as you will be searched. Anything you might wish to give to the prisoner is to be presented to reception, who will be responsible for its transfer. Is that clear?'

'Yes ... I guess.' He managed just in time to stop himself answering, 'Yes, sir'.

'There's no guarantee the prisoner will be given visiting rights, but if he continues to behave himself he should be available. Are you aware of our location?'

'No, not really ...'

'We're just outside the village of Borstal on the outskirts of Rochester. There is a bus from Chatham.'

'Thank you,' he says, but the call has already been disconnected. He stares at the telephone for a while and then ascends the stairs to his bedroom.

Everything is pretty much as he left it, as his mother promised. He sits on his bed, luxuriating in the peace and quiet and staring at the posters that adorn the walls. There's Hendrix in full flow at Fillmore East; there's the Skull and Roses poster of the Grateful Dead gig at Avalon Ballroom; and there's the poster of Tantric lovers copulating in a psychedelic world that had come free with *Oz* magazine. He lies back, gazing at the ceiling. He remembers when he was a kid tucked up in bed in their old house, before his parents separated. The ceiling and the walls, in fact the whole of his field of vision, had been painted in a pristine white so featureless that all sense of depth disappeared and he used to fantasise he was floating in an infinite white space. No wonder he'd got into drugs.

Jack opens his eyes and looks at his watch. A couple of hours have drifted past but he feels more awake. He grabs his guitar, which is leaning against the corner of the room, holds it in his lap and strums a few chords. It's a bit discordant so he tunes it up and then plugs it into his amplifier, turned down low. He runs off a quick riff that meanders between the ninth and twelfth frets. The guitar doesn't have the sustain or depth of the Fender he'd had at the squat, let alone the Monterey Strat, but it's quite respectable and it feels good under his fingers, like he's come home.

He jams around a few old standards before he feels brave enough to attempt a Devil Spawn number. When he's ready he tries out the staccato chords of *Into the Night*. The chords come to him easily, which is hardly a surprise considering how often he's played it, and before he knows it he's playing around with short riffs and runs, spiralling out from the central tune. He moves on to the more upbeat *Going for Broke*, and again he finds himself exploring new note combinations and playing tricks with the rhythm. There's no sign of the insatiable yearning he felt before, and there's no David to feed him ideas that send him off in new directions, but he does feel like his playing is looser, more creative and more confident than before. He finishes off with the crashing chords of *Road to Oblivion* and he's feeling good. Whatever else, he has gained something from being part of Devil Spawn: something he'd like to explore further; something he'd like to explore with Evelyn. Perhaps they could even get Carol and the guys from Black Knight involved.

He reacquaints himself with the guitar for the next hour or so, and then, realising he is very hungry, makes his way downstairs to see if his mother can rustle him up something.

oOo

Around eleven the following morning, Jack takes the first train to London Bridge and manages to catch the next train to Chatham with seconds to spare, pounding his way down the hard, metal steps to the platform and jumping through the door just as the conductor blows the final whistle. It's well after rush hour so he easily finds an empty compartment and settles back. He watches the blackened brick buildings slide past under a heavy grey sky, punctuated by the metal-on-metal screech of the wheels as they negotiate the forks and curves. The dingy warehouses and office blocks of Bermondsey and Deptford give way to more salubrious suburbs as the train approaches Greenwich. There are glimpses of trees and patches of green, and then they dive into a tunnel and it all disappears in darkness and noise.

Jack has always loved train journeys, particularly those that involve unknown destinations. He's often fantasised about taking the night train to Dover, just like Faylin is supposed to have done. Perhaps Evelyn's the same, and one day they could do the trip together. They'd head for Paris, and then down to Nice and on into Italy and Florence and Rome before going north to Venice and the Alps and then east towards Istanbul.

For Jack, train journeys offer a respite, a chance to step outside ordinary existence. If you're on a train there need be no backstory. This particular journey may be taking him towards an encounter that he views with some trepidation, but in the meantime he has nothing to do but sit back and relax.

As the train slips towards Dartford, never getting up much speed, he starts thinking about getting something to eat. If he'd had any sense he would have made something before he left, or got his mother to make him something, but he didn't. He works his way down the train in a direction he hopes will lead to a buffet car. After a couple of carriages he discovers a counter where he buys a cheese sandwich that doesn't look too stale, a Mars bar and a Coca Cola. He's on his way back when he spots a familiar figure.

Ania is buried in a book so she doesn't see him at first. When she lifts her head, she looks confused for a moment, then smiles.

'Do you mind?' He indicates the empty seat facing her across the table.

'No, I guess not.'

He puts his food on the table, takes the seat and smiles back at her. She closes her book and puts it down. It's a history of modern art with a brightly coloured painting on the cover that Jack thinks might be a Matisse.

'I see you've got your lunch.'

'Yes,' he replies. 'They've run out of crisps so I got this. You can have some if you want.'

'No thanks. I've already eaten.'

'OK.' He takes a bite out of his sandwich. It's dry – it doesn't even contain a spread – but the cheese tastes good.

'I guess you're on your way to visit Dean?' she says.

Hearing her voice reminds him how much he once loved her.

'Yeah, I rang yesterday and the guy said it should be OK. I hope that's not going to cause problems?'

She shrugs. 'They're pretty arbitrary about visiting. I've been three times now. First time they were fine about it – actually let the visit overrun by ten minutes. Second time they wouldn't let me see him at all, even though I'd spent a couple of hours getting there. The guy really didn't care. I guess it depends who's on.' She looks at him appraisingly. 'I don't mind if you go first. You never know, they might let me see him after.'

'Are you sure about that?'

'Yeah. Look, I know he'd really like to see you. Don't worry about it.'

'Thanks.'

He tucks into the rest of the sandwich and then moves on to the Mars bar and the Coca Cola. Ania watches him for a moment, then picks up her book and continues reading. They sit in silence for a while, each in their own world, then Ania puts her book down again.

'Dean hasn't said much, I guess in case they might be listening, but he did let slip you were there when, you know ... when he was picked up.'

'Yeah, I was there. It was right in the street. If it hadn't been for his quick thinking they would have nabbed me as well.'

'Yeah, I guessed it must have been something like that.' She looks out of the window at the passing houses. 'They did their best at Release – you know, the legal aid people – but there wasn't much we could do. They caught him red-handed, in possession. Dean thinks they might have been told; that there was some sort of snitch.'

'Yeah. What was odd, although I didn't think much about it at the time, was that both Kingpin and David knew what had happened when I got back to the squat, and that was only minutes later.'

'I think it was David. He's a nasty piece of work, and I fell for his tricks as much as anyone. I mean, I was starting to think of him as a friend, someone I could confide in, but that was just one of his games. In reality, David just wanted to add me to his collection.' She turns back towards Jack. 'But nothing happened. I left as soon as I realised what was happening.'

'You went to Magda's.'

'Yeah, and then Dean phoned.' She looks at Jack, daring him to respond. When he doesn't she continues: 'But there was something about you, too. David wanted you to come looking for me. It was all part of his scheming. I was like bait. It was something to do with his band.'

'Devil Spawn.'

'Yeah, what was that all about? I mean, I heard you were playing pretty good in the park, on Halloween, but then you collapsed and ended up in hospital?'

Jack sighs. 'Yeah, it was all a bit of a nightmare really. I can't explain what happened, but I did a few things I'm not proud of and lost a few friends along the way. And I lost you. David had a lot to do with it, but I guess I'm responsible for the decisions I took.'

'Yes, you are.'

'That time at Dillon's party ...'

'Yeah, you really cocked it up.' Once again she turns her attention to the view out of the window. It's more rural now with flat, mucky, green fields extending out to an uncertain horizon. 'You know, I was really into you, at the time, and what you did really hurt. It's like you didn't know what we had together, or you didn't believe it.' Now she looks him straight in the eye: 'You guys, sometimes it feels like you just want a girl because someone else has got her, or had her, or whatever. You're not really interested in who we really are. You're just interested in yourselves. It's just a competition for you. You might as well be trading football cards.'

'You were a lot more than a football card to me.'

'I was a winning card, Jack: the best you ever had. You played me too soon and you lost.'

'Anyway, now you're with Dean.'

'Yes, I'm with Dean, and look where that's got me. He was there when I needed him, and he doesn't put me on a pedestal. He's good to me, and he makes me feel good, but now he's in prison.'

'I'm sorry.'

'I know. It's OK.' She gives him a rueful smile. 'I guess we've both been through quite a bit since then, haven't we?'

'Yeah.'

She picks up her book and continues reading. He slowly chews his way through what remains of the Mars bar and swigs the rest of the Coke. As the train slows into Chatham station, Ania closes her book.

'There is something else you should know, about Dean. He's had his hair cut, as you do when you're in prison. It's cool, but it's a bit of a shock when you first see him.'

oOo

It's a short bus ride into the suburbs, and then a short walk through a landscape of 1950s-style semi-detached red-bricks punctuated by low-lying fields.

Jack gazes at the imposing brown brick and stone frontage of the prison's main entrance. 'Couldn't really be anything else, could it?'

'No, not really.'

'So what happens now?'

'Well, once we're through security they'll take us to a waiting room. They call out the name of the prisoner and then you go through to the visiting area. It's pretty open and there's guards standing around, so you've got to be careful what you say and do. They're really big on "no touching". Just wait 'til they call his name and then go in. With a bit of luck, and if there's time, they'll let me in after you leave.'

'OK. I guess I'll be quick, then. Just a quarter of an hour, maybe?'

'That would be good … and Jack, don't wait for me when you come out. I'd rather be alone, if you don't mind.'

'Yeah, sure. I understand.'

They walk through the heavy wooden entrance and register at reception. Ania is escorted through a side door by a stern-looking woman dressed in a stiff black uniform. A few minutes later a uniformed man guides Jack through the same door into a small room, featureless except for a table and chair and decorated in the sickly cream, military green and what can only be described as shit brown that is standard in such places.

The guard asks him to turn out his pockets, which contain only a packet of fags, his wallet and lighter, and then he is told to raise his arms and part his legs. While being patted down, Jack's glad he chose to dress in fairly nondescript jeans and shirt but the guard still spends more time than necessary around his crotch, and he's careful not to flinch at the man's pungent body odour. Once the ordeal is over he's told to exit through a second door into a larger waiting room where some eight or ten visitors sit, some by themselves and others huddled in whispered conversations. He joins Ania in the corner.

'Well, that was fun,' he says.

'Probably nothing compared to what Dean went through.'

'No, I guess not. You get the feeling they enjoy it. Being cruel, I mean.'

'Yeah,' she sighs. She nods towards the guard who is standing by an exit that presumably leads through to the visiting area. 'I've had a word, and he says he will let me through once you leave.'

'Nice of him.'

'Yeah. They're not all mean. I guess it's pot luck.'

They sit in a silence punctuated only by the occasional announcement of a prisoner's name over the tannoy. Eventually Dean's name is called. Jack stands.

'Well, I guess this is it. I'll see you around ... I guess.'

She looks up at him and smiles. 'Yeah, I guess. Thanks for coming.'

For some reason he feels like crying. He turns away before she can see and walks through the door. The visiting room is spacious and laid out with small tables spaced about six feet apart that offer their occupants at least some degree of privacy. About half are occupied, on one side by a prisoner, easily identified by their white shirts, loose black trousers and crewcut, and on the other by their visitors: despairing men and women of all ages, most single but some holding the hand of a bewildered child. The walls are uniformly painted an off-white incongruously punctuated by cheery landscapes in bright colours that look like they've been painted by children. Some eight guards, mostly male but a couple of women, stand around the walls keeping a beady eye on proceedings. In one corner a small child has broken away from her mother and is desperately hugging the knee of a prisoner, possibly an older brother, and getting increasingly upset as a female guard tries to separate them. Eventually she succeeds and the room returns to a gentle hubbub of whispered conversations.

At first Jack has trouble identifying Dean, but then he spots his sky-blue eyes and sardonic grin. He takes the seat opposite Dean at his corner table.

'So how do you like the new look? Bit of a change of style.' Dean passes his hand over the stubble that adorns his head.

'You can say that again.'

'Don't worry about it. I'm glad they did it otherwise I'd really stand out.'

With a start Jack spots a stitch above Dean's left eye, the surrounding skin slightly discoloured.

'What happened to you?'

'It's nothing. Just some of the guys exerting their manhood in the only way they know how. It's like an initiation rite; once you've been through it they leave you alone. It looks worse than it is.'

'Shit, man. It's really heavy, you being in here.'

'It's not good, but time passes. They keep you busy so you don't go completely mad, but it's mostly boring. Some of the other guys aren't so bad, and there's a couple of us that look out for each other. I mean, there's quite a few dealers in here and Kingpin's name counts for something.'

'Yeah, but seven years, man! I mean, what was it that guy said about Jagger when he was arrested? Something like "Who breaks a butterfly on a wheel?" Well, I guess you're that butterfly. And Jagger, he only got three months.'

Dean smiles. 'Yeah, but he only had a couple of pills on him. Being caught red-handed with over a hundred tabs of a very dubious chemistry is a bit different. Ania's looking into the possibility of an appeal but, between you and me, I don't hold out much hope.'

'You know Ania's in the waiting room? The guard said she could come in after I leave, so I won't stay much longer.'

'OK, it would be good to see her. But what's been happening to you, man? I heard you were in hospital?'

'Yeah, that's right. It's a long story.'

Jack thinks how much he'd like to go through the whole thing with Dean over a joint, sat out in the park liked they used to, or over a pint in the Blue Lion.

'It's all to do with that band, Devil Spawn. We were doing some shit-hot stuff but it all got a bit weird. The day after you were busted it was Halloween and we did this gig out in Abbey Park, in the ruins of the house. We were all drugged up on some powder David brought with him, and there was a bonfire and these torches burning and then it got really out of hand. I'm not sure what happened. All I know is that I woke up in hospital a couple of days later with a lot of memories of things that, as far as I can see, never took place.'

'Sounds weird.'

'Yeah, and then Evelyn tells me David and Deek – he was the bass player – have disappeared. She's still around, but the band and the squat – they're gone. Even Gina's disappeared.'

Dean smiles. 'Yeah, she does that.'

'Yeah, and now it's just me and Evelyn.'

'You and Evelyn?'

Jack looks embarrassed. 'Yeah, maybe ...'

'Well, good luck with that,' Dean grins.

'Thanks. I mean, who knows ... maybe one day it'll be you and Ania and me and Evelyn.'

'Yeah, maybe, but until then, well, it's one day at a time.'

'Yeah, I guess so.'

Jack stands up. He wants to hold his hand out; he wants to pull Dean towards him and give him a hug, but he doesn't. 'Look, I'd better go. I mean, you'd probably rather be looking at Ania than my ugly mug.'

'Yeah,' Dean laughs, and then gets serious. 'Look, take care of Ania for me, if you can. I mean, she tries to visit almost every day, but that can't continue. You and I can fantasise, but in truth she's got to move on. She can't really think she's going to wait for me.'

'Yeah, sure, man. Not sure she'll listen to me, but I'll do what I can.'

He doesn't look back as he walks through the door to where Ania is waiting.

oOo

As he steps out of his mother's flat the following morning, it feels like he's crossing a threshold into a whole new world. The sky is a light grey and the street is moist, but whatever rain has fallen has stopped. He walks past Rosie's Café to where a narrow gap between the buildings takes him into the park. If he carried straight on he would skirt the lake and eventually arrive at Riverdale but instead he turns right, up the valley floor towards the Rose and Crown. As he walks he scans the ferns and nettles to his left, and after a short while, with a start of recognition,

171

he spots the narrow path that leads up the slope and under the trees. It's more obvious now autumn has set in and the leaves have thinned out, but this is where he stood all those weeks back, dancing in the sunshine with his friends and coming up on the strongest acid he'd ever taken.

He follows the path up through the trees, the bare earth now carpeted with dead leaves. He looks carefully for the shallow depression to the left, but he arrives at the ridge and realises he must have missed it. Perhaps this is how it is going to be; perhaps the clearing and the tomb are no longer part of his world. He works his way back down, pausing every so often as something catches his eye, and he's just about to give up when he realises he is looking at what he seeks. Just ahead of him, through the canopy of dying leaves, is a clearing, and in the middle of the clearing is a slab of stone.

He walks forward and stops a few feet from the tomb. The wood is quiet but for the soft rustling of air passing through the trees and the occasional call of a bird. The stone is still blotched with moss and lichen and tendrils of ivy, but now there are clumps of small flowers growing out of the grass at the foot of the tomb, each a little less than an inch across with five cleft petals, some completely white and others tinged in hot pink. He pulls aside the ivy to read the inscription again.

He stands there for a minute or so, absorbing the atmosphere, and then ascends the path to the crest of the hill. David and Deek may be having a hard time accepting what happened, and Faylin may never have existed, but he's satisfied that Daniel, Gabriel and Lucy are resting in peace now that, in their world at least, justice has been served.

Once he reaches the top he heads to the stone bench at the end of the ridge, where he sits down, takes a joint out of his pocket and lights up. He gazes out over the lake and the Downs beyond. At last it really is over and he can get on with the rest of his life. Suddenly impatient, he extinguishes what remains of the joint and makes his way back into town. At the very least, he needs to retrieve his bag.

# Acknowledgments

My thanks to Philippa Pride for her inspirational Guardian Masterclass Free Your Creativity, Tim Lott for his Masterclass on Character Creation, Joanna Penn for Secrets of Successful Self-Publishing, and Jacob Ross for his Elements of Fiction course at the Free Word Centre. To members of the Writing! Meetup group in Bristol which helped get me started, particularly to Merlin, Cassie, Karolina, Nicola, Jerry, Stuart, Verity and of course Sandra for welcoming me in the first place.

To Jane Lee for her comments on an early draft. To Daniel Jeffreys and Ashley Stokes at The Literary Consultancy for helping me understand how to tell the story. To Louise Bolotin for her work editing the final document and for helping me see what I could leave out and what I needed to strengthen. To Alexandra Albornoz for designing such a great cover, and to 99Designs for bringing us together.

My thanks also to numerous cafés in Bristol for the quality of their coffee, their staff and their wi-fi, which over the past few years have given me the atmosphere I needed to write. Particularly notable are Crazy Fox in The Galleries, The Arts House and The Canteen on Stokes Croft, Bakers and Co. on Gloucester Road, Tincan on Clare Street (and Cafe Be-On which preceded it), Pret A Manger on Queens Road (where I finished the first draft), The Hawthorns at the University of Bristol, Boston Tea Party on Park Street, Murrays on Park Row and Twelve in Clifton Village.

And finally to Hazel, Jemma and Luke, who make it all worth while.

Printed in Great Britain
by Amazon